"CJ Hauser's *Family of Origin* is strange in that way raw honesty often is. It is sharp in its prose and in how it can so cleanly make you feel pierced through. Hauser lures us to an island and from there we learn of family and loss and the nature of our essential humanity. Funny and unforgettable."

—Nana Kwame Adjei-Brenyah, author of *Friday Black*

"In *Family of Origin*, CJ Hauser explores and explodes the most complex moments in life: those moments with a power that spirals both backward and forward in time, those moments that shift in meaning and shape us into who we are. This riveting and emotionally intricate book doesn't shy away from the deepest questions about how a family, and a species, can survive."

—Helen Phillips, author of *The Need*

"*Family of Origin* is a novel full of wonders: a heartfelt, hilarious book about the possible end of a family, and the world, and how an obscure duck on an obscure island populated by obscure scientists might just save us all. There is some serious magic in these pages. All hail CJ Hauser, who has made us a funny, tender, and hopeful book, just when we need it the most."

—Brock Clarke, author of *An Arsonist's Guide to Writers' Homes in New England*

"CJ Hauser's *Family of Origin* is unexpected and beautiful and utterly propulsive. Set in a world where colonizing Mars is a possibility, where a group of scientists and misfits believe that evolution is running in reverse, where love is strange and changeable and astonishing, *Family of Origin* reveals a new, spectacular universe. I've never read anything quite like it."

—Anton DiSclafani, author of *The Yonahlossee Riding Camp for Girls*

CJ HAUSER

Family of Origin

CJ Hauser teaches creative writing and literature
at Colgate University. She is the author of the novel
The From-Aways and the essay "The Crane Wife,"
and her fiction has appeared in *The Paris Review,
Tin House, Narrative, TriQuarterly, Esquire, Third
Coast,* and *Kenyon Review*. She holds an MFA in
fiction from Brooklyn College and a PhD in creative
writing from Florida State University. She lives in
Hamilton, New York.

www.cjhauser.com

ALSO BY CJ HAUSER

The From-Aways

Family of Origin

Family of Origin

CJ HAUSER

ANCHOR BOOKS
A Division of Penguin Random House LLC
New York

The Library of Congress has cataloged the Doubleday edition as follows:
Name: Hauser, CJ, author.
Title: Family of origin / by CJ Hauser.
Description: First edition. | New York : Doubleday, 2019.
Identifier: LCCN 2018036898
Classification: LCC PS3608.A8697 F36 2019 | DDC 813/.6—dc23
LC record available at https://lccn.loc.gov/2018036898

Anchor Books Trade Paperback ISBN: 978-0-525-56539-0
eBook ISBN: 978-0-385-54463-4

www.anchorbooks.com

146119709

For Meredith

I would enjoy flying to Mars…
I am ready to fly without coming back.

Valentina Tereshkova

Forgiveness and the future are tied together in both
directions.
Time is reversible…
The past must not mortgage the future.

The Gap of Time
Jeanette Winterson

Family of Origin

The Landing

People came to Watch Landing to forget things. They gave themselves over to its Gulf Coast fug, its boardwalk amble, its funnel-cake smell, its open-carry vodka, its fireworks every night in order to forget, because they were on vacation.

This was the summer people came to the Landing to forget their jobs, forget climate change, forget police brutality, forget opioids, forget refugees, forget their inboxes, forget white supremacists, forget tsunamis out of season, and forget forget forget anyone who took it upon themselves to remind them of these things.

The Greys did not belong here.

Elsa and Nolan Grey might have been happier if they could be forgetful, or dead, but they were not. The Greys remembered everything.

They were fondlers of old grudges and conjurers of childhood Band-Aid smells. They were rescripters of ancient fights and relitigators of the past. They were scab-pickers and dead-horse-beaters and wallowers of the first order.

The Greys had not seen each other in almost three years, but they would converge at Watch Landing because their father was dead, drowned off the coast of Leap's Island, an hour's boat ride south, and as much as they would like to forget Dr. Ian Grey, they could not.

The first sign the Greys did not belong here was that, on the bus bound for Watch Landing, Elsa was the only one not dressed for the beach.

Two girls in front of her, smelling of coconut oil, wore bikini bottoms and t-shirts and hugged collapsible beach chairs. Elsa wore green pants turned up at the cuffs and Teva sandals. Her legs itched hotly. A giant backpack rode in the seat next to her and Elsa looped her arm around it like a conspirator. The bus turned onto the bridge to the peninsula. Once she got to the Landing, there was still the matter of finding someone with a boat to take them to Leap's. Nolan, Elsa's brother, who was meeting her there, claimed this would not be difficult, but it didn't seem likely the island got many visitors, because the people who lived there were all crazy.

Elsa and Nolan's father, Dr. Ian Grey, had moved to Leap's after being humiliated at nearly every distinguished biology department on the West Coast and then losing a fellowship in Alabama. Ian's fall from grace had been going on for so long that his children thought he might never stop falling. But he had, two years ago, when he'd joined the Reversalist movement and gone to live on Leap's Island for good.

Leap's was owned by Mitchell Townes and was inhabited by seven former scientists, researchers, and naturalists whom Townes had convinced of his theories and brought to live there, free of charge. The scientists' work was dedicated to the world's smallest known sea duck, the undowny bufflehead, and the island was the species' only known nesting ground. The undowny bufflehead's existence comprised the sum total evidence of the Reversalists' core belief: that evolution had begun to run backward.

Elsa had learned all this on the Reversalists' vague though well-maintained webpage. According to a counter at the bottom of the site, she was not alone. More than ten thousand people had been interested enough in the Reversalists' theories to scroll through their manifesto. Elsa puzzled over the Reversalists' logo: the silhouette of a bearded man with a walking stick, his foot extended behind him, as if taking a step back. A caption referred to the logo as the "Darwin Walking Backward."

It seemed unlikely to Elsa that her father had believed in any of this.

And yet, by the time Ian Grey had drowned, his rumpled clothes found among pouches of seaweed in one of the island coves the past week, her father had been living with the Reversalists for almost two years, which implied that, despite thirty years at Stanford, Cal Poly, and Berkeley, Ian did believe that human progress had slowed and swung on its fulcrum. He believed that evolution had reversed its course. And he believed all this because of some fucking ducks.

The bus slowed to its final stop at the Landing and everyone got off.

The pavement was cracked. The beach-going people scattered to the ramps over the dunes, to the liquor stores, to the snack shacks and t-shirt shops, and Elsa followed them.

She was a woman whose sweat smelled of iron, and already Elsa was sweating.

She hitched her thumbs in her pack straps. Her sandy hair was roped and piled on her head, and she wore a white tank top that did not cover her soft, curved midriff. Elsa's mother, Ingrid, was a milk-pale Scandinavian nurse with very few bad moods. Elsa had inherited her paleness and little else.

There were many bars, because Watch Landing was the kind of boardwalk where people came to get drunk and stare at the ocean. No one was swimming. There were shrimp shacks and burger joints and a more formal restaurant with a long deck full of tables with white cloths, and of course this was where Elsa found Nolan.

There was a knot between Elsa's shoulders that twisted taut when she saw him. Nolan's mother, Keiko, a microbiome researcher from Kyoto, had been beautiful, and Nolan's sleek hair and open, inquisitive face were his mother's. The rest was all Grey.

Nolan's hair was to his shoulders, and he'd pushed it back with a pair of sunglasses. His long legs were jacked out from the low deck chair, and he leaned over the table as he sucked from the head cavity of a crawfish. A glass of pale beer on the table was only a quarter drunk, beaded around the rim. He wore a blue oxford, open at the neck, and linen pants. In front of him was a bowl of carcasses. He looked so much like their father that Elsa paused. She'd not seen Ian since he moved to Leap's, and Nolan on the boardwalk approximated a reincarnation.

This is mourning? Elsa called.

Nolan looked up. He stood respectfully, like a subordinate officer. His eyes were reddish and the bridge of his nose was dented from the glasses. She wanted to grab his elegant Adam's-appled throat and squeeze. Weakness in Nolan had always driven her mad. Ever since he was small and needily sucking up all of Ian's time.

Elsa drew close. Nolan's fingers in the four o'clock light were oily and spotted with red; he held them out as she embraced him, so as not to stain her clothes. He kissed her cheek, and was it possible she felt the sting of cayenne?

We're not mourning yet, are we? Nolan asked, as if he really wanted to know. As if he would not believe their father was dead unless Elsa said it was so. This pleased Elsa, and yet, why should it be up to her? They were thirty-five and twenty-nine years old, too old for this. Elsa's life was a litany of troubles caused by the various absences of Ian Grey. Why should death be any different? Probably, the ghost of Ian Grey was off plunging his big-knuckled fingers into the layers of a duck's eiderdown and squinting at whatever inscrutable thing he found there—oblivious that his disappearance had inconvenienced anyone at all.

Even this, even death, Ian would not make simple.

No mourning yet, Elsa told Nolan. She set her pack down as the waiter appeared and convinced her that a sweet, red slurry called a zombie was just the thing for a day like today. Elsa agreed. She ordered fried oysters and two sides of fries, because otherwise, she knew, Nolan would eat most of hers and she'd have to be angry at him, because she was hungry and wanted to eat them all without sharing, and there was no time for them to be angry with each other now.

The first time Elsa met Nolan, he was sitting on the blue velveteen piano bench of a Steinway that had once been hers. Inside the bench, Elsa knew, was a cupboard that held sheaves of music. Before her father left, she used to practice scales or slow pieces for him: Tchaikovsky's "The Sick Doll" and some of the *Gymnopédies*.

Now Nolan was banging on the keys.

Nolan's father was her father, but his mother was Keiko, who was beautiful in a way that made it difficult for Elsa to hate her. Nolan had downy skin and fat, childishly dimpled fists. His hair was soft and fell to his neck. They were not cutting Nolan's hair until he asked that it be cut, Ian had told her, which was stupid because Nolan was only four. No one asked Elsa anything about what she might like, and she was ten. Her mother, Ingrid, had dropped her at the door and left to take a tour of a vineyard. Ingrid did this because she was a hospice nurse and took her days off seriously—but Elsa suspected Ingrid also hoped to force her into playing with her little brother.

Elsa was marooned with her father's new family and her father was not even there. He'd been held late at the Cal Poly lab, so she was stuck with Nolan.

Nolan swung his perfect legs.

Can you play it? Elsa asked.

Dad plays it, Nolan said, and banged on the keys with his small fist to show her how.

Keiko appeared in the doorway, tumbling her hands dry on a nubby pink towel, eyeglasses on her head.

Why don't you play outdoors?

Nolan's playset was made of smooth, gray beams, not like the splinter-giving kind on the playground at school. Elsa wondered if her father had built the set for Nolan or if Keiko had done it. Her father had built things for her when they still lived in the farmhouse: a bottomless sandbox, a platform in the boughs of an ash tree from which Elsa could spy on the animals, a pony and a milk goat. That was before.

She sat heavily in a swing.

Do you want me to push you? Nolan asked. He had a gravelly voice, a child with a perpetual frog in his throat.

You're too little.

Nolan ran at her from behind, pushed, and the swing went flying. He tipped his head back when he laughed, the long hair spilling from his face like water.

Elsa stopped the swing, her feet in the dirt. The ground was black-wet and sparkling with flecks of mica.

What else is there to do? she asked.

Nolan pushed up the sleeves of his waffle tee, looking at Elsa as if he was deciding whether or not she could be trusted. He led her to a stand of cedars at the back of the yard.

Secret passageways, Nolan said. He knelt and shuffled into the hedgerow, the rubber bottoms of his sneakers disappearing.

Elsa followed him. Bittersweet vines had overgrown the property in a maze of wickery tunnels. Vines grazed Elsa's back as she crawled. Red berries in yellow sheaths peppered the packed dirt. And there was trash in the vines—a rusted kettle with a dented side, a gallon milk jug full of rainwater, a snarl of pink shoelaces. Nolan carefully disentangled these. They followed the tunnel until they came to a clearing.

There was a wide pit in the center, an old well, its stones scattered. And there was junk from the tunnels, each piece curated on a well stone: a set of horseshoes, a mangled kite, two Day-Glo tennis balls, a moldy netted hammock. Nolan selected a new stone and put the tangle of pink laces on it.

Elsa picked up the tennis balls. Secret spaces. Just the sort of thing she loved. She wondered if it was because it was the sort of thing their father loved that Nolan loved it too. That it was a kind of proof he really was her brother.

She hated that Nolan had this whole cloistered world to himself, when she'd had to leave the farm. These days, Elsa spent hours cooped up in the Potato Lake house while Ingrid was on nursing shifts, because she was not allowed to play outside by the water alone. It felt as if she was always waiting for Ingrid to return. When Ingrid did, it was wonderful; they invented word games and made newspaper ships for the bathtub and melted crayon ends in the oven, but it was not the same as it had been when Elsa was small and there had been the farm with the animals, and the tree house above the field, and the piano in the great room, and everything that she was still allowed to have when her father was there. Her father, most of all.

Elsa looked at the well hole and chucked the tennis balls inside. Nolan shouted and ran to peer over the edge.

Why did you do that? He considered for a moment, then clambered onto his belly and slid, backward, into the hole.

Elsa looked into the pit. It was only about six feet deep. Dry for years and full of dead leaves that crackled as Nolan treaded on them.

Nolan retrieved the tennis balls and threw them up. They bounced away among Nolan's other treasures. He extended his arms toward Elsa, so she could pull him out.

Elsa reached for him, then withdrew.

Can you reach? Nolan asked.

But Elsa took three steps back. Nolan's face in the hole, as she drew away, started to disappear.

Pull me out, Nolan said.

But each step she took made Nolan go away more, until finally she could no longer see him over the lip at all, and it was as if he were gone. Elsa left him and crawled back through the maze of bittersweet.

———

When Keiko called them in for dinner, it was almost an hour later. Elsa was swinging, humming a small song to herself.

Where's Nolan? Keiko asked.

Elsa shrugged.

He was playing over there, she said, pointing at all of the woods.

Keiko called Nolan's name. Paced the yard. After each call, Keiko stood very still, quietly listening for a response for almost a full minute. The fifth time there was no response, she asked Elsa again: Have you seen your brother? Elsa shook her head.

Keiko ran for the house and Elsa followed her inside. She heard Keiko call her father and tell him to come home. Elsa was pleased.

But when Ian did arrive, Elsa only saw him through the sliding glass doors. He slammed out of his car and went straight to the lawn, to Keiko. He called Nolan's name. He didn't even come inside.

Elsa went to the blue velveteen piano bench and squeezed the piping between her fingers as if it were a fat caterpillar. She lifted the seat and smelled the familiar oily woodiness of the cupboard, but it was empty. The music she used to keep in there was gone. She closed the bench and lifted the lid from the piano keys. She played as much of the first *Gymnopédie* as she could remember, but some parts she'd forgotten, and without the music she could not find her way. Hours later, her hands were stiff, and they were still searching for Nolan, their flashlight beams bouncing across the dark lawn.

———

This was the day that, according to collective tri-parental belief, everything first went wrong. Perhaps Keiko and Ian and Ingrid fixated upon the day the children went into the woods because none of them was present—and so, this plausible First Moment of Badness lay blame exclusively with the children.

Perhaps this was also why Elsa and Nolan were skeptical of the designation.

The Greys agreed that there'd been some apple-from-the-tree moment when all the good possibilities of their lives gave way to the unremarkable shit they lived in now. What the Greys disagreed about was when, when precisely, this had happened. When their lives had gone so wrong.

It was Nolan and Elsa's favorite fight, the greatest of their greatest hits, and the issue was never resolved because they were always finding the rot in different apples.

Where was that smell coming from?

Even now, the grown Grey children had the habit of counting their years backward, searching for a time when they'd been happy and the world turned the way it ought. Determining the moment wouldn't make them happy again, they knew that, but at least then they'd know who to blame.

The Greys were scientific about their misery.

I

The Island

The men of Earth came to Mars.

They came because they were afraid or unafraid, because they were happy or unhappy, because they felt like Pilgrims or did not feel like Pilgrims. There was a reason for each man. They were leaving bad wives or bad jobs or bad towns; they were coming to find something or leave something or get something, to dig up something or bury something or leave something alone. They were coming with small dreams or large dreams or none at all.

The Martian Chronicles
Ray Bradbury

Leap's Island

In the marina there were houseboats and private fishing craft, and it felt like a tailgate, music and barbecue smoke drifting from multiple small decks as half-naked people shouted back and forth. The Greys' grocery bags snapped in the weak wind off the Gulf. On their way from the restaurant, they'd bought seven days' worth of supplies.

Elsa watched Nolan lope down the dock in search of their lift, a postman who did a weekly mail-and-supplies run to the island. She was surprised Nolan had managed this. Surprised that, from this distance, she could mistake his receding figure, trim and efficient, for an admirable stranger's, not Nolan at all.

Elsa wanted to hide in one of these friendly boats so she wouldn't have to go to the island and talk to all these people who'd known her father. So she wouldn't have to spend a week alone with Nolan. Mostly, she wanted to go back home, because Elsa had better things to do. Two months ago, she'd received the letter from Mars Origins saying she'd made the second round of cuts. Elsa was one of the six hundred and sixty potential colonists being considered for a one-way ticket to Mars. The first-ever manned expedition.

Most people thought Elsa was joking when she told them she was going to settle Mars, but she didn't care. Mars Origins had sent her a plane ticket to interview in the Netherlands and that was real enough for her. The interview was more than a month away, but Elsa wanted to spend the summer preparing. Training, maybe. She desperately wanted them to pick her. Needed them to.

Elsa waited for Nolan outside the marina convenience store. Rafts and inflatable animals were tethered to the shop's awning, and she circled until she stood beneath a pink inflatable tiger raft with orange stripes. Above her head, one of his paws went *thunk thunk thunk* in the wind as he tried to escape the roping. He smelled cleanly of vinyl.

The tiger had a long mouth of teeth and narrowed purple eyes, and he was bound by ropes across his neck and midsection. It looked as if he were being punished for something he'd once done, though his face suggested that, if you untied him, he wouldn't hesitate to do it again. You'd have only yourself to blame. Who would trust a tiger twice?

She paid eight dollars to the man in the store, who gave her a cardboard box and said the tiger was inside. Elsa studied the box, disappointed. Elsa wanted to release the tiger from the awning, that tiger, she said, and so the little shopkeeper with his horseshoe ring of hair carried a step stool outside and spoke softly to himself as he unknotted the tiger from the awning.

Elsa! Nolan called. He was loading their groceries onto a small boat, at the helm of which a man in a postman's gray uniform shorts was smoking a cigarette. Elsa deflated the tiger against her ribs as she went to them.

Soon they were on the water.

The postman was cheerful and said he enjoyed the hour ride across the Gulf to the island and back. Normally, he brought a radio with him for company. No cell reception out there, he said. No internet. They don't like it.

But how do they work? Aren't they scientists? Nolan asked.

The postman shrugged. Not that kind. People are always asking me about them. I'm one of the few folks who goes out. But it's hard to describe. You'll see.

The tide was low, and whole blankets of reeds washed in one direction under the water. Soon, the bottom deepened. It got colder, and Elsa watched the marina grow smaller as she hunched over her knees. Nolan slid his sunglasses down his face. He looked like a young man about to go on an expensive beach vacation, and Elsa could not help but think of him as the New Baby. It was what Ingrid had called him when Elsa was small. *It's hard for your father with the new baby and all. He'll visit soon. It's a lot of work taking care of a new baby.*

Leap's Island had been a hump on the horizon, but as they drew closer it resolved itself into a wooded place with an irregular coast-line. Divots and inlets and coves. One side of the island was grassy, and they saw a large lodge. The other half was quite rocky, and a ways off from the rocks was a clustering of small shacks on stilts. They seemed to have popped up irregularly, like mushrooms, no neighborhood-y order to them at all. Elsa had expected a kind of colony, but as they drew closer, it seemed more like there just happened to be people living on the island. Like each scientist had set off to start her own village, ignorant of the rest.

Leap's was a private island, fifteen square miles, owned in its entirety by the Townes family for more than three generations. In the early sixties, it had been intended as a high-end hotel for beachgoers and birdwatchers, Leap's Retreat—Grand Hotel and Paradise Spa, but Townes had died before the project's completion. The following Townes had established a commune in the half-built hotel rooms and pools. Twenty-five "Leap-Backers" practiced farming and free love and preached the gospel of the "Darwin Walking Backward," a bastardization of Darwin, who served as a kind of patron saint for their belief that the world's best days were behind them. Their only hope, the Leap-Backers believed, was to get back to "idyllic preindustrial times."

Mitchell Townes owned the island now. Raised a Leap-Backer, he'd given up his father's commune values, rejecting the sloppy spiritual nature of his childhood and supplanting it with sloppy science.

It was Mitchell who had installed the Reversalists on the island, declaring it a station for field research.

They pulled into a small cove and the postman tied off the boat. Elsa climbed out, and Nolan passed her the grocery bags while the postman unloaded his boxes of deliveries for the islanders and took his sack of mail over to a set of numbered wooden cubbies with a Plexiglas front panel.

I'll be back next week, he said. He was slotting the envelopes into the cubbies rapidly. Likely won't find anyone to take you back before then. You'll be okay?

Do we have a choice? Elsa said.

It's only a week, said Nolan.

Trapped a whole week, Elsa said. She turned to the postman. Do you have any mail for Dr. Ian Grey?

Shack Seven, the postman said. He handed Elsa several envelopes. Labs in Louisiana, Georgia. She tucked them into the side pouch of her pack alongside the interview letter she'd received from Mars Origins. She would tell Nolan soon. He would be so jealous it would kill him. It was exactly the sort of thing their father would have loved.

———

They followed a path through the woods to the lodge they'd seen from afar, a place the Reversalists called the Lobby. Nolan focused on keeping pace with Elsa's pack bobbing in front of him. At the Lobby, they would meet a woman named Mariana Gates, who would take them to their father's shack.

It was the policeman who'd called Nolan back in San Francisco to tell him Ian was dead, who gave him the island phone number. Don't know if they'll pick up, he'd said. But it's worth a shot. Nolan had dialed that same afternoon, not knowing what to expect. The woman who'd answered—Leap's Island Institute for Reversalism—sounded huskily irritated. Mariana Gates had softened once he said he was Ian's son.

Nolan had told her they wanted to come to the island to collect their father's effects, and talk to the residents—

The researchers, Gates had said.

The researchers, Nolan had corrected. They wanted to speak to some of the researchers, Nolan said, and ask after memories of their father.

They won't know much about his research, Gates had said.

It's not really his research so much, Nolan said. It's more a matter of how he seemed? Before the accident.

Gates had made a sound that made it clear precisely how stupid she thought it was for the two of them to care about anything other than research and then launched into a list of all the things he could not expect the island to provide for them: cell-phone service and internet, regular electricity or private bathrooms. As Gates performed this defensive recitation, Nolan found his hand drifting into his pants, sneaking past the waistline, to cup himself. He wasn't turned on, exactly. He just sensed Gates was a woman who did not approve of many people, and Nolan felt that if he could be the sort of person who could earn her respect, he might feel something like relief.

The path to the Lobby was well tended, mulched over. It had rained, and the mulch was damp, and where the sun fell between the branches it steamed. Elsa's pack brushed the low needles of a pine, and last night's rain shook into her hair. Nolan touched a drop that hung by her ear, letting it spill onto his fingers. Elsa smacked his hand.

Nolan knew Elsa would have had too much dignity to come all the way to Leap's had he not asked her to do it. But frankly, she owed him. In the cosmic order of things, she owed him more than this.

They had not seen each other since his mother's memorial, three years ago. Before that, it had been almost a decade since they'd broken the family—ten years since the two halves had treated each other like kin.

Keiko's service had been held in the succulent house at the San Francisco Botanical Garden, because she'd loved it there and often sat reading inside the greenhouse's eighty-degree climate in shorts and sandals in midwinter.

Elsa and Ingrid had both come. When she'd found Nolan, hiding between two cacti large enough to feel like bodyguards, Ingrid had squeezed him so hard that for one moment Nolan felt his alarm at her strength replace the woolly pain that had muffled him since Keiko died. Ingrid released him.

Elsa stood behind her mother wearing a black dress with long sleeves that she gripped in her palms.

Hi, Elsa said, and then waved at him, from two feet away.

Waved at him.

Elsa seemed intent on avoiding any sort of physical contact at all. And Nolan understood that. With their parents there, with Keiko everywhere, it would have felt wrong, or dangerous.

Hi, he'd said, and waved back across those impossible two feet.

He wished she would have risked it.

Nolan had hoped Ingrid and Elsa might come back to the house afterward, but when the memorial was through they'd fled the earthy warmth of the succulent house and returned to Minnesota. Ingrid was expected back at the hospital, they said.

Sometimes, it felt as if Nolan spent his entire life trying to get Elsa to just sit down with him. To look at him and admit that what had happened, happened and that it mattered. These days, whenever Nolan tried to do something grown up, whenever he tried to imagine himself getting married or living in a house or, Jesus Christ, having children, there was a part of his brain that said, *But Elsa*. It was an excuse, he knew. Nolan didn't really want to do any of those things, he didn't think. Not yet. But all these years, it was as if a question had been posed and he still had not answered it. *But Elsa*.

They walked on. The woods around them rustled and squirrels tore across the ground. Then the path moved sharply to the left, and the walls of the forest buckled to reveal a clearing. In it was the Lobby.

The lodge-style building hulked tall and had a peaked roof covered in solar panels. A wraparound deck ringed the upper floor. From the pale blue Adirondack chairs on the deck, Nolan imagined, you could see the Gulf, but every chair was empty. An ascending flagstone path led to the Lobby's main entrance: an ostentatious rotating door made of copper. As Nolan and Elsa climbed the steps, the door spun slowly, as if they had just missed someone.

Elsa stepped sideways into the rotating door, to fit her pack, and Nolan waited for a new slice of space to spin around for him so Elsa would not smack him again.

It was clear that Leap's Retreat had been designed as a stately hotel. Inside the Lobby, the building was open all the way to the roof's peak and the deck was mirrored by the second floor's balcony, thirty feet up. Two wood-and-iron spiral staircases descended on either end. It was steamy inside too, as if the Lobby had its own climate. Banks of vegetables grew in wooden planter boxes on the main floor, and the basin of a tiled fire pit and abandoned fountain were filled with black potting soil, sprouting rows of leafy shoots. Beets, Nolan thought. Or turnips. There were signs for a kitchen, a locker room, a laundromat, and a sauna. The main hall smelled like laundry. The hot, family smell of dirty sheets forgiven in bleach.

There was no one inside.

There was a grouping of armchairs and couches in the center of the room, upholstered in what must have been considered a very jazzy fabric in 1963, when the hotel was meant to have opened. Elsa sat down in one, slinking out of her backpack. Nolan sat down across from her, his knees knocking into hers, and Elsa noticed that he smelled the same. It was a smell she had not known she remembered until there it was. A warm smell, like a good leather wallet just pulled from a pocket.

Had it been 1963, they might have been a couple drinking cocktails to ease their way out of their regular lives and into their freer, vacationing selves at this island hotel, which promised a suspension of the normal rules of engagement for nice young men and women. They might have let their knees touch, leaned in to ask for sips of each other's drinks, pressed their mouths to the same place on the martini glass.

A honking interrupted them, the sound of birds bickering among themselves, and the Greys followed the sound to a pair of frosted plate-glass doors propped open on the west side of the Lobby, one of which had a jagged chip missing from it. Elsa went in, but when she saw that it was a swimming pool, she hesitated on the threshold and Nolan pressed in behind her.

Come on, he said, giving her a little push with his knee in the back of her thigh.

The Greys approached the pool.

Elsa stood by the edge, and Nolan knelt down next to her on the yellowed tile. He trailed his fingers in the water, which was green and murky. In it swam dozens of slow, gray-eyed fish. And drifting in the pool was a family of ducks, chortling to each other as they swam in endless loops. Undowny buffleheads. The source of all the trouble.

One hundred seventy-five years since Darwin, Nolan said, looking up at her, and along comes the undowny bufflehead, fucking everything up.

It's not their fault, Elsa said. It's the people who tell stories about them.

The ducks' heads were very round and their eyes were located at the precise point where three different colors of feathers met. The females were warmly brown and gray, but the males were showoffs. A ruff of iridescent green, like shards of broken bottle, tapered into a darker cape along their backs, and a rosy sheen illuminated the space between. The rosiness dabbed inward to touch the round, black eye. There was a white cap on the back of their heads, and their bills were the color of slate, short and perfectly formed. They had pure, white-feathered bellies, smooth and sealed together at the breast, rumpled where the water permeated.

Nolan cupped some water in his hands.

That's probably filthy, Elsa said.

Nolan looked at her, wiggling his fingers as water spilled from his palms.

Don't— Elsa began, but Nolan, dirty water dripping from his fingers, grabbed Elsa around the ankles and shook her, groaning, *Graaghh!* like some B-movie Swamp Thing from the deep, ready to pull Elsa into the pool. Elsa considered Nolan's hands around her ankles.

Nolan had kissed her cheek on the Landing. Their knees had touched in the Lobby. He'd grabbed her ankles. It was stupid to keep inventory, but how long had it been, really, since they'd seen each other? Before Keiko's memorial, just the once, when she'd driven out to Carleton when Nolan was a freshman and always calling her in the middle of the night—more than a decade ago. In the time since they'd been teenagers, Nolan had mostly existed as a voice on the phone, the safety of hundreds of miles between them.

Let go, Elsa said. She stepped back, her ankles wet.

This could have been a nice place, Nolan said, admiring the tiled mosaic work around the pool as he wiped his hands on his pants. Just then, he caught sight of something rushing his way and turned in time to see a large dog. Nolan yelped and stood up. The dog raced around the shallow end of the pool, snapping at the ducks, who scattered, quacking as they waddled away in loose formation. Satisfied, the dog trotted back out to the hall, where she sat at attention.

The Greys followed.

Hey, dog, Elsa said. Look at your crazy pretty face. She plunged her hands into the long tufts of fur behind the dog's floppy ears, and the dog leaned into her touch, narrowing its eyes.

Elsa's face was too close to the dog's snout. Nolan imagined it sinking its teeth into Elsa's cheek. Be careful, he wanted to tell her. Sometimes, when people asked Nolan if he had any siblings, he said no. Other times he said yes, he had an ex-sister who lived in Minnesota and she was ten feet tall and strong as an ox. People laughed, but Elsa was a kind of mythical folk hero to Nolan. Larger than life. Taking up more space than she deserved.

A woman came clomping down one of the curved wooden staircases from the upper deck.

She's a shepherd, the woman said.

Mariana Gates? Nolan asked.

She nodded. Just Gates, she said.

Gates was tall, and Nolan noticed Elsa straightening her posture.

The dog was now leaning the drum of her stomach against Elsa's legs. She was a shaggy, piebald creature with a gray and reddish spotted coat, a wide smiling muzzle, and the kind of facial markings that made Nolan think of eyebrows. Her shag, damp now, fell in a wave beneath her sloping belly and stuck out from her back legs in pantaloons.

He called her Jinx, Gates said.

Who did? Elsa asked.

She was your father's.

He never let me get a dog, Nolan said.

Animals did not belong in the home, Ian had said, not even small ones like the Corgi in the picture Nolan had torn out of a magazine and shown to him when he made his request. This is the queen of England, Ian had said, pointing to the woman with the Corgi. That's who believes in pets. The sort of people who still think the monarchy rules.

Nice to meet you, Gates said. Sorry for the circumstances. They all shook hands. She worked a key off her own metal ring. There's really not much at the shack, she said, a couple boxes, maybe, if you'd—

I wouldn't have thought you'd need locks out here, Nolan said, taking the key from her too quickly.

Gates looked at him curiously. People are particular about their research.

Gates was about forty, her face crinkled around the eyes. Olive skin. She kept her dark hair in long bangs. She wore green khaki shorts with red-laced hiking boots and a button-down shirt that appeared water resistant. She had great legs. Nolan imagined his cheek nuzzled against her thigh. His tongue pulling at the elastic of her underwear.

Let's get your supplies put away in the kitchen, then we'll head out to Seven. She tossed her head and moved for the kitchen without waiting for assent.

Elsa snorted.

We better do what she says, Nolan said.

———

It wasn't exactly a house. A house would have touched the earth. Shack Seven was not much more than a one-room hut on stilts in a brackish inlet of the island only a short walk from the spot where the Reversalists had found the crumpled ball of their father's pants earlier that week. The spot the mainland police had begrudgingly been allowed to tramp around and investigate. The spot where, those police declared, officially, that Dr. Ian Grey had drowned in an accident.

The stilt-house was connected to the beach by a creaky boardwalk with rope handrails. Nolan followed Gates down the gangway. She smelled like lemongrass insect repellent. The mosquitos would be terrible, Nolan bet.

The only real bathrooms were in the Lobby. There was an outhouse on the shore, back in the woods, and already Nolan knew he would hate going there at night, and that he would probably stand on this very gangplank and pee into the ocean instead.

Elsa watched Nolan struggle with the two locks and the door lever, which stuck.

So the commune days are over, Elsa said. She whacked the door open with her shoulder, and gestured for Gates to go in first.

Gates walked inside. The shack was dark, but the outside light spilled in diagonally across Gates's shorts. We're a field station these days, she said. Though the kitchen and showers are communal.

Jinx trotted in and found a denim cushion in the corner that was obviously her own. She set her snout on her paws and watched.

Gates gave them a kind of tour. The ceilings were low, and there was a large battery fan in the corner behind a mattress with surprisingly new-looking white sheets and a green cotton blanket. A door on the other side of the house led to a small porch on the water, facing the horizon. There was a generator that could run a few hours before needing to be refilled with gasoline, if they didn't mind the sound. It was almost impossible to talk with the generator going. There was a water barrel in the corner. There were a number of battery-powered Coleman lanterns hanging from the ceiling, which Gates twisted on. On a long table attached to the wall was Ian's ancient iPod, a small silver square. It contained, both Greys knew, hours and hours of classical music. Bach was his favorite. Tchaikovsky a close second. He could not abide Wagner but certainly had all of the *Ring* cycle archived anyway, because he considered his dislike a personal failing to be overcome. Besides the iPod with its dead face and trailing headphones, the table was covered in papers and journals along with feathers upon feathers upon feathers. Feathers in Ziploc bags. Feathers loose in tufted heaps. Feathers sealed in jars.

Did the police look around in here? Elsa asked, picking up some papers.

Not much, Gates said. It seemed clear it was an accident. The weather was pretty bad that night. Not ideal for swimming.

Did you consider he might have killed himself? Elsa asked.

Nolan squeezed her arm violently. They were meant to bring this up gently.

Because truly, this was why the Greys had come to Leap's Island.

Yes, Nolan needed to see what his father had left him for. Yes, he had wanted to collect his father's things, because no one else would, and leaving them uncollected or thrown away seemed too sad to bear. But really, the Greys were here because Nolan needed to settle things with Elsa, who insisted that their father had killed himself.

Pure random tragedy Nolan could believe existed. It had come for him before, so many times. But suicide was unthinkable. His father was too rational for suicide, wasn't he? And so, if he had killed himself, it would have been a rational choice. And if Ian had determined that suicide was a rational choice, what was Nolan supposed to do with that? Of all the impossible things Nolan had been forced to accept that Ian had done—lost his jobs, disappointed Keiko, moved to Leap's—suicide was the one thing Nolan would not accept. He needed to show Elsa just how wrong about their father she was.

Shuffling Ian's papers, Elsa went on, Swimming in a storm hardly seems like something a person would do if he didn't intend to kill himself.

Elsa, stop, Nolan said.

Gates looked at Elsa very directly. He had no reason to, she said.

Except you all think the world is ending, Elsa said. She put the papers down, gusting feathers across the table. You can see why I might consider the climate here a little suicidal.

They think the world's going backward, Nolan corrected. Not ending.

Evolution, Gates said. Not the world.

Gates brushed the scattered feathers back into a pile with a cupped hand.

A couple of the other islanders have been wanting to come in and clean out the house, she said. I've been fending them off.

What do they want with the house? Nolan asked.

To read what Ian was working on. He'd been out on his own

observing and he wouldn't share his findings. There's a lot of interest in his data.

Isn't everyone looking at the same ducks? Nolan asked, then worried that perhaps there were huge differences in the ducks that Gates would know about and that his father would have known about and that he was showing his stupidity.

Mitchell's been trying to get everyone to come to a consensus about Reversalism, Gates said. But there are a lot of different theories. Some different kinds of research happening. Some people taken more seriously than others.

What about our dad? Nolan asked.

Everyone took your father very seriously, Gates said.

Shocking, Elsa said.

I live up in Shack Three, the opposite direction from the Lobby, on the sandy stretch. You can find me there, Gates said. Or else, leave a message on the board in the Lobby and I'll come find you.

When can we start talking to people? Nolan asked.

We can do it all tomorrow, Elsa said. In and out. She clapped her hands together.

It might take a bit longer than that, Gates said. People are busy. You can't just go interrupting their research.

She turned to go, and Jinx stood up in her bed. Stay, Gates said.

San Francisco

W hen the phone call came from the Landing policeman, looking for his dead mother, Nolan was day drinking in a bar in San Francisco with Janine, a compact modern dancer who never wore a bra, and who was, in most ways, his girlfriend. Nolan was trying to puzzle out how this had come to be so. (Certainly, his life was already a mess by this point, Ian's death only the most recent unhappiness in a long chain of misfortunes. This was too recent to be the moment things went wrong, wasn't it?)

They had met online. Janine was smart about the things bemoaned in the documentaries they streamed in the evenings, and it was pleasant to shop for organic bok choy in the market with her, or to drink too many hoppy microbrews for the hell of it. She was the resident white girl in a multiethnic dance troupe called Dance for Justice, who choreographed modern performances meant to enact social change. Their most recent performance, "I Can't Breathe," was aimed at police brutality. Every time a dancer began a solo, the others would pile onto her while one dancer ran around the stage gasping into a microphone. The *Chronicle* had called them visionary activists. A Berkeley drama professor came to all their shows and was citing them in her latest book on radical theater. In the lobby, after the shows, many people signed petitions and donated money and organized actual protests. Some cried. The whole thing made Nolan wildly uncomfortable. It seemed reductive. It seemed silly. Of course Nolan wanted police reform. Of course he wanted to see Guantánamo closed and Big Pharma shamed and the NSA out of his inbox. Nolan wanted to save the damn whales, didn't he? But he thought there was something naïve and futile about trying to do anything about it. Especially by dancing.

He and Janine often fought about this. At least I'm doing something, she said. Nolan thought perhaps there was a quiet dignity in doing nothing rather than doing something well-intentioned but stupid.

But Nolan loved the way Janine danced, how she moved. Her every daily machination was performed with a decisive purpose: selecting a lemon with a graceful tuck and bob, flinging open heavy wooden doors to enter bars with a fluid pivot. Janine always seemed to be heading somewhere in her sweat-wicking, neon-patterned sports ensembles, and Nolan admired this sense of purpose.

Still, their relationship had begun to feel accidental and mismatched, and he dreaded the idea of attending another Dance for Justice performance. Right before his phone rang in the bar that day, Nolan was wondering whether he should end things with Janine or let the days string outward in the hope that whatever tepid thing was between them would dilute itself out of existence and he would not have to do anything so unfortunate as confront her about it.

Keiko Grey? the police officer on the phone said. I'm looking for Keiko Grey?

She died last year, Nolan told the officer. I'm her son. I'm sorry.

Nolan was sorry. Sorry to be the one to tell the officer. Sorry his mother was dead. Sorry that it had taken two years in the hospital for it to happen. Sorry there was no one left in his life anything like an adult, like a safety net, like a person who could tell him what to do in situations like a cop calling you in the middle of a drunken Sunday asking for your dead mother. Sorry to be able to offer up no one better than himself. Janine looked at him curiously as she adjusted the straps of a batik halter top.

What's wrong? she whispered. Janine was alarmingly good at reading his face. Without explanation, Nolan got up and took his phone to stand on the sidewalk in front of the bar.

Outside, Nolan stared across the street. The sun glared around the corners of buildings so the people walking home from the farmer's market with their net bags of greens passed in and out of blinding spots of light.

It's about Dr. Ian Grey, the officer said. He had a soggy kind of Southern accent.

I'm his son, Nolan said.

Jesus, I'm really sorry to tell you this, Mr. Grey, but I'm afraid it looks like your father's gone and drowned off the coast of Leap's Island. Did you know he was living out there?

Yes, Nolan said. I did.

Ian had gone swimming, the officer said, in adverse conditions. The weather had been bad that night and, best they could tell, he'd gotten sucked out in a riptide. The officer gave him the number for the island phone, which he said to call about his father's effects.

After hanging up, Nolan stood outside the bar awhile. Their chalkboard had been spattered with rain, so there were translucent holes in the chalky orange lettering that announced the Giants game, drink specials, trivia night. Nolan worked for the Giants in publicity and social media. He and Janine were here to watch the game, but his father had drowned, so he supposed they should go home.

Nolan found he wanted to stay the afternoon and watch the game anyway. In fact, maybe this was the perfect excuse to send Janine home to her apartment so he could do this by himself. Maybe this was a very humane and acceptable reason for him to send her away and never call again. To never see her with their brunch friends, her dance friends, his work friends, their biking friends, to never hear them say how inspirational it was that Nolan and Janine had met online ever again, because after all, he was grieving, and so to weasel out of the relationship in this way was perfectly acceptable.

Jesus, grieving.

A woman smoking a cigarette walked by, an apricot dog trotting in advance of her. Everything smelled like wet asphalt and the spice of burning tobacco, and it was early summer, and when Nolan checked in with himself, his gut, his intuition, he did not feel much yet. But maybe it was only that Ian had died so far away, off the Gulf Coast, and so, like a lightning strike seen from afar and the thunder traveling behind, this bad news had outpaced the sound of his feelings in traveling the distance.

Nolan found himself wondering what Elsa would think when she heard. As if this might be instructive. The last time he'd heard from her, she'd still been teaching school in Minnesota. It was then that Nolan realized the policeman would not know to call her. Nolan would have to be the one to tell Elsa their father was dead.

Again, Nolan wished there was some more-adult adult whose job this could be. That he might slip back into the bar, meld into a dark and oaky booth, and watch the Giants game alone.

He called from outside the bar and gave Elsa the news. The balled-up clothing. The swimming in a storm. Ian being dead.

Not really, Elsa said.

They say he drowned.

They say, but you—what?

I don't know. I don't feel it.

No one gives a fuck about your feelings, Nolan.

Do you feel like he's dead?

He killed himself? Elsa asked.

An accident, Nolan said.

Nolan—

Are you off for the summer yet? Nolan asked. We could go.

The science quacks? No way.

They have his things, Elsa.

Isn't there someone else who could do this with you?

No, Elsa, seeing as both my parents are dead, there's not fucking anyone else.

But you're suggesting we just fly down to this island—

We have to fly to Watch Landing. And then take a boat.

Jesus Christ. And then pack up his stuff and leave?

He was working on a new article. We could see what he was doing. Talk to people.

I can't do that, Nolan. It's a really shitty thing to ask someone to do, by the way. He hasn't talked to me in ages and—

So you haven't heard from him? Nolan asked. Since he moved to Leap's?

No.

Me either, he said.

I assumed he was talking to you but not to me, Elsa said. Like always.

Well, he wasn't.

What could he possibly have been working on that would make going out there worth it?

I don't know.

What did Nolan hope to find? Evidence that Ian loved him and thought he was brilliant? Ian would never say those things. If Nolan found evidence that Ian felt this way, it would prove nothing but the fact that Ian Grey had truly and finally lost his mind.

Nolan said, They're sending his body here. I guess we should have a funeral.

Did he leave instructions?

I know he wanted to be cremated.

Put his ashes someplace and don't tell me about it, Elsa said, and hung up.

———

After letting Elsa yell at him, after letting Janine sympathize, no, *empathize* with him for hours, Nolan begged off and said he needed some time alone. He needed a walk. Janine cocked her head to the side, asking questions Nolan did not want to answer, but she let him go.

As Nolan walked the streets, which smelled sometimes of yeast and sometimes of piss and sometimes of the cool water off the bay, he panicked over being cut loose from the last real tether of his family. Ian and Keiko, both gone. There were Elsa and Ingrid, of course, but they had no real obligation to him. Not like real blood parents did.

Nolan cried. He had not thought he would, because he tended to freeze up when he knew a certain human reaction was expected of him. He was not, for example, good at peeing in public restrooms. But it turned out the double-think of his brain extended only so far, and he did cry, just like anyone else would, and this, at least, was a relief.

He walked and cried until it was late and he was exhausted, and when he took stock of his location, meaning to find a route home, he saw the Giants stadium in the distance and realized he'd been on autopilot, heading for work, yes, but also heading for the stadium because it was the closest thing his family had to a cathedral. Nolan rounded the stadium to pass McCovey Cove, where he and his father had come the night after Keiko's memorial, the day Elsa would not touch him.

Because the Giants stadium was on the bay, when home runs flew high enough above the bleachers, they splashed into the cove. The night of Keiko's memorial, Ian and Nolan, unsure what else to do, had chartered a small boat and bobbed among the other hopefuls in their kayaks and small craft. Nolan remembered that everything had smelled of diesel that night and that rainbows of fuel had played in circles on the surface of the water. When the field lights flooded on in the evening dimness, Ian had toggled the radio, and then there were the familiar voices of Miller and Kuiper, gently shooting the shit, starting the game.

Nolan conjured the image of his father as he had been in their boat that night. What if he was already forgetting? He would remember his father's long face. His crooked nose. His wire-rimmed glasses, which were unfashionable, Keiko always said, because they made him look like a scientist. I am a scientist, Ian would say, and Keiko would sigh. That night, Ian sat with his back tall and his hands braced against his knees. He wore Keiko's Yomiuri Giants hat, and he was waiting.

Their odds of a splash ball were bad, still, the night Keiko died, Nolan and Ian sat in their boat with their heads tilted toward the lip of the stadium. Anticipating something that might or might not appear each time a Giant came up to bat. A light in the sky. A freak chance plummeting down.

Elsa was wrong. Ian was inherently hopeful. He couldn't have killed himself.

Nolan turned his keys in the stadium's staff entrance and made his way into the office. Inside, he flicked on the lights. It was late.

He and Ian hadn't known how to lose Keiko, but at least there had been two of them. Alone, Nolan wasn't sure what to do. He pushed on the stadium door and found it unlocked.

The concrete labyrinth behind the stadium smelled of fried-dough oil, peppers and onions, the blue juice of bathroom cleaner. He entered the stadium through section E. The lights were not on and it was dark in the valley of the field, but the media monitor was enough to see by. The screen faced away, but when the LEDs flickered, Nolan knew the slideshow was flipping along, a phenomenon that always reminded him of his childhood Viewfinder, plastic goggles Ian had given him for his seventh birthday, into which he'd slotted slides of the wonders of the world: Easter Island, the Hanging Gardens, the Pyramids. The monitor scrolled the Instagram posts of people using the GIANTSLOVE hashtag.

The media monitor had been Nolan's idea, and he'd been roundly treated as a genius for coming up with it. Nolan wasn't quite sure what this meant, because his job was, essentially, being young. Being a person who worked for a baseball team who understood social media and how it worked. Most days, as Nolan sat at his desk, trying to think of anything less than lame he could post to the Giants baseball page, the feed of other people's faces scrolling past him, he felt as if he was doing nothing.

Nolan hopped the fence. He walked onto the field, past the third base line. He took off his sneakers and rolled up his pants. The grass was perfectly mowed in stripes, and it felt like dense carpet. He balanced on one foot. The other. He had played left field, briefly, as a child, and he gravitated to that space. It felt like a home.

Nolan's parents had fallen for each other because they both loved baseball. They had named Nolan, in fact, after Nolan Ryan. This was because Keiko and Ian could not agree on a single major league baseball player they both liked *except* for Ryan, who'd played for neither of their teams but was the name behind the *Nolan Ryan Baseball Super Stadium* game that both Ian and Keiko loved playing on Super Nintendo. Ian supported the San Francisco Giants, Keiko, Tokyo's Yomiuri Giants—but there was a fundamental understanding between the two scientists that when variables interacted with other variables for long enough, they sometimes yielded surprise. That after hours of uneventful nothing, sometimes something unlikely or wonderful might happen on a mud-red diamond. That baseball was the place for giants.

In the field now, there were deep blue patches of shadow drawn long across the field, and from them, Nolan imagined Titans rising. The monsters had long limbs, rounded bellies, and hands too large for their arms. They were the Giants of Nolan's youth. Because when Ian and Keiko talked about Giants baseball when he was small, this is what he had assumed them to mean. That there were monsters tame enough that they could be trusted around people.

Even now, Nolan was not surprised he'd believed in this. His parents had seemed just as fierce and magnificent as any Titan he'd dreamed up for the San Francisco team. The first time Nolan went to a game and saw the men on the field, he was bitterly disappointed for three innings. Sulking in disbelief that these men were who Keiko and Ian had talked about with such reverence.

Then, in the fourth, he saw Marvin Benard steal third base and forgot he'd ever imagined anything better.

In the womb of the stadium that night, Nolan felt very small. He knew that the blinking lights in the sky, planes or satellites, could not see him. He could run the bases and lie in the grass and shout himself hoarse all night and no Giants would come. The very best Nolan could hope for would be for the security shift to begin and Bill Parsons, the chief, to come swipe his flashlight beam across Nolan's face and pityingly explain why he could not be out here at night. And even if he was caught, barefoot and shouting in left field, he knew he would not get in trouble, because even to Bill, Nolan was not worth the bother.

Leap's Island

Elsa and Nolan sat on the deck that night. It was getting dark out and the shack listed like a fat man transferring his weight. Nolan sank into the netting of a red camp chair that was stretched, he imagined, to the curve of his father's back. It was hot and he stripped away his sweaty shirt. They'd bought a bottle of vodka and a can of pineapple juice at the landing and drank warm cocktails from waxy paper cups.

The buffleheads honked softly, clustering near the deck. Elsa was feeding them scraps of bread.

The ducks bumped each other, competing for waterlogged scraps. The bread hunks flowered open, soft in the water.

You're interfering with science by feeding them, Nolan said.

I'm not too concerned with their science. Elsa tossed a piece of bread long, distracting an aggressive male mallard who'd been mooching off the buffleheads. Once he'd bolted, she tossed a larger piece right in front of it, and a smaller bufflehead glided in to claim it.

You're welcome, she said. The bird tossed its head back and choked the bread down.

And then, as if it knew they were waiting for a show, one of the undowny buffleheads came and performed its oddity for them. The duck perched on the deck railing, its wings held out, crucified, bedraggled chest feathers pointed toward the last of the sun. There it was: a demonstration of the Reversalists' entire reason for being on Leap's Island.

He's drying his feathers, Nolan said.

So?

Because their down isn't waterproof. His down—Nolan pointed at the fat mallard circling Elsa after being tricked—is waterproof, but the buffleheads' isn't. Or it used to be, and now it isn't. That's the whole thing, Nolan said. Reversalism.

I read the website too, Elsa said. But she hadn't studied it closely because she'd grown too furious thinking about her father believing such bullshit. *This duck* made him think the next generation was empirically worse than the last? *This duck* signaled evolution running backward? Water dripped from the lowest fringe of its matted chest feathers, regular as a leaky tap, and the little bird shook itself. It was a ridiculous creature, but it didn't seem bad enough to make a person run away and live on an island for the rest of his life.

She frowned at Nolan. What exactly did Dad think this proved?

If it wasn't on the website, I don't know it.

I thought maybe he talked about it, before he left.

Nolan shook his head. He would have loved to lord this over Elsa. Tell her anecdotes about Ian confiding in him about his work, his fears. But Ian would never have done that. Before Keiko died, Ian had talked with her. The two of them stayed up late fighting and laughing about their work, and they would just wave at Nolan when he entered the kitchen to get a glass of water or a dish of ice cream. Sometimes, Nolan would stand, leaning against the kitchen counter, until his spoon clicked against the bottom of the bowl. He could listen to them, but when it came to science, they were a closed circuit and never thought to let him in.

He's got a lot of notes in there, Nolan said.

Elsa shrugged.

Don't pretend you don't want to know.

What?

If Dad thought the world was going to shit.

The world is going to shit.

If Dad thought *we* were shit.

Let's just go to bed, Elsa said. She made to stand, but Nolan put a hand on her thigh, pressing his thumb into the soft spot beneath her knee. The bufflehead was still in position on the railing, stuck in its posture as the water ran from its chest. The duck closed his eyes and rosy feathers pressed in around the seams of his black lids.

Nolan said, You really don't think him coming out here has *anything* to do with us?

And of course this was what Elsa was afraid of. She shouldn't have been surprised that the thought had occurred to Nolan too.

How could Ian's belief that mankind's progress was in retrograde seem like anything but a referendum on their own disappointing existences?

Of course Elsa wanted to know what was in Ian's notes.

But that Nolan could so easily admit his need to know was repellent to her. There was nothing more humiliating to Elsa than her own desires.

So she shrugged. I don't think he thought about us very much, Elsa said.

Nolan released her leg and slumped forward like a kid, his belly creasing, and Elsa felt bad.

He pointed at the sad little duck on the railing and said, If we look through his notes, I bet we'll find something.

Elsa knew he meant: Find the precise tone and tenor of Ian's disappointment. Find out why he left us. Find out what we could have done better.

Fine, Elsa said. She was getting near the bottom of her drink, and she tipped back the cup and drank the dregs. The liquor had settled, and the syrupy end of the cup was strong.

———

Their father's bed was made neatly. The green cotton blanket was rolled over at the top. The sheets were unwrinkled. Their father's bed was low to the ground, and it was too small.

Nolan unfurled his sleeping bag on the floor and slunk into it. He clicked off the lantern and the dark was absolute.

Elsa stripped down to her tank top and underwear and lowered herself onto the bed. She brushed debris off her feet, bits of leaves and sand, before tucking her feet under the blanket and pulling it all the way up over her head. It smelled person-y, a bit like unwashed hair, but not unpleasant. She was too hot and pushed the blanket down again.

Birds were calling in the woods beyond the shore. The Gulf slapped at the stilt-house, and Elsa heard the slow drip of water running from the moss beneath the walkway back into the sea. She heard the teeth on Nolan's sleeping bag unzipping, and then there was pressure on the bed, the weight of Nolan next to her.

She turned and felt around in the darkness.

Elsa patted and grabbed until she felt his thin wrists. He lay on his side, facing her. She cupped his face, tugged the sheaf of his hair.

Why did you say that earlier? Nolan asked softly, though there was no one to hear them.

What? Elsa stayed very still and stared into the darkness where Nolan's breath was coming from.

About Dad killing himself. You said it when I called you too. Right away.

It didn't occur to you?

He wouldn't have.

He joined a doomsday cult, Elsa said, flipping over and away from him. People who think the world is ending don't have great life expectancies.

Nolan was quiet a moment and then pulled the blanket back up from the bottom of the bed where Elsa had kicked it, spreading it over both of them. He smoothed the cotton over Elsa, beneath her arm, the slope of her ass, the backs of her legs.

Nolan, Elsa said.

Good night, Nolan said, and he turned away.

Elsa was not sure which one of them fell asleep first. The last thing she remembered thinking was that she would not last a whole week on this island. It was so warm beneath the blanket Elsa thought she might pass out if she didn't kick it off. But she didn't, because if she did, she knew Nolan would pull it back up again, would touch her again, and so she sweated in the heat until she fell asleep.

———

In the morning, Nolan walked out onto the porch. Elsa was in the Gulf, drifting in small orbits on the pink tiger float. She was wearing an athletic-looking bikini and sunglasses. She was reading a *Scientific American* with Mars on the cover. She smelled of sunscreen but already looked blotchy, the whitest kind of white girl.

You're burning, Nolan said. Jinx leaned against his bare legs and sent a cold nose investigating up his shorts.

It was ten o'clock and light filtered through water the color of strong tea, the soft and murky bottom sending motes of dirt toward the surface in return. A weak breeze tunneled across the water and small waves merrily crashed themselves onto the shore. The tiger spun Elsa in a wide arc.

It's morning sun. Not even strong yet, Elsa said. She took her sunglasses off. Elsa had lost herself a bit last night. In the presence of Ian's ghost, Ian's things, Ian's dog, she'd felt herself being pulled back in time to when all the Greys had been together—she'd felt Nolan trying to pull her there.

We should pack up his things, Elsa said.

They had six days before the post boat returned, and this seemed to Elsa an eternity of time to be stuck on the island with Nolan.

She knew what happened to people who stayed in close quarters for more than a couple days. Performances dropped away. Honesty took hold. Bullshit could no longer be kept under wraps. And so Elsa would pack Ian's things quickly. Maybe Nolan could be rushed along. Maybe they could phone the mainland and try to find a way to leave sooner.

They began sorting through the shack that morning, but as they put Ian's things into the two large duffels Nolan had brought for this purpose, the Greys found themselves distracted by small mysteries.

When had Ian gotten a San Francisco Symphony t-shirt with Beethoven's face on it? The rubber sandals found outside the door couldn't possibly be their father's; he claimed sandals were a conspiracy to inhibit motion. Even the handwriting in Ian's journals seemed wrong—too legible, almost elegant. The man who lived in this shack was not quite Nolan and Elsa's father. He was a kind of almost-Ian.

At the table, Nolan read through stacks of papers as Elsa crammed the duffels. Jinx—the most confounding part of their father's kit— dozed in her bed.

Nolan read the long, neatly lettered rows.

This is a roster, he said. Of ducks. He banded some of them.

Just pack it up, Nolan.

Thirty in total, but he seems extremely excited about Duck Number Twelve.

Define excited.

Nolan flipped the page over and showed her three exclamation points next to the reports concerning Duck Number Twelve. There were lists of places the duck had been seen. Behaviors the duck had displayed. Most of it seemed obvious and boring, but a few bits were so technical as to be indecipherable. There was a list of tests Ian had requested for the duck, though there was no facility to perform such tests on the island.

Nolan, it's nonsense, Elsa said.

Nolan shook his head. He wouldn't have come out here if there weren't something to figure out.

He didn't *come* here, he *left* everything else, Elsa said. And I can tell you from experience, the sooner you stop hoping for good reasons Ian leaves, the better.

Nolan looked wounded, but Elsa couldn't help it. Nolan had been defending Ian their whole lives and it drove her crazy. Ian had changed, Nolan always said. But people didn't change. They just ran away from everyone who knew them too well so they could start over and do a better job of obscuring the worst parts of themselves.

And now here she was in this ragged shack, clinging to the coast of nowhere, surrounded by jars of feathers, revealing that what Ian had given up everything in his life for was just a squalid heap of nothing. The island confirmed that, with each choice, each fall, since Ian had left Elsa, he'd chosen things that were worse and worse. And every time it felt like he was saying: Even this I choose instead of you.

I think we should just pack up and go, Elsa said.

I need to eat, Nolan said.

———

On their walk to the Lobby, Nolan pointed out a lone stilt-house above the rocky outcropping on the west side of the island. The shack was listing toward the sea, as if even this island were not far enough away.

———

In the Lobby kitchen, there were long steel tables and industrial sinks. It had been built to service a hotel of eighty guests with a three-star restaurant. Now there were masking tape labels on cupboards that said things like JIM'S GRUB! DO NOT TOUCH!

Elsa scrambled eggs and did not offer to make any for Nolan, who poured some of the cornflakes he had purchased into a bowl.

They brought their food to the dining room, a tall-ceilinged space with a chandelier and a dozen round tables with pink linens on them. Gates was at one of the tables vivisecting a grapefruit. She had a stack of toast next to her, cut into triangles.

It's nicer in here than I expected, Elsa said, sitting down next to her.

Mitchell renovated some of the facilities, Gates said. The kitchen, showers, pool. The upstairs is mostly uninhabitable.

It's not that bad, said a man entering the dining room, weaving between tables to greet them. I live up there, after all.

Elsa set down her fork.

Mitchell Townes had heavy brows, a dark mustache, and a silver goatee. He was lean in the way of former addicts, a tall man with bright eyes and a sunburned Anglo complexion. He wore a t-shirt, the sleeves rolled up, unlaced boots, and dirty jean shorts. Across the back of his left calf was a wide, toothed scar that cut crosswise across the bulge of flesh. An empty woven laundry bag was slung over his shoulder.

Mitchell, he introduced himself, and they all shook hands. Then he remembered the circumstances of their meeting. My condolences, of course, he said. Your father was a brilliant man.

Elsa could tell that Mitchell did not mean this. Or if he did, that he'd found Ian's brilliance something irritating, too precious, and she liked this about him.

Elsa had expected a certain kind of man when she'd read that Leap's was privately owned. Someone idle and stupid and entitled. She was surprised by the man in front of her. His face was deeply creased around the eyes and mouth and on his right bicep was a tattoo of a ship framed by a banner that read: HMS *Beagle*. She considered what it might mean for a man to live his life on an island. To not need anything from the mainland, or desire it. How this was not unlike living on Mars. She was curious about the kind of man who could do this.

We appreciate that, Elsa said. She smiled. Nolan put his cereal bowl down on the table and looked at her.

We were hoping we could talk—Nolan felt himself about to say, to some of the quacks—to some of you. About our father.

If you'd like to hear remembrances of your father— Mitchell said.

It's his research we're interested in, really, Nolan said.

Mariana frowned.

Did you introduce them to Esther yet? Mitchell asked.

Gates shook her head. I was leaving that to you.

I'm sure Esther Stein would talk to you. She's been hoping to meet you for some time. Gates will show you the way.

What about the others? Nolan asked.

I can't speak for everyone, Mitchell said. He wrapped his laundry bag tightly around his hand. But why hurry? Enjoy the island. If people want to offer their condolences, they'll find you. He saluted them and left.

That this island was a place to be enjoyed was an absurd thing to say, and yet Elsa thought Mitchell might believe it. He spoke Southern, his accent hard to place. He was a commune kid, and it sounded like a dialect all the island's own.

Elsa said, I thought Mitchell was rich?

Rich? Gates said.

She nodded.

Mitchell's grandfather was rich. The past two generations worked their way through most of the money. The Leap-Backers in particular. Communes are expensive if you don't know what you're doing.

So if the money's gone, Nolan asked, not that it's any of my . . . but how— He had finished his cereal and wished for some of Elsa's eggs.

A tax exemption is the only thing keeping us afloat right now. We have to refile as a scientific organization this year. Which is a headache, because we need to show publications as proof we're working "in the public interest." Mitchell's got an editor at *Nature* interested in a kind of soft feature—which is amazing, but even *Nature* can't publish the feature if we don't come to some kind of agreement about what exactly is going on with the ducks.

People disagree? Elsa said.

You could say that.

What did our father think was going on? Nolan asked.

Gates placed her spoon across the hull of her grapefruit. Were you close to your father? she asked.

There was no good way to answer this.

Nolan would say yes, of course. Nolan would say that his father had talked him through every decision of his life, had made every decision of his life for him, really, except a notable few that were Elsa's doing. He would say that he could sketch his father's face, his posture, from memory.

But if this were true, then how could Nolan explain the fact that he was on an island on the Gulf Coast with no idea what his father was doing there? How could he explain Jinx and the Beethoven t-shirt, which surely belonged to a more lighthearted man than he knew Ian to be? What could he say to account for the fact that, since his mother had died, the only thing he and his father could reliably talk about with any kind of ease was baseball? That they had held things together in the little Bay Area house—which never seemed to run the right temperature or smell quite right with Keiko gone—by endlessly speculating over the Giants' home versus road abilities and whose arm was about to fall off in the bullpen. But when the season ended, and the off-season hot-stove reports provided so little, they'd lapsed into silence. It was not long after this silence had left them unable to access each other that Ian had left. And moved to this island. And Nolan could not even begin to say why, but he suspected that if he'd just been able to keep talking about baseball, then maybe Ian would have stayed and maybe Ian would be still alive.

Not really, Elsa said. We were estranged.

Estranged was a stupid, dramatic word, and Nolan hated her for using it, particularly because he supposed it was the word she used for him too. He could imagine Elsa, a few drinks in at the bar, leaning in close to some cowboy or lake rat, saying, Yes, I have one brother but we're estranged.

Or maybe that was wishful thinking. Probably Elsa never spoke of him at all.

Sorry to hear it, Gates said, with the impassivity of someone who has already known something to be true. You can ask Esther about his research. If she knows anything. Most of us don't.

Who lives in the shack on the western shore? Nolan asked. The tilting one at the very edge?

That's Remy St. Gilles, Gates said.

Nolan put both his palms on the tablecloth and tried to remain very calm.

The British science fiction writer? The Asterias series?

Gates nodded. He also has a master's in evolutionary biology and an ABD PhD in cosmology. But yes, the writer.

Nolan had read all eight of the Asterias novels. The series followed a spaceship on a mission to discover a new Goldilocks Zone home on other planets for earthlings, but at every stop, they discovered a new species, evolved "perfectly" for the conditions of that planet. Every time, after some hijinks, the crew decided, no, still not right for us. Ian had read Nolan the first two books, *The Great Space Sea* and *Stardrift*, about Mars and Jupiter, when Nolan was small. Ian had scoffed at all the implausible details (You know a ship could never actually land on Jupiter, right? You know the ice-moss people's agricultural system could never really feed a population that large? Yes, Dad. Read another chapter?), but by and large, even Ian found the books irresistible. The fourth book, about Pluto, was now a collector's edition, because St. Gilles had demanded they stop printing it after Pluto was designated a dwarf planet. The ninth and final book of the series, about Earth, had yet to be released. Readers had been waiting for it for seven years. Nolan had heard that St. Gilles had left London, gone mysteriously missing, and was presumably at work on the novel. But to come here? To Leap's?

Is he working on the last book? Nolan asked.

I wouldn't ask him about that, Gates said. If you really want to talk to people, I'll get you to Esther.

Park Rapids

M aybe Elsa did it because she'd had to rush to grade all the last spelling tests before class that morning and the tests said things like *bux*, which was *books*, and *werl*, which was *world*, and *srpry*, which was either *surprise* or *sorry*. She could use a word that meant both those things at once.

Surprise! (I'm Sorry.)

Elsa put stickers that smelled like strawberries or licorice on all the spelling tests, even though some children had gotten everything wrong.

Maybe Elsa did it because Dylan had left her a month ago to the day and it didn't seem like he was coming back. Or maybe it was because she'd slept hardly at all. Or because it was the last day of school. Maybe it was because Nolan had called her the day before and told her that their father was dead.

(This was a bad day, but it wasn't *the* bad day. Elsa would have to look back much farther to find the first gonging of her unhappiness.)

But probably it was because Elsa thought of James Peacock as a particularly sensitive kid that she thought she should tell him the truth about the dead bird.

James was a quiet, apocalyptic child who did things like stare directly into the sun and then report to Elsa that it made cool fire in his eyes. He was the oldest in the second-grade class and a source of great worry among the teachers: What to Do with James? He'd been held back a year because he "lacked emotional maturity," but Elsa didn't think that was true. Sure, James acted babyish sometimes, but it seemed to her a defensive strategy, as if he knew that growing up was a bum deal and was trying to opt out.

Part of the problem was that James's emotions were enormous and tended to move across the schoolroom like weather systems. Several times a day something would set him off—a wasp trapped between the windowpanes, a crooked carpet square—and he would sob or scream and want to press his damp face against the female teachers' chests. Good news was equally distracting. Whenever James was proud of something he had done, he would climb the highest available structure—a desk, a chair, a slide—and shout out his own name.

In fact, right before they'd found the dead bird, James had won an elaborate playground game involving six jump ropes and promptly climbed to the top of a jungle gym to pump his small fists in the air and shout: James Maxwell Peacock!

He'd fallen off a moment later and scraped himself up.

He trundled over to the teachers.

I am looking for the nurse, he said.

I'll take him, Elsa said, when her co-teacher rolled her eyes.

James didn't cry over falling; this was not the sort of thing that made him sad. He was philosophical about pain. On top of the world one moment, bleeding and headed for the nurse's office the next.

You're being very brave, Elsa told him, and he nodded.

They were as far as the cracked basketball courts when James said, What is that?

There was a turbulence of birds at the three-point line. They complained as Elsa and James waved them off, wings popping, all chattering beaks and squawks.

What was left was most of a dead grackle. It had obviously been hit by a car, one wing at a terrible angle. Its eyes were partly eaten.

What happened to it? James asked.

Let's look and see, Elsa said. This was her first bad idea. But James seemed so calm.

A red tangle of guts had been pulled from the grackle's belly like party streamers. His intact eye was oily. The other was punctured, leaking some kind of fluid. His talons were overextended, as if launching off and away.

Why does it look like that? James asked.

Elsa said, It's dead.

She felt that this was an opportunity to have James reckon with the realities of the world. A teaching moment. He could handle it. If people just told him the truth for once, maybe he could put all the small miseries that set him off into perspective and growing up wouldn't seem so terrible.

Do you think he was really old? James asked.

No, Elsa said, I think he was about… a teenager bird.

Should we take him to the nurse, James asked, and see if she can help him?

Sure, Elsa said, why not.

She scooped up the bird and put it into his hands.

It seemed like a healthy impulse.

They arrived at the nurse's office looking like Hitchcock extras, James already bleeding from his knees and now also carrying the mangled bird, its body in his right hand, the wad of its mangled intestines balanced neatly in the palm of his left. And at this point, Elsa was actually feeling pretty proud of James. She was feeling like this experiment was a success. James had not felt too many feelings or been immature or too sensitive. Here he was, reckoning with something really grown up. The nurse screamed.

For Elsa, the screaming nurse wasn't the worst part. It was the way James Peacock calmly looked at the bird in his hands and then at Elsa. It was as if he had decided that they, calm, bloody, were right, and the nurse was wrong, and as she saw this terrible idea cementing into a lesson in James Peacock's mind, Elsa wanted to say, No, no, please forget this. Don't learn from me. I'm sorry. This was the wrong answer. I am always the wrong answer.

———

If it weren't the last day of school, I'd make you take a leave of absence, her principal had said.

I don't know what I was thinking, said Elsa.

Just have a good, long summer, the principal said.

———

At the bar that night, the teachers celebrated the end of the school year, and they could not stop laughing at Elsa for what they considered a kind of ballsy last-day stunt. It was a shitty bar. They'd been feeding quarters into the jukebox all night, trying to get something danceable to come on, but the same sad-sack old country music kept coming out of it, and Elsa suspected they were actually just listening to the bartender's phone. He was young, in his twenties, slinky black t-shirt, skinny ribcage, and a too-large rodeo buckle at his waist. She would have said a standard-issue farm boy, but he had exquisitely beautiful blue-inked tattoos of a squid snaking up his forearms.

Soon, the teachers were drunk.

So when her phone rang again, Elsa picked up ready to tell Nolan that no, she would not help him plan a funeral for a man who obviously didn't want either of them in his life. She pressed a hand to her ear and wandered away from the teachers' table and stood in a back hallway next to crates of soda and a mop.

I need to know if he killed himself, Nolan said. I just don't believe he would have.

Of course he would have, Elsa shouted over the bartender's horrible music.

You owe me.

Don't pull that.

It's true. You owe me more than this, Nolan said. The least you can do is come out and just help me get his stuff and talk to a few people. Figure out what he was working on.

And if he killed himself.

No, no matter how crazy he went, I don't believe he would ever do that. He wasn't like that.

You mean he wasn't like me, Elsa said. You're just mad because I understand why he would do it.

Are you drunk? Nolan asked. Where are you?

It's the last day of school.

So you're free, then.

You're really calling this in? Elsa said. Because I'm telling you, if you're going to pull this I Owe You shit, you only get to do it once. This is it.

Nolan laughed. You think something else is going to come up? That someday I'll be in trouble and be just waiting for you to ride in and—

Okay, okay, okay.

Good.

I hate you.

I know.

Elsa hung up the phone and leaned against the wall. There was math to be done. As children, she and Nolan had always seen each other a couple times a year. Holidays, birthdays, graduations. But then, when everything went wrong—how long ago was it? She had been nineteen, which made him thirteen. Or no, fourteen, because it had been the fall and his birthday had just passed and her twentieth yet to come. Jesus, he'd been fourteen. That was the year their parents forbade them from seeing each other anymore. After that, Nolan called her sometimes. She'd driven down to Carleton once, when he was in college, when he'd begged, which must have been a decade ago. And then at Keiko's memorial. But these were cursory meetings. Since they'd met in earnest? It had been a while. It had been a long time.

———

It was eleven-thirty and the teachers had been on the tequila. The night had acquired its own kind of momentum. They had drunk enough to forget almost everything, and they were feeling good.

Elsa had just returned from the bar with new drinks for everyone when the PE teacher said, Of all the kids, James Peacock. What a basket case.

He's not, Elsa said.

The gym teacher jumped up on his chair and raised his arms.

James Maxwell Peacock! he shouted, and all the other teachers chorused along with him, arms in the air, laughing.

They were still shouting and laughing when Elsa slipped away to the bar's back porch. You couldn't even see the lake from it, just the parking lot. Elsa sat on the railing, legs swinging, and finished her drink.

Poor James Maxwell Peacock, she thought.

Elsa could not be trusted around people, was what she was thinking. Trust your gut, people said. Just be yourself. But whoever had said these things was not thinking about Elsa when they said them. Did not know how far afield her gut could lead her. Every good thing she touched turned—into what? Wounds. Her ideas never panned out. She'd always end up hurting people.

This was why she had to go to Mars. She couldn't bear to look over her shoulder and see one more sad, wounded bird laid out behind her.

Mars began as a joke, a dare to prove to Dylan how little she needed him. How little she needed anything, not one thing on the whole planet.

She and Dylan had watched the *60 Minutes* story about the Mars Origins program together while drinking beers and eating pizza and they'd both been fascinated. Had both laughed about it. People would live in domes? There would be people willing to go, knowing they'd never come back?

I could do it, Elsa said. I don't have so many ties.

Dylan swiped his hand along her thigh.

You're as caught up in this planet as the rest of us, he said.

That's it, I'm going, Elsa said. You heard it here first.

Dylan continued to stroke Elsa's legs as she typed all her information into her phone, requesting materials for Mars from right there on the couch.

Within a week, a packet arrived in the mail. Elsa read it out loud to him over breakfast. She left it between the salt and pepper shakers.

One day Dylan said, Can I throw this away?

No, Elsa said.

Cut it out, Dylan said, which meant she'd got under his skin, which meant she couldn't stop.

By talking about Mars, Elsa hoped she was making Dylan insecure, was making him realize he loved her more than she loved him, because if that were true then Elsa was safe. As long as his side of their love had more ballast to it, she felt in control and like he would not leave. Everyone left Elsa, and so she needed to be sure.

Surprise! (I'm Sorry.)

After she made the first round, Dylan started having dreams. He had a dream about Elsa in an astronaut helmet where he knocked on the shield and could not bear the sight of her face behind glass. He had a dream of Elsa choking to death on red dust. He had a dream where she was floating upside down and eating dehydrated ice cream and missing him while "Space Oddity" played in the background.

Elsa suggested that Dylan had invented these images and that they were not dreams at all.

Dylan suggested that Earth was not over.

When Elsa made the second round of cuts, she received in the mail a pair of undeniably real airline tickets to the Netherlands to interview for the trials.

She showed them to Dylan.

Cut it out, Major Tom, he said.

I'm doing it. I'm going to Mars. I'm serious, she said.

It turned out, this was the last straw. She'd found it.

Kicking her heels against the porch railing on the last day of school, drinking behind this terrible bar, Elsa wanted to cry. Dylan had been gone for a month and her father was dead and she wanted to tell James Peacock he needed to grow the fuck up and cleave every sorry soft bit of himself away, and fast. She wanted to float away to Mars and be held in her spacesuit and map the finite borders of her own longing.

The bartender came outside and lit a cigarette.

You okay?

Elsa nodded and hopped off the railing.

Give me one of those, hey?

As he lit her a cigarette, the bartender's face was suddenly so close it seemed inevitable. Elsa dropped the cigarette from between her lips and kissed him.

Whoa, he said. Elsa moved in closer. She grabbed his belt buckle and twisted it, pulling his jeans tight at the crotch. She bit his neck. He groaned and it sounded like old country from the jukebox.

The bartender grabbed Elsa by the arms and turned her around. The bartender pinned her to the wall. He pressed himself against her, his hands holding her wrists against the vinyl siding that smelled of bleach. He drove his knee between her legs.

Is this what you want? he said.

A truck's lights briefly passed over them as it pulled out of the parking lot, spitting gravel.

You want this? he said again.

But Elsa could not have anything she wanted. The things she wanted were lost or impossible or unnameable or would collapse under the weight of her need for them, so no, she did not want this, but this, at least, she could have, and so it was yes.

Leap's Island

The southside beach Gates took them to was nicer than Ian's. There was surf, and pipers ran along the shore like urgent children. Esther Stein and Gates were neighbors, and both of their shacks were raised on tall stilts, decks built out in front. The steps to the decks were warped in a way that suggested the tide ran up them. Esther had an ancient canoe tied to a post with a mezuzah fixed to it.

Ahoy, Greys! Esther said as they approached.

Esther spoke in the strong honk of a Long Island accent.

The Greys waved at the small, wrinkled woman in a deck chair who was looking at them through binoculars. She sat next to an inflatable baby pool, neon blue, bulbous, and patterned with beach balls.

Hello, Gates, Esther said. I haven't seen you at home much. Are you camping out?

Gates waved at Esther without saying anything and headed for her own house, which had a bright yellow kayak tied out front.

Children, come! said Esther Stein, and the Greys climbed the water-warped stairs to meet her. They were adults, yes, but there was a part of them that longed for someone to make them small again. To send them back in time to when mistakes had not been made and relieve them of their own agency. And so, when Esther called them children, the Greys obeyed. *Children.* It made them young. It made them Ian's.

———

They sat in low chairs next to Esther's patio table with the baby pool on it. They crossed their hands in their laps, trying to be deferential as they had been taught to do with the old and the insane. Esther was eighty if she was a day. In a bin next to her chair were a pad of lined paper, multiple pairs of binoculars, a stopwatch, a mess of pens, and a small device that looked like a miniature fan.

Well, I think it's wonderful you want to talk about your father, Esther said. Such a charming man. Such a loss.

We're mostly interested in his research, Nolan said. Elsa rolled her eyes, but he continued. Did you know much about it?

That's rich, you asking me. Esther poked Nolan in the chest. You're the one who has all his notes.

We aren't biologists, Nolan said. They don't mean much to us.

Esther shrugged. I don't know the specifics, but you've got seven scientists out here trying to show how screwed we all are and then Ian—

Esther cut herself off and lifted her binoculars. They were on a long beaded chain that sparkled pink and green. Elsa suspected Esther had made this chain herself.

Ian what? Elsa asked.

Oh! Esther said, spying something delightful. She handed Elsa a pair of binoculars. Sweetheart, I'm going to need you to help me with a behavior sample. She thrust a pad of paper and stopwatch at Nolan. You log.

Nolan took the stopwatch. It seemed rude not to. We don't really know anything about birds, he said. We just had a few questions about—

Esther gestured to Elsa. Quickly, dear. Do you see them?

Elsa found the binoculars enormously heavy. I don't really know how— she said, although this wasn't strictly true. When she was small, Ian and Ingrid had taken her bird-watching on Sanibel Island several times. Elsa wondered if Leap's had ever reminded Ian of those summers.

Scan the shore over there. Do you see the pair? Esther said.

Elsa lifted the binoculars and scanned. The sight was fuzzy, and it felt as though the lenses were too far apart. Or like her eyes were set too close together. But Elsa pushed the barrels together and twisted the focus and there were the buffleheads, standing on the shore, dripping wet. Their white caps looked smooth, and the green around their necks was striking when wet. Elsa could see beads of water like ornaments in their wings. What had become of the binoculars Ian had given her on Sanibel? They'd been pink, she recalled; she had picked them out at the gift shop, pink instead of functional black, a choice Ian had disapproved of. Still, he had written her initials on the nylon cord in Sharpie, and she remembered feeling inordinately proud of this. To be trusted with equipment.

I see them, Elsa said.

Nolan, are you ready? Esther said.

I don't know, he said. Nolan felt panicked. He liked to be prepared for tasks. He didn't like being bad at things, and without preparation he was bad at most of them.

Just write down whatever I say they're doing, Esther said. Comfort, Resting, Locomotion, Interaction, Alert, or Foraging. There are two ducks, so I'll tell you two things and just write them on a fresh line.

This seems like a lot, Nolan said.

Set the watch, Esther said, and every fifteen seconds, I want you to call out "Mark" and I'll give you data, okay?

I'm ready, Elsa said.

Go, said Esther.

Nolan set the watch. It beeped. At fifteen seconds he said, Mark?

Resting, Resting, Esther said.

Nolan wrote down *Resting*, twice, next to the time on the watch. Mark?

The second bufflehead was pecking at something along the shore.

Resting, Foraging, Esther said.

Because the second one is eating? Elsa said.

Exactly, Esther said.

They went on like this and soon fell into a comfortable rhythm. Elsa found she enjoyed Esther's narration of the ducks' activity.

Locomotion, Locomotion.

Locomotion, Alert.

Locomotion, Foraging, Esther said.

Elsa said, The second one isn't eating. He's biting his feathers.

Good girl, Esther said. Locomotion, Comfort then. He's preening. You take over with your young eyes. I'll check you.

In spite of herself, Elsa was proud. Her arms ached from holding up the binoculars, but she didn't dare put them down or she'd lose her sight of the ducks.

Mark, Nolan said.

Alert, Resting, said Elsa.

Alert, Comfort.

Comfort, Comfort.

Nolan notated the actions. After a while, he realized it would be easier to divide the sheet into two columns, one for each duck, and to list only the first letter of the word Elsa said. He revamped the sheet and between observations he scrawled a key at the top of the page. He numbered out the time slots in increments down the page. It was quicker this way, more efficient.

Foraging, Comfort.

Comfort, Comfort.

Resting, Alert.

The stopwatch beeped. That's it, Nolan said.

Well done, children! Esther said, letting her binoculars rest against her chest.

Elsa put down her binoculars and the immediate world swam up to meet her: Nolan chewing on his pen, sweeping his hair behind his ear as he studied the notes he'd made. How much easier it was to look at something through the scope. Detailed, tiny, and comfortingly far away.

Nolan handed Esther the pad of paper.

What have you done here? Esther said. Is this shorthand?

I made a key, Nolan said. It's much faster, which means it's more accurate too. You could make copies of it even, and just have the template ready to go.

Esther frowned. I'll just transcribe the notes over, don't worry. You did a good job.

But don't you eventually have to log this information anyway? Really, you should have a digital spreadsheet open, with the template in there. That way, you could immediately calculate percentages.

I appreciate the spirit of ingenuity, Esther said, but I've been doing observations this way for twenty years.

Let her do it the way she wants, Nolan, Elsa said.

But it's better this way, he insisted.

Esther laughed. Every generation wants to reinvent the wheel, she said.

I was just trying to help, Nolan said.

Charming, helpful millennials, Esther said, and took out the small fanlike device. She began taking a reading of the wind speed.

Nolan asked, What do millennials have to do with anything?

You're neither of you much like your father, you know, Esther said.

Are you saying we're dumb? Elsa said.

She's saying we're not as smart as Dad, Nolan said.

Well, everyone knows that.

Yeah, but—

Don't even. We're so much dumber than Dad.

Esther sighed at Nolan's sheet and put down the fan, notating something.

Do you need us to do it again? Nolan asked. I can do better notes this time.

Elsa said, Don't be a sore loser.

I'm sorry, Nolan said. Are you under the impression you just won?

It's not really a win/lose outcome, Esther said. It's data collection. She was now staring through a tiny black sight at the ducks.

What exactly are you trying to get out of this? Elsa asked.

Information about shifts in the ducks' behavior, Esther said. To support my theories.

You really moved here for these ducks? Elsa asked.

Nolan handed back his stopwatch, but Elsa found she didn't want to give up her binoculars.

Everyone says they moved for the ducks, Esther said. But it's not for nothing that you wind up out here. We're all a bunch of old kooks, if you ask me. Don't tell the others I said that. They've been trying to kick me out for years, but I'm the only one who publishes anything, so they can't.

What have you been publishing? Elsa asked.

Bird counts. And an analysis of mallard migration shifts last year. They fired me from the Audubon Society board in ninety-eight, but I got my degree at Cornell, and the alumni community is tight, so some people will still publish me.

Cornell? Elsa said.

Don't act so surprised, sweetheart, Esther said, it's unbecoming.

It's just, if you went to Cornell, what are you doing here?

So Esther Stein told them her story. Everyone on Leap's had one.

———

A lifelong birder, Esther Stein had a PhD in ecology and evolutionary biology from Cornell University. She was a vice president and chief scientist on the board of the New York Audubon Society. She could have taught anywhere, but chose to teach environmental biology at a high school in Ronkonkoma, because she loved where she lived and loved children. She often received letters from former students about the hikes they had taken and creatures they had seen; leaves and bark rubbings fell out of the envelopes. Her students' innate curiosity and enthusiasm for the natural world, Esther claimed, was what kept her going.

But recently, the children were changing.

In her Enviro Bio classes, Esther was famous for making her students run to their various study sites to maximize class time. She shouted: Be light, be quick, keep up or you will be culled from the herd! Previously, people had found this charming.

But this winter, when she made the students run out to the field of their second-rate football team and take off their mittens and press their hands into the snow to imitate the tracks made by different types of animals, the students complained. They showed her their hands, wet and red. It hurts, they said.

Everything good hurts, Esther wanted to say, but relented.

Let me see your fisher cat tracks and then you can go back inside, Esther said. And the kids toppled over and waddled in their designer coats until they'd made some semblance of the tracks. Then they pointed at the divots in the ice crust and said, Can we go now?

Can we go now. It broke Esther's heart.

Esther decided she needed to take action. The problem was winter, she decided. The children were not unenthusiastic; they were just short on sunlight. They needed a reminder that spring was coming.

That day, it was windy. Twenty degrees. Two boys in the last row of the classroom kept using a pencil to lift the back of one of the girls' sweaters so they could see the top of her thong. The other students were texting under the table, as if she could not see this, as if Esther were somehow not a person, with eyes, at the front of the room.

Outside, Esther said.

I have a doctor's note, the girl in the thong said.

I said outside, *now*.

Esther's plan was to march them up to the ridge, and from there they would see the whole of town laid out in white-blanketed patches. She would show them the thawing lake. From the shore, the lake still looked frozen, but from above, a black melted pit appeared in the middle. The first sign that spring was nigh. She would give them this moment of hope. It was a forty-minute class period. She had just enough time to hike them there and back.

Except for one kid in rain boots, the students did not have proper footwear. One of the girls was wearing yellow canvas sneakers. One boy wore boat shoes with no socks.

How did you even get to school like that? Esther said.

I'm just moving from one heated space to another, the boy said.

Esther had a large purple down coat ribbed in fat sections. She had a fleece neck warmer and an ear band and thick gloves and a hat with a knitted flower on it. Her wire-rimmed glasses fogged when they pushed the door open and headed outside.

They marched silently at first, dutifully, but as Esther continued to give them no idea what they were walking toward, and the hill grew steep, they revolted. My ankles are so cold, boat shoes said, slipping. This is bullshit, said one of the boys. The girl in the canvas sneakers was quietly crying. But Esther would show them. They would be grateful. This is what it meant to be really alive.

They reached the peak. Twenty-five minutes, longer than Esther had planned on it taking them.

There, she said. And it was just as she hoped. The fields of white. The supreme quiet with the low drone of obscured traffic below. And the black heart of the lake: a wobbly kidney-shaped hole thawed through at the center. Irrefutable.

Do you see? Esther said.

See what? the students said.

The thaw is coming, Esther said. Look.

The children looked.

We walked all the way up here to look at a motherfucking lake? a boy said.

A hole in a lake, the crying girl said miserably.

But one of the boys, the only one wearing boots, was staring at the hole in the lake like it might save his life. He was a sickly kid, hacking with bronchitis all winter, Esther now remembered. He was the only one who looked at her, radiant, and nodded. Justin, she remembered, his name was Justin.

For Esther, Justin was enough. Fuck the rest of them. Just this one kid.

As they headed back down the slope, the children grumbled that she'd lost her mind and they were going to tell their parents about this. They heard the bell ring from the schoolyard. They were running late, but they were almost back.

But then, Justin, her beacon of hope, fell and went sliding down the slope. He would have been fine had the stream not been at the bottom. Had the stream top not partially frozen over and his leg not broken the ice crust when he hit. His boot plunged into the water of the tributary stream, the heavy coldness filling it, and he yelled. It was the first real noise she'd heard out of him all year. He was pulling and pulling to get his boot off, but the weight of the water was too much and the suction of it was keeping him in. The water must have been freezing.

Justin, calm down, Esther said. We can get you out if you stay calm.

Help him! one of the other boys yelled.

He's going to be fine, Esther said. Just let me empty his boot out. When she'd got him free, she saw that the crust of ice had cut his leg. Just a little, but there was blood. She poured the freezing stream water from his boot; there was more than she'd expected. Justin cried when she returned his wet, empty boot and told him he needed to put it on. We'll be back soon, and you'll be fine, Esther said. We'll get you warmed up in the nurse's office.

They returned to the school building twenty minutes late.

Justin was fine. He was sick for a week, but Esther didn't believe that could really have been a result of the boot incident anyway. Justin's mother turned out to be less reticent than he was. She called the office and told them Esther had death marched those children in the snow in the middle of winter.

People can go outside in winter, Esther said. It's not toxic outside, it's just cold. But at the end of the year, it was made clear that perhaps Esther's time for retirement had come. They had been wanting to cancel Environmental Biology for years.

That summer, at a board meeting for the New York Audubon Society, Esther was slated to present in her capacity as chief scientist. Her presentation concerned the work of a group of scientists studying a population of undowny buffleheads in the Gulf, whose research she thought might be applicable to their own local species of duck. A study was in order, Esther claimed, and she hoped the board would greenlight the project so it could be determined whether northern species closely related to the undowny bufflehead might also be showing evidence of backward speciation.

After some awkward laughter at what the other board members assumed to be a joke, Esther suggested that this was a bellwether that should not be ignored. It was the beginning of the end.

The board members stopped laughing. Esther was fired the next morning and moved to Leap's three months later.

———

It's because of all these kids and their video games, Esther said. They never go outside anymore. They can't identify a tree for shit. Every year, they have less and less to do with the world outside. Their bodies don't even look the same. Pale skinny kids wearing shorts in winter. Soft fat kids bringing me notes saying why they didn't have to go outside. Allergies. Suddenly everyone has allergies and they want me to teach environmental science without ever going out of doors at all. I don't know what our natural habitat is anymore.

My students all have allergies, Elsa said.

Esther sighed. Of course they do, she said.

Do you ever see Duck Number Twelve? Nolan asked, and ignored Elsa when she whipped around to glare at him.

Twelve? Oh, the banding, Esther said. That was your father's thing.

No one else has been banding the ducks? Elsa said. At all?

Esther blew air. Before she could answer, the children heard the flapping of wings. One of the buffleheads came and landed in the plastic kiddie pool on Esther's deck, splashing a little.

One of your friends? Nolan asked.

Shhh! Esther said. She hunched over and gestured for Elsa and Nolan to follow her. They crept as she did, suddenly feeling like disciples.

They stood at the periphery of the baby pool, and the duck tensed like he was going to fly away. They remained still, and eventually the bird began paddling around in the water, his webbed feet tocking rhythmically like a toy's, clearly visible against the pattern of beach balls on the neon baby pool's bottom.

Do you see? Esther said.

See what? Nolan said.

The water, look.

Nolan and Elsa watched, unsure what they were looking for.

The water, Esther repeated.

Nolan squinted. Behind the duck he saw a pearling in the water. There were beads forming on the surface in its wake. Oils, separating from water, warping and bending and beading away.

Esther lunged at the duck and grabbed him around the middle. He quacked vociferously, but Esther lifted him, shaking the creature so water dripped from his tail and back into the pool. The duck was unbanded, Elsa noted. Not one of their father's ducks. Though what difference would it make if it was?

Esther inspected the water, the duck, and then violently threw him over the railing. Elsa squeaked, but the duck picked up flight and took off, honking.

Jesus Christ, Elsa said. Did you need to do that?

What is that? Nolan asked. In the water?

Oils mostly. Waterproofing. That's what keeps their feather down from getting wet. They're losing it. Shedding it every swim. Esther pulled a plastic flacon with a rubber stopper from her pocket and dipped it into the water, collecting the duck oil. She plugged the flacon and handed it to Nolan.

Elsa rolled her eyes. For a minute, she'd started to believe Esther was sane because Elsa's students also seemed soft and strange these days. What had happened to all the paste eaters and bug collectors? Gone. At show-and-tell, students brought in handheld games and princess franchise merchandise. So, yes, Elsa saw what Esther saw, but it had nothing to do with evolution, or ducks. It had to with Elsa, failing at her job. Because what business did she have telling her students this world would provide them the safety and happiness and love that Elsa knew probably wasn't waiting for them at all? Her job had started to feel like lying, and the lies Elsa told the children were the same lies she'd believed when she was small, before Ian left and Nolan came. Elsa had been promised the world was otherwise, and sometimes, she thought that if she'd only been told better truths at the outset, she could have been ready for every rotten thing that came later.

Nolan lifted the flacon. Inside, the oil beaded in the water. He turned the tube over and the golden beads drifted to the surface.

Why are they losing the oil? Nolan asked.

Esther said, My analyses have been inconclusive. I think we've lost our biological imperative to adapt to environments. Living the way we have for so long, it's stopped impacting selection. We're no longer good at adapting to things in the natural world because it's too hard to tell which parts are real anymore—as she said this, she gestured to the baby pool—so we don't know what to adapt to.

You're saying this is happening to us? Nolan asked, lifting the vial.

I don't know what it is we're losing, Esther said, but it's got to be worse than this.

Nolan looked mind-blown as he handed the vial back to Esther.

Esther, Elsa said. Our father, was he depressed? The police said his death was an accident but—

Oh no, honey, Esther said. Ian wouldn't have killed himself. It wasn't in his nature.

It's just that you seem to think everything is going so wrong and I wondered if he—

Esther shook her head. None of us would be on this island if we had the nerve to just kill ourselves.

She turned the flacon over and watched the oil droplets migrate, pushing past one another to the other end of the tube.

He was such a brilliant man.

———

On the hike back, they were quiet. It was nearing three o'clock and the ground steamed. Nolan stopped to catch his breath, bracing his hands against his thighs. Elsa snapped a hair elastic around her wrist, watching him.

I wish you'd stop talking about Dad killing himself, Nolan said. You're upsetting people.

Everyone who lives here is already totally and deeply upset, Nolan. Dad was obviously some kind of upset too. He wouldn't have been here if he hadn't become the kind of weird misanthrope who believes ducks are spelling out doom and millennials are ruining the species with video games and—

Actually, so far it seems like everyone thought he was just a wonderful guy, Nolan said. Which frankly is weirder than hearing he was suicidal.

Elsa sighed. She could smell her own body. Her armpits, her cunt, the oil in her hair. She would have to go swimming again or try the showers in the Lobby. Yes, it was weirder, but that didn't mean he didn't do it. What Elsa wanted to say was that she was never surprised when someone killed himself. She was only surprised by her own animal perseverance day after day. What Nolan was failing to understand was how much their father had been lugging around with him for so long *because of them.* How there was no way Ian didn't blame himself. How it was a miracle he had lasted this long.

What she said was, Just because Ian seemed happy doesn't mean he wouldn't have killed himself.

Jesus Christ, Nolan said. Okay but, like, what was that in the water? There was *something* in the water.

Are you that stupid? Elsa said. It could be anything! Boat diesel the duck swam through or natural oils from a plant. I mean, I don't even know for a fact that all ducks don't go around leaking oil all the time. What the hell do I know about ducks?

There was that David Attenborough segment about the undownys from the Reversalists' website, Nolan said. He's not a Reversalist.

Wasn't that special called *On the Fringe*?

But it's true they're less waterproof, Nolan said, pointing at Elsa like he'd caught her. We *saw* that duck drying himself on the porch.

That's not how evolution works, Nolan! If the ducks were actually going backward, they would just be born with feathers that were less and less waterproofed every generation, Elsa said. They wouldn't be actively leaking their oils into Esther's kiddie pool.

Nolan shoved his hands in his pockets.

How are you the child of scientists?

I don't know, Nolan said. I don't know why I'm not like them.

Maybe that's for the best, Elsa said, and started walking again. Nolan hustled after her. There are other ways to be.

Other than brilliant?

———

They arrived back at Shack Seven. The water along the shore was scattered with small fallen leaves.

I'm getting in, Elsa said. I'm dying.

Before she'd even unbuttoned her shorts, Nolan had pulled his shirt over his head and kicked off his shoes. He dove into the shallow water, and it was clear enough that Elsa could see the whole form of him, hands pointed out in front, black hair streaming behind, shorts waterlogged, as he shot through the weak tide, graceful in spite of himself.

Nolan seemed, to Elsa, a picture of normalcy and health. He wasn't brilliant, but he was fine. Wasn't he? Every moment they were together, she could not help but watch to see if he was okay, and for every moment he was, Elsa wanted to run away before she had a chance to learn otherwise. She let Jinx out, and the dog raced along the shore, peeing on the reeds.

Elsa's pink tiger was tied to one of the shack stilts with a nylon cord. She undid the knot, undressed to her suit, and waded with the raft into the water. She hugged the tiger to her chest, her legs paddling, her back warm in the sun.

Nolan swam toward her underwater, trailing silver bubbles from his nose that ran behind him in chains. He broke the surface just next to her, and his eyebrows were mussed. She reached out from the float and straightened them, one at a time, with her finger.

Nolan grabbed on to the tiger float and hung from the other side. Just tell me once that you're one hundred percent certain Dad killed himself, and I'll stop asking, he said.

She could feel how badly he needed her to tell him some kind of lie about their father, but Elsa was done with that. She wanted out of the business of comforting half-truths.

Underneath the float, Nolan tangled his legs with Elsa's. Their shins knocked and then Nolan caught her legs between his like a vise. He squeezed and Elsa felt an unwelcome clutch at the base of her stomach.

They stared at each other across the float. There was so much that was not allowed that the island seemed willing to permit. Things underwater. Things offshore.

Elsa stretched her legs and made to pull them free, but Nolan clamped on to her again.

Elsa said, The alternative is that he went swimming in a storm.

But at least if it were an accident he still believed in his research, Nolan said.

I guess, Elsa said. Nolan's knee was pressed hard against her thigh and she was lightheaded. This island was a ruse. It was a way of pretending the world was other than it was.

Stop, Elsa said.

Nolan released her legs. He drifted from the float and burbled water. If he still believed in his research, he had a good reason to leave us, to come here, Nolan said.

Elsa's float began to drift away in the current. She kicked away from him.

Nolan grabbed the tiger paw and pulled her back.

This matters, Nolan said. Please don't pretend not to care.

I'm just trying to be realistic, Elsa said. She pinched the plastic seam of the float.

You said you'd help.

There were two fat brown fish metronoming in the water beneath Elsa, unworried by their feet. She pointed her toe at them, and they adjusted course.

I just don't know what to do about it, Nolan. I feel like you want me to take care of things, but this whole situation is fucking weird. I don't understand what you want from these people. I don't understand what you want from me.

The what was hard to pin down. Nolan felt as if there was something Elsa had of his, and he wanted it back. Some long-missing something that she had stolen from him and which would be returned only if Nolan could name it. His sister's shoulders were burned, a red saddle across their breadth, and he stood up on the sandy bottom and pressed her sunburn, dragging a line across her shoulders with his finger and watching the skin turn white, then flush.

He looked so morose that Elsa actually felt sorry for him.

She said, Honestly, the thing that really bothers me is the clothes.

Nolan had thought of this too but was surprised that Elsa had. It felt like a private detail only he would notice.

Their father's clothes had been left in a bundle the size of a baby on the beach. The clothes were rumpled together, and there was a kind of horror in this for the children that was not unlike what the sight of a damaged body would have prompted. Because Ian Grey would never have left his clothes that way. He was a man who believed that everything had its place and should be returned to it. He trained the children to always put away their things. A pair of underwear left on the bathroom floor, a book crooked open across a chair's arm, any object not properly returned to its place was, to Ian, like a sentence left half-complete, trailing off in ellipses. If Ian had gone swimming, he would have folded his clothes. They would have found them stacked neatly on the beach.

I didn't think you'd remember that about him.

The sun was sinking toward the waterline, its orange-popsicle color bleeding across the clouds like a stain. I remember, Elsa said. As well as you, anyway. She lifted herself up on her elbows. The float wobbled.

When Elsa remembered Ian, she remembered him in her childhood living room, at the farmhouse, playing the Steinway. Nothing solemn. Scott Joplin, maybe. He would do the jaunty little head bob he did when he thought he was playing especially well. Elsa remembered sitting on the floor, next to his non-pedal foot, and pressing her ear against his leg as he played. That piano was long gone. Gone like the farmhouse. Gone like Ian. Maybe it didn't matter if he'd drowned or killed himself. Her father had been taken from her over and over again, and Elsa was tired of coming up with new ways to suffer in his absence.

———

That night, they made no pretenses about the sleeping bag and slept cupped like shells in their father's bed. They'd been sleeping an hour when Elsa heard a noise at the door. The handle jiggling.

You just have to lift it while you do that, she heard a voice say. No, you have to stick it in, then lift it so it will catch.

Nolan sat up, awake. He looked at her.

Hello? Elsa said.

Is someone in there? the voice said.

Shut up, just get the lock, the other voice said.

Yes, someone is in here! Elsa shouted. Nolan wished Elsa wouldn't shout. He wished they had said nothing and could hide.

Fuck, the voice said.

Let's go, let's go.

Elsa got up. She was wearing a tank top and underwear and no bra. She strode over to the door and flung it open, turning on a Coleman lantern as she went. Jinx was up and growling low, curled around the side of Elsa's legs.

There were two men running down the ramp.

Elsa, close the door, they're leaving, Nolan said.

What do you want?! Elsa shouted.

Palo Alto

I t was the week Ian lost his job at Stanford that Keiko first
saw the rat in the lemon tree. They were still living in Palo Alto
that summer, even though Ian would not be returning to the
Biology department in the fall, his tenure having been denied after
he'd written an apologist's defense of a recent article published by
the Reversalists. The op-ed appeared on a pop-science website,
and the headline the editor had attached to it read: "Just Because
They're Crazy Doesn't Mean They're Wrong."

Have you seen this? Keiko said, thrusting her phone at their son.
She was a microbiome researcher. The Greys had prided them-
selves on being a kind of macro/micro power couple for as long as
Nolan could remember.

Nolan was twenty-six and lived in San Francisco and was beginning to regret coming home for the weekend. He had come to complain about his job and be coddled by his parents. No, Nolan had
not seen this.

I never said that, Ian said, taking his glasses off. What I told
her was—

The trouble is that you told her anything at all, Keiko said. Half
of this country doesn't even believe in evolution. Why would you
muddy things with nonsense?

It's not nonsense if it's true.

Your father is losing his mind, Keiko told her son.

———

That was the night Keiko saw the rat, Milo.

Nolan named the rat in an effort to lighten the mood, though both Ian and Keiko had frowned at him when he did it, which at least made him feel as if things were normal again. Keiko had been in the yard picking lemons, thinking to squeeze a wedge over their salmon dinner, and she'd just grasped one when she saw the rat—gray, slinky-bodied, white gullet and long whiskers—trying to disengage a fruit of his own. He touched the lemon all over with his paws, grasping at it like a too-large dance partner he could not quite accommodate.

The sight of his touching and touching the skin of the fruit repulsed Keiko. She dropped her lemon, walked inside, sat at the table, and put her face in her hands.

Then she made her demands.

Ian told her that where there was one rat, there were probably many. Statistically, he said, to get rid of one rat would do nothing.

Nolan knew that what Keiko actually wanted was for Ian not to have aligned himself with crackpots, not to have humiliated himself by losing his job. But this was impossible, and so she was desperate to extract from him instead an infinity of smaller, possible things.

Get rid of it, Keiko said.

Ian complied, less out of understanding and more because she had posed to him a problem, and he was in the business of devising solutions.

He bought a Havahart trap.

At dinner, they ate their salmon quietly and without lemon.

That night, Ian set out to catch Milo.

Keiko had gone off to bed at ten o'clock, in a mood. Defensively, Nolan had tried to do the same. If he could go to sleep now, he could make today end, and in turn tomorrow would come quicker and he could flee to the city. Perhaps his parents, who never fought, would work things out and their life would return to normal while he wasn't looking.

He was half-asleep on the couch when he heard Ian in the kitchen: cupboards clicked, a glass rang on the counter, a cork popped free of a wine bottle. Ian crept past Nolan's pullout couch with a glass of wine and a flashlight.

Nolan got up. He was wearing boxer briefs and a Giants t-shirt worn soft and holey at the armpits. He had grown his hair out again and was vain about it. He'd tied it up in a small bun for sleeping, but now pulled it loose. He poured himself a glass of a decent Petit Syrah he couldn't believe Ian would open for just himself and grabbed another flashlight from the kitchen junk drawer.

Ian was sitting in a plush chaise longue. The red patio tiles were still warm from the day.

Nolan sat on the chaise next to his father, balancing his wineglass on one steepled knee. After a moment, Ian clinked his glass against Nolan's.

The tree was overgrown, fat lemons dangling like moons over both sides of the fence. The plastic Havahart was balanced on one post, baited with peanut butter. Next door, their neighbors' mother, an elderly woman with dementia, had been sent out to smoke her last cigarette of the day beneath her grandchildren's unused basketball hoop. From beyond the fence they could hear her quietly talking to herself in Spanish. At the edge of the patio, Keiko's potted succulents were purple in the semidarkness. The rosemary border was oily and fragrant.

They played their flashlight beams along the top of the fence where the lemons hung, two spotlights dancing around a stage, anticipating a marquee performer. Nolan ran his fingers through his hair as they drank and waited.

The rat appeared.

Nolan was quiet, but danced his flashlight rapidly to draw his father's attention. Ian caught Milo in his beam. Nolan noticed the rat's pink nose and pearl-gray fur and thought he looked quite clean. The rat trotted efficiently along the rails, sniffing the lemons, then caught the scent of peanut butter. As Milo hesitated, deciding, Nolan found himself wishing he would avoid his fate. Go for the wildness of stolen lemons.

The rat let out a small squeak as the door to the Havahart snapped shut behind him.

Ian picked up the trap.

What are you going to do with him? Nolan asked.

Release him in the strip mall.

What if he doesn't like it?

He's a rat, he'll like it, Ian said.

Nolan knew Ian didn't really believe this and felt sorry for him. He'd never felt sorry for his father before. Keiko and Ian had always been so competent that, even in his late twenties, Nolan considered it agreed upon between the three of them that he was the one to be sorry for—it had been a heavy pour of the Syrah; Nolan threw pity parties when he drank—but really, what was all this for? Maybe it was crazy, but was it wrong if Milo wanted to waltz with fruit when the moon was clear? Wanted to preen his pearl-gray fur and forget the rest of the world as he rolled in Keiko's rosemary and admired himself? Wanted to sink his teeth into a lemon's neck and suck all the juice from the evening?

Just Because They're Crazy Doesn't Mean They're Wrong.

He looks quite healthy, Ian said, inspecting Milo through the mesh.

Must be all those lemons.

Ian jangled his car keys.

———

Nolan got into the passenger seat still wearing his boxers. Brought his wine. Ian gently buckled the boxed rat into the backseat.

They drove, their windows down, the night sweet. A Sibelius

concerto was playing quietly from the stereo. Nolan sipped his wine, drinking in the car a slight thrill.

They didn't talk, but as they drove, Ian began a kind of monologue addressed to Milo. He spoke to the rat as if Ian were a mafioso driving a failed accomplice to the bus depot. He told Milo that their current arrangement was untenable. He had no personal problem with him. He would bring Milo to their destination safely, and no harm would come to him provided he stayed there. But Ian did not want to see Milo again. Not in his yard, not in his lemon tree. If Milo returned, well, then there would be trouble. Ian couldn't promise Milo he would not come to harm if he returned. Was he understanding him? *Capishe?*

Nolan inspected his father. He knew Ian would have spoken like this whether or not he'd had company in the car, and Nolan found this charming. But he was also thinking about Keiko saying that Ian was losing his mind. Keiko, so adamant that this rat who had crept into her garden was the thing spoiling it. (But surely things had been spoiled in other ways before. Surely Nolan's unhappiness had not started with the rat.)

They slowed, pulling into a strip mall, a line of dumpsters behind its restaurants. Several other rats scattered as they approached and idled, but they did not look so clean, so nice, as Milo.

The open driver's door dinged as Nolan watched Ian set the Havahart by the dumpsters and unlatch it. He heard his father softly talking to the rat again but could not make out his words. Milo did not leave the trap.

Nolan finished his wine and cradled the empty bulb in his hands.

Leap's Island

What do you want, Elsa repeated, holding the Coleman lantern high, so it cast half her face in light.

The men stopped. Looked at each other, then started back up the ramp.

We heard Dr. Grey was dead, one of them said.

We didn't think you'd be in here, said the other. There are rooms at the Lobby that regular people stay in.

Who are you? Elsa said.

Jim, said the one.

Mick, said the other, swiping off a faded green baseball cap that read FARMS = FOOD.

We're sorry for scaring you, Jim said.

I wasn't scared. Elsa gestured for the men to come in but remained in the doorway so they had to brush past her naked legs as they entered. Elsa felt them sizing her up, but she didn't mind. Elsa was never afraid when she was meant to be. Stillness was frightening, because it meant you were waiting for the other shoe to drop. So long as you ran headlong into trouble, it could never take you by surprise.

———

They were rusty-haired with Irish blue eyes, but leathery and tanned. They were lean and their legs were so ropy it felt indecent to look at them. Both men wore t-shirts that read HERITAGE FARM NETWORK.

Mick and Jim sat at the table while Elsa poured vodka and pineapple juices and Nolan introduced himself.

Brothers? Nolan asked. Mick nodded.

Siblings? Jim said tentatively, pointing from Nolan to Elsa, as if it seemed unlikely.

Elsa said, What exactly did you want from the house?

The brothers looked at each other. His logbook, Mick said. Everyone on the island wants to publish, but no one's collected any data worth a damn. We thought if we could give it to Mitchell, it might buy us some goodwill.

We were also hoping for a note, Jim said. He had opened one of the Ziploc baggies of undowny feathers on the table and now began arranging them in size order.

A suicide note? Elsa said.

He would have left one, if he were drowning himself, Jim said.

What makes you so sure? Elsa said. She didn't like these boys theorizing about her father. If there was anything to be theorized, she and Nolan would have done it already.

We took him out on our boat for count days, Mick said. We were close.

Well, there's no note, Elsa said, gesturing around at the shack. For you or anyone else.

Then it was an accident, Jim said. Plain as that. He'd now arranged a dozen tiny feathers on the table in a kind of mandala wheel.

Nolan was pacing around the shack, obviously irritated, tripping over the edges of the braided rug. Jinx followed at his heels.

That doesn't mean anything, Elsa said. You don't have to leave a note to kill yourself. She couldn't stand the way people on this island described Ian so intimately. The man she had known had always felt a million miles away, and it made Elsa feel dizzy and furious.

You seem young to be Reversalists, Nolan said.

Truth, Mick said. That's the trouble. Most people out here, they came to get away from us.

Us? Elsa said.

Millennials, man, Jim said. Millennials.

———

Mick and Jim Riordan were, unbelievably, New Yorkers. Born a year apart to a trust-funded expressionist painter father and a "pure math" mathematician mother, they went to a prestigious private school where, based on the promise of their finger-painting and precocious reading skills, they were subjected to a series of intelligence tests that soon confirmed what their parents had always known would be true: their children were geniuses.

They graduated from high school together at ages twelve and thirteen; from Penn, magna cum laude, at fifteen and sixteen, having written a joint honors thesis about the evolutionary advantages of the pupa cage-building practices of the Arctiinae moth (as compared to the small log-cabin structures of the bagworm moth's more attractive but ultimately inferior larval shelters). They were immediately accepted to the PhD program at Stanford to pursue their research into the evolution of larval shelters. And they would have, except that the year Mick turned twenty and Jim nineteen, the wooly dusk moth went extinct.

The brothers had wanted to study the wooly dusk moth because it had, to their mind, one of the most advantageous larval structures. It built, in essence, a perfect geodesic dome of leaf bits, attached and shellacked by an excretion that rendered the leafy dome shiny, impregnable, and perfectly disguised. The dome was usually found suspended by a viscous filament, leaflike, from a branch. But deforestation in Brazil had cut the wooly dusk moth's habitat in half, their number precipitously declining, and when the moth suddenly appeared on the endangered species list, it became impossible for the brothers to get specimens. Mick and Jim were beside themselves with the news. Because of their dissertations, but also because they loved the genius little builder.

They were drinking beers in their shared apartment one night, debating what course to take, when Mick said, Let's just go. We could observe it in the wild.

Much to the dismay of their advisors, the brothers left in the middle of the spring semester of their first year of the PhD, dropping from classes, TAships, and two different research projects they'd been assisting, and went on an observational trip to Brazil. The brothers had no delusions that they would actually find a now-endangered wooly dusk moth in the wild, but they had to see what they could learn before the wild was gone.

They trekked with a guide from the Sao Paulo Biosciences Institute for a month, then extended the trip to three. They saw more species in those three months than they'd seen in the whole of their careers. Cocoons made from what looked like indigo wool. Dusty wingspans as wide as a man's face. Phosphorescent eyespots. They saw species they knew nothing about, and fully half of them were on the verge of extinction because of deforestation. The wooly dusk moth itself never manifested, and by the same time the following year, it was declared extinct, the particular tree it made its larval cages from a prime victim of logging.

Mick and Jim returned to Stanford in the fall with enough observational notes on rare and endangered species to write about for the rest of their careers. But when they thought about returning to the classrooms, the labs, they couldn't bear it. What was the point of studying these things when a year from now they might not even exist anymore?

They considered moving to Brazil. They considered becoming advocates for forest preservation or anti-logging lobbyists (child geniuses often have an inflated sense of their own capabilities). They considered joining the Earth Liberation Front. But ultimately, they were so depressed by these conversations they decided to do nothing.

They came into their trust funds at age twenty-one and used the money to buy a farmstead in Ohio, where they started the Heritage Farm Network, trying to backward-engineer frankenseeds, contaminated by drifting Monsanto GMO species, back to their original DNA. They grew and cultivated a dozen heritage seed strands. They sold their heritage seeds to other farmers and their produce to a local CSA. They lived alone, ignored phone calls from their parents and from professors who said they were squandering their talents. They spent most nights watching horrifying documentaries about the vanishing honeybees and fracking. They compulsively read every environmental doom-and-gloom think piece published and were infamous on a dozen different conspiracy subreddits. They had always been casual weed smokers, but around this time, they made it a daily habit.

Their appetite for consuming information grew exponentially, and their belief in the possibility of doing anything about the problems they researched dwindled. They were manic, ravenous, despairing, and high. They googled and googled more bad news.

And then, following a particularly pessimistic thread of internet forums down the rabbit hole, they found the Reversalists' website.

They knew it was their place. They sold the farm. They ignored Mitchell's application procedures. They packed up a seed kit, a bag of clothing between them, and bought a boat.

When they arrived at the island landing, the first person they saw was Ian. He had thinning sandy hair and glasses, and when they spied him, skinny-chested and shirtless on the wharf, the collars of at least three different sunburns were outlined on his chest.

That your boat? Ian asked.

The brothers nodded.

Then we're going to be friends.

A meeting, chaired by Mitchell, was called to deal with their unexpected arrival, because even though the islanders were egalitarian in most things, it was Mitchell's island and it was Mitchell's money, and so he dictated who belonged. Despite the small draw of his movement, Mitchell refused to let in just anybody. The brothers had ignored the application procedure. Typical millennials.

Most of the islanders considered the brothers members of a younger generation they were trying to forget existed. In fact, most of the Reversalists' research had started not with the ducks, but with their abiding sense that something had gone unstoppably wrong with the world, and that the generation of young people rising up were the cause of it. At best, the millennials were stupid, lazy, entitled narcissists who could not be trusted. At worst, Mick and Jim and the whole of their generation were an evolutionary step backward for humanity. An insurrection of idiots who would trample everything the Greatest Generation and the Boomers had achieved and doom the species permanently.

The Reversalists felt this to be true, and so they set about proving it. They would find, in the undowny bufflehead, a science to match their sentiments.

They wanted to send the brothers back immediately. To deport them. And this was when Remy St. Gilles suggested the non-millennial policy. Everything that was wrong with *out there*, St. Gilles said, was because of millennials. Millennials had been trolling him about his books for years, demanding faster publications and e-books and generally ruining his career. Millennials didn't take anything seriously.

Like your old asses aren't the ones who fucked everything up in the first place, Jim said.

Like you all weren't smoking cigarettes and building SUVs and making bubble after bubble and destroying the world economy, Mick said.

Like you guys aren't the ones who clearcut forests and removed mountaintops and drilled and drilled, Jim said.

Literature, St. Gilles said. Who killed literature?

But it wasn't only St. Gilles who wanted the millennials out.

Gwen Manx, the reproductive scientist, called them a sexual threat. She wore baggy athletic shorts and a gray t-shirt with a picture of a horse on it and chainsmoked Virginia Slims. The way she looked at the boys with her arms crossed and her cigarette piping upward, they could not imagine they seemed very threatening to her but felt too timid to say so.

Esther Stein, ever traumatized by her years as a teacher, wasn't crazy about the idea of the brothers either and worried they'd be wild, possibly noisy. They're going to want to install the internet, Esther said.

It was only Ian who'd motioned they could stay.

These boys have degrees from Penn and could be at Stanford right now. But they want to be here. They have experience with reverse engineering seed cultures. You'd be foolish to let them go. If you can't stand these two members of the next generation, boys who came to you, who believe in what you believe, then who can you stand?

St. Gilles had snorted at this.

If we hate our own children, Ian continued, it's no wonder everything is running backward. That is precisely the opposite of how things are supposed to work.

Mitchell had been silent. They're farmers, Dr. Grey. They're no longer scientists and this is a community devoted to research.

You're not a researcher, Ian said. And no one spoke for a good long while after that. Because Mitchell took great pride in spearheading the "scientific" endeavors of the island. He proposed experiments and selected which papers might be sent out for publication and stopped by people's shacks to offer feedback on their work. And they all let this happen and said nothing, though everyone knew, of course, that Mitchell was the wealthy son of a wealthy son of a real estate developer and hotelier, and everyone knew that he was a commune kid who'd never left the island except for a few lost years as a teenage junkie, but everyone also knew that Mitchell had a temper on him and didn't appreciate it when people pointed out any of these facts.

That's right, Mitchell said finally. But I pay the bills.

Everyone laughed tentatively.

Unless you can prove you have some research need specific to the undowny bufflehead that validates your residence here, gentlemen, you'll have to go.

They'll be my research assistants, Ian said. I'm in need of help.

And what exactly is it that you're working on, Ian? Mitchell said. You skipped our past two performance-review meetings.

My work is still in its early stages, Ian said. With the boys' help, I'll be able to report back to you quite soon, I'm sure.

And so the boys moved in, and this was how they came to be indebted to Ian.

It was Ian who suggested the nesting pod project. True buffleheads nested in holes made by flickers and woodpeckers up north, species that didn't exist on the island. So when the original ducks had been imported to the island, they'd had to find alternative cavities for nesting. In the Reversalists' time, the buffles had been found nesting in everything from dead oak cavities to suitcases, shipping boxes, soup pots, wardrobes, mail cubbies, empty ovens, and oversized decorative vases. They were scattered across the island, with no central nesting ground.

It's not exactly larval cages, Ian said, but maybe you could design them new nesting structures? In one concentrated area?

The brothers began sketching. Work revived their enthusiasm, and soon they felt that nesting practices might be the key to the whole thing. Maybe it was because the ducks lived in these totally unnatural spaces that something was turning back their evolution. Mick and Jim had grown up in a New York City penthouse forty-five floors above the street, on a block where northern mockingbirds imitated car alarms and sirens, singing their ruined world back to the men who had built it.

At their first all-island meeting, the brothers presented their sketches to the others. It was a series of geodesic domes made of lumber and canvas, fusing the designs of two larval cage structures. Pods for the ducks to nest in.

Jim said, If you live in an apartment complex long enough, you don't even feel like a person anymore, because you never really have to interact with the natural world or see anyone. You don't have to work together with people.

You don't commune, Mick said.

Mitchell said, Do you really want to talk to me about communes?

But the sketches were good, and no one could deny the buffles needed a better nesting ground. So the brothers were given funding for supplies and started building the pods.

In the same spirit, the brothers were also the ones who started farming in the Lobby. They called it the Hippie Reeducation Program. They taught the generation who had gone to Woodstock and believed in the hypothetical recycling of materials and the practical smoking of weed how to compost with earthworms. How to indoor-irrigate. How to grow tomatoes upside down in hanging baskets that saved space. They turned the Lobby into a greenhouse full of plants grown from colonial-era seeds.

None of this is particularly revolutionary, the older Reversalists said.

That's exactly what's wrong with all of you, the brothers said. You only ever wanted to fix problems in ways that felt exciting. You thought you could make the world a better place by talking about it. Fucking about it. Marching about it. You need to learn how to do shit, they said. Then you need to work your asses off. Then you need to get a dozen other people to do the same. That's the only shot we've got.

We don't have any shot, the Reversalists said. The Earth is kaput.

That's easy for you to say, the brothers said. You'll be dead soon.

You'll be dead too, by the time it gets really bad.

Maybe it's not us we're worried about, the brothers said. Have you thought about that? The people who are coming next?

The Reversalists tossed their hands up, as if these unborn people couldn't possibly be worth the trouble. They grumbled. But they ate the brothers' produce. And it was good.

———

It's like they didn't even realize they were living on a commune, Jim said.

There's a real dearth of communing going on, Mick said. It's like, they're bad at the things they invented and then they're mad when we're better at them too.

He really said that? Elsa said. About children?

The thought of Ian saying the word *children*, speaking passionately about kids, felt far removed from the man she knew. Probably she and Nolan were no more who Ian had so vigorously defended than the other million kids born in their generation. But even so.

Yeah, he was really passionate about not shitting on the next generation and all that. He kind of adopted us, Jim said.

Don't say that, said Nolan.

It doesn't feel good to be replaced, does it Nolan? Elsa said.

Jinx was at Nolan's feet and rolled over with her legs bent in the air, offering her belly to be scratched.

Did you help our father with banding at all? Nolan asked. Do you know anything about Duck Twelve?

Duck Twelve, the brothers said. They caught each other's eyes and laughed. He's a trip. Your father was really into him. But it's hard to predict where Duck Twelve will be. Doesn't think like the other ducks.

Jim stood up, and the feathers he'd laid on the table blew out of pattern. He went over to the bed and lifted the mattress. He pulled a blue waterproof logbook and a green waterproof field journal out from where they'd been hidden.

These are all the places we went on count days, Jim said. He flipped to the later pages. And here you can see which ducks we sighted those days. This is what we came for.

Why was he keeping them under there? Elsa asked.

Mick said, You know Mitchell has already been through here looking for this, right?

And he didn't think to look under the mattress? Elsa said.

Only teenagers with TVs know to hide things under mattresses, Jim said. Mitchell was a Leap-Backer. Commune kids. Different kinds of secrets.

What exactly was our father looking for? Nolan asked. Do you know?

He was tracking factors that influenced the ducks' lives, Mick said.

The children tried to follow what the brothers told them:

Imagine ducks with anatomy and physiognomy so complicated that the majority of their caloric energy was devoted to maintaining and developing said bodies. Then, a mutation. The waterproofing was the most obvious change, the origin of the undowny, but there were others. The sum effect of which was that the undowny bufflehead was a duck simplifying its physiological structures, internal and external. Over the past ten generations, the average UBH voluntarily consumed 8 percent fewer calories, an astronomical amount, but maintained the same level of general health and fecundity. Their simplified bodies required fewer calories, which in turn meant the duck spent less time tracking down food, which in turn meant they were able to spend more time on other endeavors.

Endeavors? Nolan asked. What else does a duck have to do?

Your father seemed to think they were meditating, Jim said.

Meditating?

While they're drying themselves in the sun.

That's insane, said Nolan.

And isn't it a time suck? Elsa said. The opposite of becoming more efficient?

Jim shook his head. He wasn't saying their lives were more efficient. Almost the opposite. He was saying that their bodies were more efficient so their lives could be less survival-oriented. He was working to show the beneficial impact of the shifts in bufflehead physiognomy for the population as a whole—not in measures of sheer population growth, but in the overall health of the next generation: life-span and less traditional variables that collectively amounted to what he called a superior "quality of life." Essentially he was asking: Even if efficiency and survival are high, at what point is the "quality of a life" too low to validate existence?

The Greys stared at the boys. Ian was a man who wore the same ratty workshirts day after day because they were perfectly fine. Who left a spoon balanced on the side of the sink all day so he would not have to use a second one later, despite their having dozens of spoons and a fully functional dishwasher. Ian was a man who never sat still to watch a movie because it was a waste to do only one thing at a time. Less efficient? Quality of life? It sounded impossible that this could be Ian.

Nolan said, So he was just watching the ducks and thinking: they're having a ball!

It's not that simple, Jim said. What he was looking for was something bigger—

It sounds exactly that simple, Nolan said.

Dude, don't be stupid, Jim said.

Don't call him stupid, Elsa said, gesticulating and knocking several feathers off the table. Nolan felt gratitude well up in him. *Stupid* was what his parents had never said out loud but what he had always heard. That he wasn't like them. That he was as unextraordinary as everybody else.

Jim pressed the baggie of feathers into one of the books and handed both to Nolan. He said, He was the only one here who fought for us.

Thanks for this, Nolan said, lifting a notebook. Nolan wanted them gone.

Absolutely, Mick said. Small island and all that.

Nolan showed the brothers out and noisily locked the door behind them. He resented being frightened because Elsa let strange men into the house, when they were in bed, undressed, and had no way of knowing whether it was safe. He hated how it felt to hear Mick and Jim talking about Ian, like they knew him.

Because of course Ian would adopt boy geniuses. That Nolan had never resolved into such a thing, with parents like his, had been a mystery and a disappointment to everyone, not least of all Nolan himself. His childhood had been full of aptitude tests and advanced placement committees. He spent weekends with strange pencil-chewing women who took notes as Nolan failed to rotate 3-D objects in his mind. Nolan could not solve elaborate word puzzles or determine the number of snakes in cave Y. Nolan was unable to decipher the numeric patterns in endless Sudoku grids. Later, his parents thought there might be a psychological reason Nolan was not yet a genius and began taking him to psychologists instead. But in the Rorschach tests they gave him, Nolan saw only spilled ink.

Elsa was sitting cross-legged on the bed. I really wish you hadn't let them in like that, Nolan said. He sat next to her.

They showed us the logbooks, Elsa said. You should be excited. Now you can research away. She tossed the books onto the floor a little too hard. The baggie inside poofed open and undowny feathers escaped in a burst. They floated slowly back to the floor, some of them traveling over the mattress, toward the children.

Nolan snatched one out of the air. I can't believe Dad spent time with those idiots. That doesn't sound like him, does it?

Elsa said, You didn't pan out, he moved on; stop being surprised, Nolan.

Nolan lay back on the bed. He breathed and counted his breaths. He counted to five.

Actually, Elsa said, this is the first story that sounds like him at all. Dad giving up on a family, moving on, finding someone new. She flopped over backward next to him.

Elsa, Nolan said, looking at her. Don't. She was baiting him. It was easier to be angry than to be sad. Two small feathers had landed in her hair.

You started it, Elsa said. She ducked and pressed her face against Nolan's ribs. She bit him through his t-shirt. You're the one who made us come out here, she said. You're the one who wanted to open everything up again. She buried her face in his neck and bit him again, gently, on the neck. Less gently on the shoulder.

Fuck, Elsa, stop.

Elsa crouched and looked at him. You wanted this, she said.

Nolan pushed her and she tumbled over onto the mattress.

The years before you came were the only good years, Elsa said, sitting up.

Nolan felt miserable and crazy. He sat up and pulled at his shorts. I know you thought I was the end of the world back then, but you can't possibly believe it now, he said. It's never me, he said. It's never about me at all.

Are you going to cry? Elsa said. Nolan—

She reached for his hand, and he pushed her again. I'm not even enough of a person to be that bad, Nolan said, too loudly. I'm completely benign and insignificant. How could I possibly have been the one to ruin everything?

Elsa hitched herself up. She straightened her tank top and rested her hands on her thighs. Okay, she said.

Nolan sucked a breath in, too hard.

Are you okay, New Baby? Elsa said. Besides Ian?

I'm fine, Nolan said. I just meant— He rubbed his eyes.

Why are we here, New Baby? We could try to call the postman. Maybe we should just go home.

No, Nolan said.

He didn't know what he was playing at, and it was getting out of control. He'd dragged her to this island because he felt like everything they'd been through was unresolved and keeping him from being whoever he was supposed to be. Someone smart and good like Keiko. Someone worthy of his father. But all being here was doing was making him feel like a stupid teenage boy who wasn't in control of anything. Who was going to let things get fucked up in exactly the same way all over again because he still didn't know how to be a fucking person. There were feathers all over the mattress.

Janine was always telling Nolan how wonderful he was. How much good he could do if he just thought about his job in the right way. He was connecting people around something they loved! And it didn't have to be baseball and Twitter, Janine said. He could find another job. She was so enthusiastic. Upbeat. Nolan knew Janine expected him to be some kind of phenom, whatever he did, and when she said she loved him, he felt sick, as if he were somehow hiding from her that he was already over. A blown flower. Nolan wished he could return to a time before anyone had any expectations for him. Back when he was still *becoming,* his parents watching with rapt attention, waiting for him to unfurl into someone remarkable.

Elsa poked him. You know that if Ian's dead, we're allowed to not be okay, right? When someone dies, it's basically the one time when it's completely acceptable to be awful and empty and not okay in any way.

Sure, Nolan said. I know. He flopped back onto the bed and rolled over. Elsa gently squeezed his shoulder where she had bitten it. She tugged at his t-shirt collar so it pulled against his Adam's apple, but he didn't move. Nolan was so tired. He fell asleep with her tugging like that, with the lights on.

———

Elsa heard Nolan's breaths grow even. She felt like she was coming down from a fever.

She got up and retrieved the two waterproof books from where she had thrown them. Choosing the field journal, Elsa leafed through pages of her father's handwriting. Before he'd become a Reversalist, Ian had worked in some of the best-outfitted labs and universities in the country, with teams of interns and grad students and million-dollar software at his disposal. That his work could now be contained in two slick Rite in the Rain journals was pathetic.

PERSONAL FIELD JOURNAL OF DR. IAN GREY

*Duck Number Twelve is significantly smaller than its brothers
and sisters, and yet, its wings are much longer. They are
awkwardly long, and when extended, appear unwieldy, as
if flight would be a burden and not a freedom. Duck Twelve's
bill is perforated with not one but three sets of holes, one set
at the typical spot, close to the beak's origin, and the other
two farther down the beak. The purpose for these holes is
unknown. The duck has uncommonly wide feet, which enable
it to swim not faster, but in greater bursts of power, so the effect
of this specimen is one of undecided motivation but great
conviction.*

*Whether Duck Twelve is a freak among its peers, an
anomaly, or represents an indicator of a coming evolutionary
advancement is unclear at this stage. He may simply
be an aberration. But I confess I suspect his physiognomy
and perceptive profile will endure at least another
generation.*

*There is not a scientific way to categorize the difference
between the way in which Duck Twelve lives its life
compared to the other undowny buffleheads, but I hope
that through observational notes, the differences will become
clear. I have begun to think of Duck Twelve as the Paradise
Duck, a name born of its seeming joie de vivre. I know a
duck cannot be happy but I think the Paradise Duck might be.
Might, in fact, be demonstrably "happier" than its peers.
I cannot, as yet, determine why this might be. The Paradise
Duck has, as best I can tell, no partner, no offspring, and no
role of any significance within the group dynamics of its clutch.
And yet, it seems to take more joy in the daily mechanics of
living.*

It broke Elsa's heart to see Ian write like this. All "Dear Diary, today I saw..." He sounded like the crazy Florida birders they used to mock on vacations to Sanibel Island.

Ian taught Elsa to have nothing but disdain for the birders' personal quests for Big Years. At the hotel breakfast, they'd see old people at neighboring tables checking off roseate spoonbills and bertuffled sharpshinners in their guidebooks, which they pored over while picking at yogurt and fruit. To Elsa, it seemed the birders were so empty of life they needed to catalogue the living things they'd spotted: beautiful or ugly winged creatures who couldn't care less about being seen. Be the bird, Elsa thought. Be the bird, not the crazy old lady watching it.

And now here was her father, journaling about a duck he had named. It was everything he had once loathed. Joie de vivre. Jesus Christ.

Elsa was about to put the journal away when she had a thought. A stupid one, but she could not resist. She flipped to the last page of the journal and skimmed the final entry. It was from the day before her father died.

It was about Duck Number Twelve, the Paradise Duck. He had observed it splashing gleefully in a hidden inlet where the other ducks did not go. "Playing alone!" he wrote, and mentioned that he had successfully taken blood samples from the duck earlier in the day and sent them to a lab in Louisiana. That was it.

Elsa shut the notebook and clicked off the lantern. She got into the bed. Nolan was radiating heat beside her and the blanket did not feel right.

Had she hoped for some kind of clue? Dear Diary, today I watched some ducks then decided to off myself?

She'd spent so much time hating Ian, but at least she'd hated him because he was so large, so great. Elsa had always thought she might manage to become something like Ian. When she'd applied to Mars Origins, she'd been banking on the fact that they would see the Ian-ness in her. But what did that mean now? The man in these notebooks, in the Reversalists' stories, was sentimental and idiotic.

They would never pick her. They were looking for explorers and adventurers, brave and brilliant souls.

The night birds were calling. In the bed, Nolan was asleep, his hair looped back in a bun. She raked her fingers along his skull, pulling his hair free, and it spilled across the pillow.

Park Rapids

Elsa was squeezing limes, and Ingrid was washing the blender. The screen door to the lakehouse was open, and they were making margaritas to celebrate the end of Elsa's school year. Her mother was still wearing turquoise scrubs from her nursing shift, and she chewed on ice as she washed the dust from the blender, which had not been used since the last time they'd been in a celebrating mood, a time Elsa certainly couldn't remember.

There must have been something we celebrated, Ingrid said.

If you can't remember, it didn't happen, Elsa said.

I don't think that's true at all, said Ingrid.

The limes Elsa was squeezing stung her cuticles in a ringing kind of way.

They make juice, Elsa said. It comes in plastic bottles. Shaped like limes.

That's not the same. Ingrid crunched her ice. This is real.

The juicer was made of milky green glass, and wrinkled fetus-y seeds floated inside. Elsa split one between her teeth. Sour. The rubber watch Elsa wore was ticking quietly.

I'm thinking of going to Mars, Elsa said.

A staccato laugh from Ingrid, because Elsa was always saying things to bother her mother on purpose.

Me too, Ingrid said.

Really, though. There's this program. For people to go.

Like tourists? Ingrid said. Sounds expensive.

No, for good.

What's for good?

Like, forever.

Forever?

Well, until you die.

But that's absurd, her mother said. Why would they want someone like you in space?

Thanks a lot, Mama.

I'm totally serious. Don't you need to have an awful lot of training to do something like that?

They don't want to waste people with training. The idea is to be colonists. If you make it. And for them to test the effects of the trip. On our bodies. To gain information.

Elsa, frankly, if you were going to kill yourself, I'd think you'd have the good sense to jump off a cliff or take pills or whatever people do, and not bring the whole US space community into it.

I don't want to die, Mama.

Well, that's what it sounds like. Giving up and killing yourself in a way that pretends to be heroic. She clicked the clean blender into its hub.

It's the opposite of giving up, Elsa said. This planet's not going to last forever. And if we don't settle Mars someday soon, we'll never be ready in time.

In time for what?

In time for people to colonize it, to continue the human race, when the Earth is over.

Earth is over?

When we can't live here anymore.

You're being an alarmist.

What about global warming and the hole in the ozone layer? What about the oil crisis? What about all those storms and disasters getting worse? I don't understand why people always call you an alarmist when you're pointing a finger at something that is genuinely fucking alarming right next to you.

Well, I refuse to believe anyone would let that happen. We have a lot of smart minds in this country. Someone will figure something out.

Like who? Like Dad?

Frankly, I think that if the Earth were burning before his eyes, your father would sit there and fan the flames, Ingrid said. She pulsed the blender. That was always his way.

Ingrid wiped her hands on the apron. This was the closest to a negative thing Elsa had ever heard her mother say about Ian. Not when he left. Not when he got remarried. Not when Elsa and Nolan got in trouble and he reacted so badly. Not ever.

Like Dad's some kind of nihilist? Elsa asked.

No, Ingrid said. Not like that. He's just so interested in what might happen, what it could look like, that he makes it so without thinking about the outcomes. And then later, when the thing is done, he makes that face, like, Hey, how did I get here?

Did you like that about him? Elsa said.

I liked everything about him, Ingrid said.

Elsa sighed.

So you think everything's going to be just fine. A-okay, Elsa said. You're not worried at all for the generations to come?

Are any generations to-coming? Ingrid said. It doesn't look like it. How is Dylan, by the way?

He's fine, Elsa said. And he was. He was better than fine. He was the only reason Elsa could imagine for staying on Earth and not floating away to Mars at all. Ingrid, on the other hand, did not need her. Elsa knew her mother loved her, but if Elsa left, Ingrid would be sad for just the right amount of time, and then she would grieve in some very healthy manner, and then she would be returned to the bloom of health and high spirits.

Her mother tipped the bottle of tequila into the blender. She took the lime juice from Elsa and poured it down the blender spout.

She said, Unless you can promise me there will be future generations to care about, I find the concept terribly abstract. Ingrid ran the blender.

———

They drank their margaritas sitting on the back patio, staring at the lake.

Cheers, Ingrid said.

The margarita was sour and chemical and sweet too. It had that medicinal tequila taste that always made Elsa feel better as soon as she'd sniffed it.

How can you just give up on the planet like that? Ingrid said, patting her thigh.

You say *give up* like there's something I could do to fix it.

There's always something to do.

But Elsa could not believe in her mother's cheerful insistence that everything would turn out sunny. Elsa truly believed that, when she looked at every blooming thing on Earth, she was seeing it for the last time. That this generation was the last to have the privilege of seeing its green planet in an uncomplicated way. She thought of her students, seven and eight, and how much they would hate her when they got old and realized how fucked everything was and how little she had done to stop it. How little any of them had done. Her generation. Grown-ups, she supposed they were grown-ups now. Their parents were still alive, but they were old and so all of this could no longer be their fault. It was hers now.

The kids in Elsa's classes had been brought into this world under auspices of ignorance, in the hope that things would go well, in the face of all the evidence that it would not.

Sorry, babies, Elsa thought, like a mantra, all day while she was teaching them spelling words or watching them on the playground or siphoning Elmer's glue into wax Dixie cups so pompoms could be attached to the construction paper hats for snowmen. Sorry, babies, sorry, babies. Sorry we couldn't do better. Sorry no one planned ahead. The only thing Elsa could think to do to help was to go to Mars. Surely there were better people to go; she knew this. But Elsa was not good at sitting back and watching other people do things.

Her mother slipped out of her shoes. Rubber flats with nubby insides. Her toes were painted a pale metallic coral.

Tell me about something good, Ingrid said.

This was always what her mother said. Ingrid shut her eyes and lay her head back on the chaise. She held her margarita in one hand and the other she tucked snugly into the marsupial front of her apron pocket.

This margarita is very good, Elsa said. She stuck her tongue out so part of the salty rim came away.

No margaritas on Mars, I bet, her mother said. I bet Martians live their lives stone-cold sober.

———

Dylan picked her up. In his truck, the windows down, Elsa pleasantly buzzed, they drove down straightaways, through fields that were warm in the evening light and smelled toasted and rich like hay. She reached over and rubbed the crotch of his jeans with the palm of her hand. He kept one hand on the wheel. With the other, he took her hand in his and held it tucked into his own fist.

Holding hands instead. That's what things were like with Dylan. He understood that sometimes when Elsa thought she wanted sex, what she really wanted was something else much smaller. He knew that she was afraid to ask for small things like this because the need in them did not seem big enough to draw attention. That she was afraid her small needs would go unnoticed, and so she made plays at bigger ones instead.

Dylan was wonderful in bed. Squeezing every part of her like he was taking inventory. Really and truly fucking her sometimes, and then lingering and waiting and stroking patiently other times, and Elsa never knew which Dylan she was going to get and that was what Elsa liked. Because Elsa was never so bored as when she felt she could predict exactly what someone would do and when. Mostly Elsa always thought she could predict what people would do, because Elsa was very smart—not brilliant like her father, but smarter than it was good for a person to be. The kind of smart than ran interference on happiness.

But maybe Elsa was not as smart as she thought she was, or she would have realized that sometimes you know what people are going to do because that's just how people are. Good people, anyway, are creatures of habit and dependable wants, which you needed to be in love, because otherwise, you found yourself short on synchronization points.

And Elsa wanted but did not want to be in love. The word *love* made Elsa feel nauseated, like everything was so common and commoditized and trampled on that there was nothing new or good in the world at all. Except for maybe the things that were not good. Things that were bad, but freshly and surprisingly so, having been spared people trying to define them or make them their own. And so these were the things that were left to Elsa.

They drove on, and in the fields the hay had been baled in whorls and the bales sat like quiet giants. Dylan released her hand, and Elsa drew her legs up in the seat and hugged them to her.

Would you want to go to Mars? she asked him. Really. If you could.

Probably not, Dylan said.

Why? Elsa asked.

I don't imagine you can move around much out there. I think I'd feel all cooped up in a rocket. Not enough space.

All there is, is space, in space, Elsa said.

But you couldn't get to it, Dylan said. That would make me even crazier. There's no place you can go on your own two legs.

You'd be better than legs, Elsa said. You'd be floating. Forget legs.

Forget these legs? Dylan smacked her flank a few times. Never.

What if I were going to Mars? Elsa said.

If you were on Mars, Dylan said, I guess I'd have to consider a visit.

Leap's Island

They did not wake until after noon. Still lying on her back, Elsa smelled her armpits.

I smell like pineapple vodka.

Maybe drink less, Nolan said.

I'm on summer vacation! Elsa stood up quickly. This is how I spent my summer vacation.

When does school start up?

Maybe never, Elsa said. I might not go back.

Really? Nolan said. What would you do instead?

Elsa unzipped the side pouch of her bag and took out the letter from Mars Origins. She passed it to Nolan.

She had her first in-person interview with the Mars Origins people in one month. She'd already booked her ticket to Amersfoort in the Netherlands. If Elsa advanced to the next round, she'd be one of the Mars 100 who would get tested in training situations in simulated settlements. She would get herself together by then. She wouldn't smell so much like vodka. She would work out and look like the kind of strong but compact person you'd want to share a spaceship with. She would teach herself a little farming. A little code. A little Russian, just in case. She'd make an amazing mixtape of songs to play in space. Mix for Mars: David Bowie, Elton John, Misfits, Rob Zombie (Ian would suggest Langgaard). By the time she went to the Netherlands, she would be the sort of person the selection committee would see and think: a woman like that should never be left behind.

Oh my God, are these those colonization people? Nolan asked. I heard about this.

Mars Origins, she said. I have an interview.

You're not serious, Nolan said.

I mean, there are two more rounds before it's final, Elsa said. But if they pick me, training will start next fall, so I won't be able to teach.

Training? Elsa, this is ridiculous. He flapped the envelope against his palm. You're fucking with me right now, aren't you?

When are they expecting you back at the park? Elsa asked. Isn't it peak season?

They're not. Seriously, Elsa, you don't really believe in this, do you?

What do you mean, they're not?

They said if I left now they'd fire me, so I quit.

Elsa stared at him. The calico curtains were flapping into the room so that light flashed across the floor in hot intervals.

Nolan, she said. They must have some sort of policy for deaths in the family. They wouldn't give you any time off at all?

I didn't ask.

You didn't tell them he was dead?

Nolan shook his head. There was something about naming Ian's death—in the ballpark, of all places—that had struck him as impossible. It was a place where Nolan could remember Ian, in his jaunty ball cap, as uncomplicated and enthusiastic, boy-like, almost an equal, and to invite death into the bleachers would spoil that one good thing.

They told me I should work remotely, he said, but there's no internet, so—

So you have a job until they realize no one's been running any social media for them.

I guess, Nolan said.

What are you going to do? Elsa said.

I have to figure out what I want to be doing, Nolan said. Then I can look for the right kind of new job.

I mean about money, Elsa said.

I have money.

How could you possibly have money.

Blood money.

Be serious.

My mom listed me as the beneficiary for her life insurance.

What about Ian?

Nolan shook his head. When he lost the Alabama gig, she changed the policy.

Elsa got out of bed and looked out the window. It was windy and the Gulf was choppy.

Do you think Dad had life insurance? Elsa asked, sounding almost wistful.

Nolan started laughing and did not stop until Elsa shouted at him that she was going to take a shower in the Lobby and did he want to come or not.

———

They walked in the water along the beach. Elsa picked up shells as the wind snatched at her hair and Nolan carried his sneakers. The morning was cool, and the water was warm, and broken shells and snails tumbled over Nolan's feet.

You're not really serious about this Mars thing, are you? Nolan said.

Elsa shrugged.

After James Peacock had learned the wrong things from her, after she had failed to decipher meaning in the patterns the truck head-lights played against the vinyl siding as she fucked the bartender on the back porch, after Ian died, Elsa had recommitted herself to Mars.

The brochure for Origins said that the colonization mission was to ensure the survival of the human race, and yeah, that sounded stupid and dramatic but maybe it actually was that simple. Maybe it was that big.

Because if Mars Origins was part of saving the human race, then going was a decision that was clearly good. It was a choice she could make and be certain about.

Elsa felt the opposite of certain when it came to everything else in her life. Whatever inner thing guided normal people in their choices—a diviner's stick in the ribs, a magnet of the hips, a compass of the skull—Elsa's was broken. Nolan had been her first wrong choice, years ago, and as much as she'd have liked to pretend that she was different now, that it had been a stupid teenage mistake, there was too much other wrongness that came after. Dozens of dubious choices she'd made later that all seemed to bloom outward from that first moment. Dubious because Elsa was never sure what was the right choice and what was the wrong.

Was driving Dylan away the right choice or the wrong choice? Had she been empowered by having sex with whomever she chose on that porch—or was she a bad feminist giving her body cheaply? Her body, sprawled out in her adolescence and unclaimable ever again—wasn't she supposed to practice self-love and self-care and accept her body no matter what it looked like? Or was she supposed to go to the gym every day and prove she could master it? Had she been helping James Peacock by telling him the truth about death or hurting him? Was teaching a valuable way to spend her time, or was she just hiding out from doing whatever hard work a good person would actually be doing to save this sorry planet?

Which was the right choice and which was the wrong choice?

Sometimes, it seemed to Elsa that the era of certainty was over. Past generations had seemed so sure of their goodness. The Greatest Generation fought the Nazis, for fuck's sake. They had known this was a good thing. What must that have been like?

Her generation had Iraq and Afghanistan. Her generation had the internet. Her generation had globalization. What was the right thing and what was the wrong thing?

Mars was a clear moral choice, and if she made it, Elsa thought it might wash away all the smaller, less certainly good and obviously bad choices she had made in her lifetime. Maybe it would even neutralize her complicity in all the generational crimes she'd be on the hook for if she got old enough to see her students grown.

Mars could be a new era of certainty.

And at least if Elsa went to Mars, she wouldn't have to stare down every forked decision yet to come in her life.

She didn't need to explain herself to Nolan. Elsa pushed him in the shoulders, and Nolan stumbled in the surf. He caught his balance. She changed the subject.

She said, One of those journals is a field diary. It has proper entries.

Does he say anything about us?

Elsa almost pitied him. It's about the ducks, Nolan.

Right. Of course.

He was writing about Duck Twelve again. He named it. The Paradise Duck.

Because?

His notes are insane. Because it seemed *happy*?

Nolan made his mouth a stiff line and said nothing.

Elsa knew how disappointed he was, but he was faking it admirably. It was a remarkable trick, the way Nolan now looked like a man. He carried his tall frame with a swinging confidence. He was handsome, and well put together. She imagined someone meeting him for the first time might suppose he was a kind of dandy. Confident, arrogant even. But it was a cover. Elsa knew Nolan was desperately sensitive and loving. That he could be easily swayed. That he brooded over small hurts, tending them like pets.

It occurred to Elsa that with Ian dead, and Keiko dead, she and Ingrid might be the only ones left who knew Nolan in this secret, softer way. The intimacy came with a responsibility, and as she considered this, she felt as if she'd lost a game of hot potato. Because being there for Nolan was not her job. It couldn't be. After all, she'd been redacted from Nolan's history a long time ago. Elsa's whole life, she felt, was a series of events in which she'd been redacted from the lives of people she'd been tricked into loving. Kicked out of stories she'd been stupid enough to think were her own. Ian, Nolan, Dylan. But it didn't matter now. This time, she was going to redact herself. From the planet, even.

The shoreline grew reedy, and there were foamy clusters of insect eggs clumping grasses together. Nolan tripped over a piece of driftwood.

How is a duck happy? he said.

How is anyone? Elsa said.

———

The Lobby was full of breakfast smells, but the main room was empty again. There was a sprawling oak reception desk at the back of the room, between the helixing staircases. Behind it were twenty feet of paneled mirror, speckled with rot.

Elsa approached the desk and leaned cross-armed on the counter between a set of princess telephones. Nolan followed. He picked up one of the receivers, listened, then pressed the phone to Elsa's ear, covering her other with his palm. His hand was warm, and the hum of the dial tone surprised her. She closed her eyes to listen so she would not have to look at the two of them in the dappled expanse of mirror.

Hey, look, Nolan said. Elsa opened her eyes, and he was pointing. Just before the entrance to the men's and women's locker rooms was a sign that read: SAUNA.

You want to? Nolan said.

Hell yes, Elsa said.

They got towels from the locker rooms, and when they met inside the sauna, it was damp and hot. There was a basket of steaming rocks and benches and the deep smell of wet wood.

Nolan fingered the edge of Elsa's towel, and Elsa recognized it as a dare.

Elsa was never the first to say no, and so she took the towel off and handed it to him. Nolan took off his own towel and tossed them onto the bench.

The Greys sat across the room from each other. This was different from how things had been in the dark.

Elsa watched Nolan and he watched her and each felt the other taking in the ways that time had changed them. How did fifteen years hang on a body?

They were daring each other to notice. Daring each other not to care.

Nolan's eyes started watering in the heat. He felt sweat running through his hairline, behind his ears, down his neck. His whole back was coursing. Nolan ran his fingers through his pubic hair, which was damp. His shins, when he rubbed them against each other, were slick.

Elsa leaned against the wall, the wide white insides of her legs flattened against the bench. Her bush was enormous and pale. Sweat beaded at her temples, but it did not run and instead seemed to hang there like embellishments around her eyes.

The Greys closed their eyes and tried to be still as the sauna did its work and the poison began leaching out of them.

Nolan tried to think about nothing, but Nolan had not been on the internet for three days. His phone didn't work, and he knew there were things happening in the baseball world and he was not posting about them. He was sure he had emails from vendors and coworkers whose going unanswered was suspicious and would cause him trouble later, if he still had a job when he got back. Anything could happen on the mainland, and he wouldn't know about it. A fire, a political coup, a celebrity gaffe—whatever. Though maybe if he didn't know what was going on, it was not his problem. Maybe that's why the Reversalists were so happy out here, living in a state of willful not-knowing. If they *were* happy. Nolan wasn't sure about that. In truth, everyone they'd met seemed miserable. Had Ian been? Nolan was sure Janine was calling.

Elsa sighed, and it sounded as if she had never been so content.

I'm going to shower, Nolan said. Elsa kept her eyes closed. He stood up, wondering if she would open her eyes and look at him, but she didn't. Not even when the boards creaked beneath his weight.

In the men's locker room, there was a long bank of open showers along the wall. The tiles were white and blue and mosaicked into Mediterranean geometric patterns that reminded Nolan of waves. He imagined the kinds of guests the original Towneses must have anticipated hosting here. Rich family men who wanted to take saunas and leave their children at the pool. People so rich they could afford a beach hotel on a private island that ensured there would be no one to shame them for their excesses. The hot water tap screeched as Nolan turned it. Here was Nolan, lanky, sweaty, flecks of seaweed and sand kicked up along the backs of his legs, alone in the showers. Townes would have hated him here, and Nolan enjoyed this thought.

Nolan soaped himself all over. He soaped his balls. He soaped his feet. He scrubbed the back of his neck. He washed his hair until it squeaked when he ran his fingers through it, the way Ian had showed him meant it was clean when he was a boy. He soaped away three days of sweat and booze and sea salt. He thought about how he and Elsa had been naked together as children and how it was the same now. He tried not to think about her low-slung ass. How it hung like heavy fruit. Without him wishing it, his dick started to harden and arc. It had been three days without that too. He couldn't do this here. But he reached down. He chose to think about Janine's dancer's body, but then he was thinking about how he and she together were so light the bed hardly bucked at all, no one getting any good momentum, and how Janine was always moving, never staying still, in a way Nolan guessed was sexy— maybe someone better would think it was sexy, but sometimes he wished she would just stay still so he could fuck her properly, and he felt bad for wishing this. He thought about a porn he'd seen once where a woman had been pinned down and tickled until she screamed. Laughing so hard it was violent. He thought about Gates's legs.

He stroked his dick. He pressed his forehead against the cool tile wall. He pulled upward, tightening his grip, jerking off until he came against his stomach in several warm bursts and the water, forgivingly, washed it away.

He toweled himself dry and dressed. He should have brought fresh clothes. As soon as he'd got his shorts on, he felt dirty again. When he came out of the locker room, Nolan meant to seem bored and uninterested with Elsa, but she was already in a small group of people who were shouting, including Mitchell Townes.

————

From a distance, he saw the Reversalists tighten their circle around Elsa like one organism. They were all talking at once, Mitchell Townes trying to calm a Slavic-looking woman in swim shoes who seemed to be yelling at Elsa. She was waving around a pack of Virginia Slims, and Esther Stein was shaking her head at the trouble. An older black man who, Nolan realized giddily, must be Remy St. Gilles, seemed unfazed.

Nolan stepped between Elsa and the woman.

Don't fucking yell at my sister, Nolan said to Mitchell, who had not been yelling at all.

They fell silent, taking in Nolan at his full height. Elsa's light hair was darker for being wet. It lay against her shoulder and was soaking a spot through her t-shirt.

No one's yelling, man, Mitchell said. Be cool.

She was yelling, Elsa said, pointing to the woman with the cigarettes. She wants to experiment on us, she told Nolan. The woman was in her mid-forties. She had thick brunette hair elaborately plaited down her back and wore a black t-shirt with a wolf on it. Her swim shoes were crusted with dried mud. She had a dozen tiny silver hoops pierced along the cartilage of her left ear.

Gwen, the woman said, offering her hand to Nolan. When he

didn't take it, she said, It's a simple test and it just won't take that long. Half an hour, tops. She pointed at Mitchell now. I specifically told you I needed to work with them as soon as they arrived before the island climate affected their olfactory range and you promised—

I promised I'd ask them, Gwen. He was pinching the bridge of his nose as if Gwen's very presence was giving him a migraine. He wore a gray t-shirt with the sleeves cut off and pulled at the collar of it. So now here we are, asking.

Well, the answer is no, Elsa said. I don't want anything to do with whatever it is you're trying to prove out here.

Certainly not what she's trying to prove, Remy said.

Gwen was the reproductive scientist who had suggested Mick and Jim might be a "sexual threat," Nolan realized, and suddenly wanted very badly for Elsa and him to head back to their shack alone.

They've said no, Gwen, Mitchell said soothingly, as if to a small child. Your work is a vital part of the project and at the next intellectual trust meeting we'll give it our full attention and see if we can't make up for any data—

Gwen snorted. You just want to table anything you don't agree with.

Your research is being considered very carefully, Gwen, and I'm sure it will be nominated to go out next submission cycle if it doesn't get included in the *Nature* piece.

Blow me, Mitchell, Gwen said. She walked out through the rotating doors.

Mitchell laid a hand on Elsa's arm. I'm very sorry about that, he said.

He looked at Elsa, and she wondered what it must feel like to be in charge in this way. To be in control of an island and everything on it and not worry about anything beyond its borders. Mitchell's hand was warm and he was sure in his grip, and Elsa felt as if she wanted to lean into him, to relax into any kind of certainty at all.

Gwen is just very passionate about her work, Mitchell said.

We all are, Esther said. But you don't see us running around like maniacs.

You don't have to work with Gwen, Mitchell said, ignoring Esther, his hand still on Elsa's arm. Just come see me before you leave, and bring any of your father's research you find along with you.

But, with the papers, what if we want to— Elsa was going to say "keep them." She hadn't wanted them before. But now that someone else did, she was reluctant to give them up.

Well, thing is, it's all part of the article for *Nature* we're working on, Mitchell said. All research and material generated during residency at Leap's is part of the institute's intellectual trust. There is only communal work on the island.

It's very important, dear, said Esther. You don't want us to get the hook, do you?

Mitchell shot her a look. Esther, don't be dramatic.

We all know it, Mitchell, no use pretending, Esther said.

Agreed, said Remy St. Gilles.

Nolan turned to Remy St. Gilles.

Is your novel part of the intellectual trust? he asked. I mean, you'll still publish it? Won't you?

Remy St. Gilles studied Nolan through a pair of very expensive-looking tortoiseshell glasses, which surprised Nolan, because St. Gilles had never worn glasses in any of his author photos. St. Gilles wore leather sandals and a linen shirt with two pens in the pocket. Pens! Certainly the man was writing the last book. Nolan could not believe how close he was to the author of the Asterias series. St. Gilles's close-cropped hair was gray at the temples; he must have been in his early seventies.

You don't look much like Ian, St. Gilles said to Nolan. He spoke with a soft British accent. He turned to appraise Elsa. He said, In fact, neither of you look at all like him.

Nolan stepped closer to St. Gilles. He could hear blood rushing in his ears.

Nolan had spent a lifetime listening to this bullshit.

Nolan saw Ian in his own face. He knew he was there. But he had spent his whole childhood having people look at him and Ian strangely when they were out together without Keiko. His Asianness, Ian's whiteness—people sometimes asked them if Nolan was adopted and it made him want to throttle them.

It crushed Nolan that, of all people, Remy St. Gilles, a man who'd invented a universe of possibilities Nolan loved, a man who could imagine sentient matriarchal insects on Mars, could fail to find Ian in Nolan's face.

It made him furious.

Who asked you? Nolan said, stepping closer again. St. Gilles looked alarmed. But Nolan didn't care. Let him feel alarmed.

Really, who the fuck asked you? Nolan said.

St. Gilles stood up straighter, visibly prickling.

Mitchell was still holding Elsa's arm. She broke free from his grip and grabbed Nolan's shoulder. He's an idiot, she said. You look so much like Ian. Why you're so hot to admit it I don't know, but—

Nolan took a breath. He stepped back.

You don't behave much like him either, St. Gilles said.

Remy, Esther said. They've lost their father.

St. Gilles scoffed but didn't say any more.

Let's go, Nolan said. Elsa nodded, and they left the Reversalists to their huddle. Elsa saw Mitchell watching her as they went. He looked relaxed, unbothered by the commotion.

Both children crowded into the same cube of revolving door space. They pushed outside and found Gwen smoking a Virginia Slim.

I'm surprised you're allowed to do that here, Elsa said.

It's not allowed on the main campus but fuck him, Gwen said. You want one?

No thanks, Elsa said. Nolan shook his head.

A whole generation has given up smoking overnight. If I weren't already so freaked out about everything, nothing would freak me out more than that, Gwen said.

The children shrugged.

Not to harp, Gwen said, but it's really not so far to my observation deck, and it's a ridiculously simple test and—

Nolan interrupted, I don't really know if we're comfortable—

He looked at Elsa for backup, but Elsa was staring back through the revolving doors. The crook of her arm felt alive where Mitchell had touched her, and Elsa knew this kind of tingle was a message from her body's early warning system. It was a bad sign.

Come on, Elsa said. Let's just get out of here.

Follow me, Gwen said.

———

They followed Gwen and the land grew marshy, the perimeter muddy.

Gwen had laid wooden planks across the deepest pits of mud, and they followed her to an enormous oak with boards nailed into the trunk in ascending ladder steps. Gwen went first, balls of mud dropping from her shoes as she climbed, her legs powerful in her spandex.

The structure they entered was half tree house, half duck blind, at least twenty feet up and big enough that they could all fit snugly. Tacked to one wall was what looked to be an organ, butterfly-pinned and left to dry. It was musky with rot, and Nolan felt bile in his throat.

Mitchell hates me, Gwen said. She was wound up, pacing the shack. He uses jargon about the intellectual trust to make himself seem like he knows what he's doing, but it's all a lot of shit. He's playing scientist, and I won't pretend otherwise, so he stuck me back in the swamp. Like I care. The boys are installing the new nesting pods halfway between here and my shack, so now I have two observation decks exactly where I need them.

What exactly are you researching? Elsa asked. She'd been eager to get away from Mitchell, to weaken the magnetic something she'd begun to feel back at the Lobby. It was the feeling she got right before she did something reckless and stupid, and Elsa was done with that. But she'd just traded one sort of discomfort for another, because now Gwen was gesturing to the organ on the wall.

Gwen's project was a mapping of the female bufflehead's uterus. A phenomenon that didn't sound necessary unless you knew that ducks had one of the most complex and nonsensical uterine systems in the animal kingdom and that the undowny bufflehead's was more complex than most.

It's a labyrinth in there, Gwen explained. These ducks, these female ducks, really, are making it harder and harder for the males to impregnate them. Making it harder for them to reproduce. Think about that for a minute. Years and years of evolution based on procreation and mating to ensure survival, and here's a species that is physically, reproductively evolving to lower the chances of conception.

Why would that happen? Nolan asked.

It's an arms race of ducky sex equipment, Gwen said.

If this has anything to do with the test, I'm out, Elsa said. I am so far gone.

Only indirectly, Gwen said.

———

Gwen wanted to have a baby. Really any baby, but they kept denying her adoption applications because Gwen was epileptic. She had intense full-body seizures where she clenched her jaw and rocked on the floor. She told the Reversalists, as she had told a train of roommates and colleagues before that: Don't do anything. If I have a seizure, just leave me alone.

But what about holding your head? What about putting a wooden spoon in your mouth?

Nothing, Gwen had said. For fuck's sake, why doesn't anyone know anything that's not on TV? If I seize, I need you to do nothing, and wait with me, and be calm.

This is why they wouldn't let Gwen have a baby.

So Gwen began having sex with strange men. She did not ask

them to use condoms. She was surprised at how few of them suggested it themselves. They came inside her. Sometimes they came in her mouth and she swallowed, but always Gwen thought about the waste of it. Life! She picked up men at bars and parties. She went to weddings she normally would have talked her way out of because there was always some groomsman loitering at the open bar as it shut down. She would take them back to her Holiday Inn Express room and they would fuck, Gwen bent over the mauve-and-gold polyester coverlet that scratched like everything synthetic in the world. Gwen would say, I want you inside me, I want you to fucking come in me, and they did, most of them. Gwen got no one's phone number. She did not call or write. And neither did they. Sometimes Gwen thought about how, had she been interested in these men, she would be engulfed in sadness. Luckily, she had no interest in the groomsman with the dimples and vodka cocktails, or the karaoke-bar loner who sang Journey all night, or the man in loafers and khakis who'd seemed tame until he got her back to his house and threw her on the bed in a way that made Gwen think he did not like women very much at all.

Gwen did not care. As long as they came inside her.

But there was no baby. She was as empty inside as a scooped-out melon. No matter how many times she felt the hot twist of possibility, inside, there was only what had been there before. Only herself. And that was the magic, after all, she knew, to make something out of nothing. From so little.

Gwen was forty-seven. She had waited too long. She knew this, of course. She had a Master of Science degree in breeding and genetics from the University of Florida and a PhD in the physiology of reproduction from Texas A&M University. She worked as a consultant to cattle ranches and bull breeders for a decade before being wooed by her alma mater's Department of Meat Sciences. She lasted only a year because she could not bear to see the title printed on a business card.

The year she turned forty, Gwen went back to school at UC Davis to become a large animal vet. Gwen's clients were a strip of dairy operations and small farms. She delivered calf after calf in the night. She saw how people, strapped for money, kept breeding their cows even when they were too old, and how the older they were, the more the calves came breech, were still, were strange, were needing to be killed so shortly after they'd made it into this world. So yes, Gwen knew. She had understood the clock of sand that held her eggs, and yet, she had waited. Stupid old cow.

When Gwen was young, she'd thought that because she knew all this, things would work themselves out. Her boyfriends would eventually become the right boyfriends and her work would calm down and start paying enough money—all these hoped-for factors would just materialize and then she would go off her birth control because then she would be ready and would decide to make a baby happen and then it would happen. She was a scientist. She was in control of her fate.

But after she and the last boyfriend had broken up, she did the math—how long it would take her to meet someone new, and how long after that they might be ready to have children, and how, by then, it would be too late. And this was when Gwen started sleeping with strange men.

She lost most of her vet clients after repeatedly showing up hours after she'd been scheduled. After not answering late-night phone calls when she was needed. She was a vet out of work.

Gwen found a new job at a petting zoo in a local park, and this was where she learned about ducks. As a large-animal specialist, they had never been in her purview before. But now, here she was, in her terrible khaki safari outfit helping children feed quarters into the animal-feed dispensers, and here were the ducks, and what Gwen learned was that ducks were really big on rape. That a male duck has a penis three times the length of his body in the form of a corkscrew. That he wedges himself inside a female and that the corkscrew shape is such that, once he has mounted her, there is no way for her to get free until he is no longer erect.

This phenomenon in the males, historically, caused female ducks to evolve some tricks of their own. The uterine passageways of an adult female duck were designed to not let the wrong sperm in. The uterus was essentially booby-trapped. There were dead ends that a male might enter, thinking he was impregnating the female, only to be shooting into an empty decoy vagina. There were many passageways that led nowhere and only one that led to life. The female duck had a keen sense of this, so if the wrong duck mounted her, she could wriggle and manipulate him down the wrong road, often avoiding egg fertilization, until the right duck came along.

All this meant, of course, that it was more difficult for the duck's eggs to be fertilized. It meant that fewer eggs were laid and baby ducks born. It meant too that more of the baby ducks that were born were the product of pairings desired by the females. And Gwen knew that this likely had to do with mate preferences such as size and dominance and had little to do with power, but when she watched the female ducks being brutally mounted in the petting zoo, she could not help but think that, maybe, they understood the difference between the children you wanted to have and the children born because that's who happened to come inside of you that day.

Gwen became obsessed with the idea of a species evolving toward a more difficult path to procreation. She talked about it to the other petting-zoo workers. She talked about it to people who came to the petting zoo (who grimaced and led their children away from Gwen's fenced pond). She talked about it to her friends until they said they couldn't hang out with Gwen anymore unless she stopped talking about phantom duck vaginas.

But Gwen could not stop talking because Gwen had no baby. She had done everything else right. She had done well in school and worked hard and gotten a good job because she lived in a world that told her she could have it all. But by the time Gwen looked up from achieving everything she'd been told was good, she'd missed out on the one thing she'd really wanted. Because everyone told her that being a mother was an unremarkable thing that anyone could do. It was so easy, teenagers did it by accident. She had been told that smart professional women waited.

And when Gwen thought about it, it was women who had told her this. Her mother. Her mentors in school. Her colleagues. Her bosses. It was women who pushed her to lean into her career. And it was women Gwen found in the online fertility forums and adoption message boards she trolled late at night. A whole generation of women who had cheated each other out of using their own bodies.

So Gwen called Diana, one of her professors from veterinary school. Didn't it seem crazy, like evolution was running backward, that a species would evolve to become less fertile? Did it seem like a sign that everything was falling apart? The end of humanity?

Diana pointed out that it wasn't necessarily a step backward; it was just a more selective step forward, a choice for more intentional procreation.

No, Gwen said. That's not how evolution is supposed to work.

So you're an evolutionary biologist now? Diana said. You specialized in ungulates.

But isn't it about life? Gwen said. Any life? Let all the selection in the world take place afterward, so long as life found a way in first?

Are you talking about ducks or are you talking about women? Diana asked. You're oversimplifying. Talking metaphorically. You sound like one of those fringy Reversalist people.

Gwen said, Who?

Carleton College

NORTHFIELD, MINNESOTA

TEN YEARS BACK

I t wasn't the way Nolan thought it would be. He had chosen Minnesota because of Elsa, but of course his parents had suspected this and fought him. Yet Nolan had all the Carleton brochures, the pictures of the labs and resources that would be at his disposal as a biology major, and so they had caved. It was almost four hours away from Park Rapids, after all. His parents moved him in that fall.

He had been calling Elsa since he got accepted to school. At first, she'd sounded panicky and tried to get off the line with him as quickly as possible. It had been almost five years since they had spoken, but he was older now and he wanted to talk about it. His parents wouldn't talk, and who else could possibly understand?

Once, he'd caught her asleep, and she'd been too drowsy to yell at him and they had talked for twenty minutes about nothing, really. A dream Elsa had been having. And they'd felt almost like real siblings until she told him to stop calling her, to forget about her and just go to college like a normal fucking kid.

I'm not a kid, Nolan had said. I'm not normal, he might have said, had Elsa not clicked off the line.

Nolan wouldn't call Elsa again for a little while, he told himself. He wanted to grow older first. The objectionable and boyish parts of him would be shed in those first weeks of college, he was sure. He was going to have sex with girls. And then he would call Elsa.

But instead, every night, Nolan found himself traveling the campus in packs of young men. The women had their own packs. They roamed campus in their enormous coats and hats and scarves in the relative safety of their respective herds and the burbling warmth of new alcohol. Every trek was the same cold shuffle, terminating in a dorm, behind whose metal door was only another pack of boys. Games with beer in red plastic cups. Admiring the posters they also had in their own dorms. Door after door opened and never were there any women. Never was there any promise of him feeling any more adult any more quickly.

Nolan wondered if he had allied himself with the wrong pack too quickly, but everyone Nolan met seemed the same. Nolan felt sure that he was different. Nolan came from twinkling, urban San Francisco, and his parents were brilliant, and then there was Elsa, an experience that he was sure the other boys could not even imagine. Nolan held his own life close to his breast and felt superior and disappointed in the other boys for not being more interesting or grown than they were.

They were all of them nineteen.

It was November, and they were on the trek, and it was freezing already, and Nolan was taking off his scarf as one of the members of his pack pushed open the dorm door to yet another night of trying to pretend they were living exciting young lives—then Nolan smelled perfume. The door opened and the warm radiator stink that came from all the dorms in winter hit him first, but then he could smell something . . . gardenias . . . Nolan's mother had taught him about flowers. And sure enough, when they pushed into the dorm, too eagerly, their fat plush coats squeezing each other together, there were the girls. All the girls were wearing skirts and stockings; a few even had bare legs. Clothes that could not possibly keep them alive outdoors. They had shed their coats like chrysalises. There was a heap of jackets on a bed in another room and they smelled like all kinds of different shampoos and perfumes, and as Nolan took off his own coat, he inhaled. He still made out something of gardenias, and he stiffened a little in his pants, imagining taking someone into that nest of coats. It was possible.

He loitered near a wall with a cup of bad vodka and orange juice.

There was a girl sitting on the arm of the couch. She was wearing a swingy black skirt and black stockings with rips in them. It was the rips that got Nolan. They were so neat—clean lines, flaps hanging open. It was like she had done it on purpose. On one very white knee there was a bright pink Band-Aid.

Nolan sat on the couch. He touched her cold knee. The Band-Aid.

What happened? he asked. He could not believe he was saying anything. That he was touching her. But this was an emergency. He could feel that it must be tonight or the girls would be lost back into the frozen campus, never to be heard from again.

I cut myself, the girl said. She leaned over and took the edge of the Band-Aid between her fingernails, sloppily painted. She peeled the Band-Aid away. There was a red line there, a small, totally straight cut. The flesh was dewy and sticky-looking where the Band-Aid had been.

How? Nolan asked.

She shook her head, embarrassed. Her hair, short to her chin, dyed a deep bottle red that was almost purple, danced around her face and Nolan smelled it. Gardenia. It was a perfume they sold at malls, strong and cheap, that Elsa's mother wore. Elsa was forever stealing sprays of it so that when she visited, she wafted into the house smelling of her mother in a way that made Ian look unhappy.

I was cutting the holes in my tights and I slipped, the girl said.

It looks pretty janky, Nolan said.

Thanks.

But I can help, he said. He pinched the rim of the ripped hole and tugged, the long expanse of her calf visible in the gape, until the edge of the tear gave way and a run sprouted and laddered its way to her shin. Now, he said. That looks right.

———

Later, as they picked their jackets from the mound, he said, Don't you just want to crawl inside and sleep there?

What? she said.

Nolan never-minded her because everything he said sounded strange and wrong these days, and he'd found that repeating himself seldom solved problems. The problem was the things he said in the first place. The problem was him.

They walked in silence, bundled in their enormous coats, back to Nolan's dorm. He'd left his roommates at the party, ensuring the room would be empty. The sidewalks were icy, so they had to high-step through deep snow, and by the time they'd gotten back to his dorm, they were exhausted.

Inside, he undid her zipper and then his own coat and then he wasn't sure what to do next. She should do something, Nolan felt, though he wasn't sure what. He didn't know what to do because there had only ever been Elsa that one time before and Elsa had known what to do. But he wanted something of his own, that wasn't Elsa's, so he had to try. She got everything first. His father, sex. Before he had even known what these things meant for him, they had been hers, and he wanted to take them back from her.

The girl in the ripped tights looked nervous. She was clutching her hands together and looking at the floor like she was waiting for Nolan.

They made it into the bed, but they didn't take off their clothes until they were under the covers, which was difficult in Nolan's single. Once they were naked, Nolan grabbed onto himself like he was dying. He assumed she would do the same. But she didn't. So he took her hand and moved it to her clit. But the girl snatched her hand away. It was in this moment that Nolan realized everything he thought he knew was wrong. The porn he'd watched was wrong. The one sexual experience he had spent five years replaying over and over in his head was wrong. What he and Elsa had done was not what everyone did and maybe it was even awful. Of course, he had been told this before. His parents had yelled and then broken apart the family and then refused to ever mention that night again. So Nolan had known it, factually, yes. But it was not until this moment that Nolan considered that maybe what happened *had* actually ruined him in some way. That in some other, better version of his life, this would have been the night he lost his virginity and bumbled around sweetly with this broody, shy girl who smelled of gardenias. But it was too late for that, and Nolan understood now that he would never have a chance to do things right the first time.

(Had this been the moment when everything went wrong? Nolan sometimes wondered. But no, there was a difference between realizing how wrongly he'd been made and the moment the wrongness actually happened. And so it was before this. It was further back.)

The girl took Nolan's hand and put it on her, and she took ahold of him. He yelped. Her hands were so cold.

The girl with ripped stockings tried to stroke his dick with her freezing hands, and Nolan wriggled further under the covers, because he felt like he was going to cry and did not want her to see. He was hard, but he hated it. He got up on all fours, crouched over her, and said, Is this okay?

I'm on birth control, the girl said. For my skin. And Nolan guessed this meant yes.

He took himself in his hand and tried to press into her, but he could not find the place. She did not help to guide him. Elsa would have helped. But this was his job now, he understood. He was supposed to take charge, and Nolan realized that he hated this. He wanted to be led places. To resist and then give in to desire. But he did not know how to tell the girl what he wanted. It was too embarrassing to ask, and he didn't really think she could give it to him if she tried. Nolan searched again for the place, but failed, and collapsed next to the girl, who had begun to cry.

I'm sorry, she said.

It's okay, Nolan said. Why are you sorry? I'm sorry.

After he'd walked her back to her dorm, it was almost midnight, and Nolan was walking in alternating patches of darkness and spotlight along the campus path, breaking the ice crust on the banks of fresh snow that had been rained upon and frozen overnight.

The streetlights reflected glossily on the ice crust. Nolan bent down and punched a fist through it. He thought it would feel satisfying to crack the shell. That his hand would go cleanly through. But instead, the top layer shattered like glass and sliced his wrist, once on the way through, and then again on the way out. The cut was not deep but it sang hot and cold as the snow melted. A tiny bead of blood welled up and he sucked it clean. Nolan stood there, watching the next bead of blood rise to the surface, and sucked it clean again. He was so miserable. He would stand here all night until he froze. He would suck every drop of blood from his body until he died.

He took out his phone and called Elsa.

Hello? There was bar noise, but she was up. She was out.

Where are you? Nolan asked.

Are you crying? Elsa said. Come on, New Baby, what can be that bad?

Can you come here?

You know that's a bad idea, Elsa said.

Where are you?

A bar in Little Falls, she said. There's a mechanical bull and a bunch of jackasses who think they're cowboys. They're all wearing flannel shirts even though their fathers are all soybean farmers.

That's close, Nolan said. You're close. You could come.

It's not, Elsa said. Nolan.

Please, he said.

———

More than two hours later, Elsa parked outside Nolan's dorm. She texted and he came down.

She was leaning against the ticking hood of her truck, wearing a green Carhartt coat and a gray wool cap pulled over her hair, which was longer than he remembered. There were empty coffee mugs on the dashboard and empty packs of cigarettes. Five years older than the last time he'd seen her and she was so obviously not a college student, so obviously older than him, a woman, that he felt as if he'd summoned a dangerous demigod, and he no longer knew what he'd intended to do next.

This is a bad idea, Elsa said again. Do you have any coffee?

We can't go up, Nolan said. My roommates came home and they're sleeping.

I drive all the way out here and we're going to freeze our asses off?

We could sit in your car, Nolan suggested.

Elsa yanked her truck door open. Nolan pulled the passenger-side handle three times before Elsa unlocked it.

The truck's heat smelled plasticky, as if something was melting inside. The radio played low guitar music and an orange streetlamp beam was cutting across the parking lot. Nolan felt bulky in his coat. He unzipped it.

Elsa unzipped her jacket and slipped her arms out of it. She lay back against the seat and twisted against the headrest to look at him. Her hair was staticky and danced around, silvery in the dark.

So what's wrong, New Baby?

Nolan began to cry.

Jesus Christ, Nolan.

It's all your fault, he said. You did this to me.

Let's not.

It's like you pressed the fast-forward button on my life and made me do things early, but now I'm here and I've already done everything, but I did it weird, and I don't know how to do things the normal stupid way like I'm supposed to. He sniffed.

You could have just yelled at me on the phone, Elsa said. I was in a warm bar and a man named Dylan was buying me drinks.

Nolan continued to cry.

All I'm saying is, I had a good situation going. I'm a twenty-five-year-old woman in bumfuck Minnesota and I've got to take good situations where I can find them.

She opened the console and took out a rumpled plastic baggie with two joints in it. Nolan calmed a little.

Elsa dug a lighter from her pocket. You had a good situation going earlier? Is that what this is about?

Why—

Your shirt's on backward.

You don't even care, Nolan said, pulling his sleeves.

I'm here, aren't I? Elsa said. She cracked her window and lit one of the joints. I drove over two goddamn hours so you could yell at me in person. She took a hit and exhaled out the window slit. You want some? she said.

Does this mean you're staying? Nolan asked.

I can drive fine.

He reached for the lit joint, but as he leaned in to take it, he found his face close to Elsa's and it had a kind of gravity to it, so Nolan leaned in and kissed her, palming her face with his cold hand, hooking his thumb beneath her jaw.

Her mouth was soft but he felt her tense up and recoil almost immediately and she pushed him back across the cab, hard.

Aw, fuck, Nolan. No.

They sat there for a long while.

Elsa took another hit of the joint. The radio was playing cowboy songs.

He leaned toward her again. He wanted this to make sense. If Elsa didn't make sense now, then what did that mean about everything that had happened before?

Nolan, she said, and drew her elbow back, like she might hit him, but she looked afraid.

I know, Nolan said, and he took the joint instead.

Leap's Island

See? Gwen said.

Down in the mud and reeds, a male duck had mounted a female and was beating her with his wings, pinning her still as he entered her.

A mosquito whined by Elsa's ear. Gwen, in her muddy swim shoes, without a baby, with a duck uterus nailed to her wall, gave Elsa a crawling feeling all over her skin.

The ducks were still fucking.

They're really going at it, Nolan said. He was leaning over the wooden railing, heimliching himself on the beam. Elsa felt like grabbing him and saying: Stop messing around. You're not a little kid. That was the problem with Nolan: he would always be younger than her. The New Baby. And somehow, this meant that she would always be more responsible for the two of them.

Have you ever seen a duck banded number twelve? Nolan asked.

His Paradise Duck? Gwen said. He could have been here, but I wouldn't know. I'm not interested in tracking males. I'm focused on the choices made by the females, and the repercussions for the ducklings. And, of course— She pulled them closer to the uterus, a sketched map in progress next to it.

This was your idea, Nolan whispered hoarsely near Elsa's ear. Let the record reflect, I did not suggest this.

See this? Gwen said, pointing at something fleshy that meant nothing to the Greys. Goes to nowhere. Nowhere! All these, she insisted, will not result in fertilization. Gwen was staring at the uterus as if it might have something to say in its defense.

Elsa had expected the Reversalists to be crazy. Legitimately mentally ill, or else crackpot hippies. But instead, Elsa found them willfully alone, playing out their misery in weird scientific pageants without audience. It had been a long time since she had seen him, but Elsa loved her father. She was proud of the elastic strength of his mind, uncluttered and expansive. The possibility that this was what had become of Ian was too much.

Sit! Gwen said suddenly, perhaps sensing she was losing them, and the children sank to the floor, cross-legged. Gwen dragged an Igloo cooler over to them.

So, are you ready? she said to Elsa.

Sure thing, Nolan said. Ready.

Actually, Gwen said, I'm only interested in female choice for this study.

I thought you were only interested in ducks, Elsa said.

Nolan said, I thought the whole reason we trekked out here was to be in your study.

I don't need you, Gwen said. But as you may have noticed—she gestured around at the island—I'm pretty short on female test subjects. So are you ready? she repeated to Elsa.

That definitely depends, Elsa said. How involved are my ovaries?

Only very indirectly, said Gwen. She rooted around in the Igloo cooler. From it she pulled five Ziploc bags with what appeared to be gray t-shirts inside them. She set them in a row in front of Elsa.

Sniff, she said.

What? Elsa said.

I'd like for you to smell each of these shirts, and then describe its smell to me in terms of intensity, pleasantness, and sexiness.

I'm sorry, sexiness?

This is a classic test, Gwen said.

What are you testing? Nolan asked.

Can't say. It would affect the results, Gwen said.

Nolan was intrigued. He had been to Sonoma once and the sommelier, a South African woman in a low-cut dress, had told him he had an excellent nose. Janine said the sommelier was just flirting with him, but Nolan had been proud when the somme-lier confirmed that he did indeed smell fresh cherries, and pipe tobacco, and fresh-cut grass. Whatever this test was, he was sure he'd be good at it, and it seemed unfair that only Elsa would get to participate.

Smell, Gwen told Elsa again, pointing to the first bag.

Fine, Elsa said. She'd got them here, she could get it over with quickly. She took out the first shirt and smelled.

I mean, it smells like a sweaty guy wore it, Elsa said. It smells iron-y like sweat and maybe a little funky too. Herbal.

Gwen twirled her pen at Elsa, requesting further information.

Elsa sighed. I would say the smell is very intense, not that pleas-ant, and largely unsexy, she said.

Okay, Gwen said. Next one.

As Elsa pressed her face to each soft shirt, she ultimately had to admit that there was something sexy about smelling mysterious men's clothing. One smelled like rising bread. Another like tomato soup and the can it came in. The fourth smelled like orange peels gone slightly rancid. The last shirt Elsa smelled, then balled up and smelled a second time, and a third, before she said: It smells like pond water. It smells like someone maybe wore it into a pond.

He didn't, Gwen said. The subjects just slept in them.

Well, okay, it smells like pond. Kind of vegetable and fresh.

How would you describe the intensity and sexiness?

Jesus, Elsa said. I mean, it's not that intense. That's what's nice about it, I guess. It's only a little bit there, in a way that makes you want to smell it again to make sure. That's sexy, I guess. Sure. This is the sexiest-smelling shirt. Is that what you wanted to hear?

Wow, Gwen said. Yes, absolutely. So just to be clear, shirts two and five are somewhat pleasant smelling and only shirt five you would describe as sexy.

Yes. Put it down for posterity, Elsa said. Are we done?

We are, Gwen said, closing her notebook.

Nolan, still feeling left out said, Now can you tell us what you were testing for?

Sure, Gwen said. In mate selection, traditional data show that women prefer the smell of pheromones from men who are significantly genetically different from them. It gives offspring a better chance of avoiding genetic diseases and increases viability. And that translates to the smell response to their pheromones.

Wait, Elsa said.

But in my case, what I'm looking for is a decrease in the overall rate of positive response. Gwen gestured to the ducks. I'm looking for a downward trend that trumps any genetic dissimilarity.

Are those t-shirts from—

The men on the island, sure, Gwen said.

Was one of them Ian's? Nolan asked.

Number five, Gwen said.

Oh God, Elsa said.

Two out of five is slightly lower than average, Gwen said. So depending on how the comparative DNA tests come back, it likely supports my hypothesis.

That's a horrible thing to have done. Not telling me that, Elsa said. She had her hand to her mouth. Nolan was gaping.

Remy's shirt was number two, which makes sense. Mitchell and the boys could be similar or not…She tapped her notepad with her pencil. The Grey shirt is confusing. Huh. Well, I'll just need a DNA sample from you so we can confirm, Gwen said.

Elsa didn't move.

How many do people normally find sexy? Nolan asked.

At least three, Gwen said, sometimes four, according to the original study. But they all smell terrible to me. That's the whole problem. That's my point.

Nolan said, I want to smell them.

It doesn't really work with same-gender samples, Gwen said. The biological reproduction element isn't in play.

Nolan said, Shuffle them around so that I won't know which is which.

Elsa said, Nolan, can we just— I'd like to go home.

I can't believe you didn't realize it was him, Nolan said. I have a really good nose, and his smell is so particular.

That's not really what the experiment is for, Gwen said.

Just do it, Nolan said. He slid across the floor, closer to her.

Gwen shuffled the shirts.

Nolan smelled each shirt twice. On the second pass he picked out the third shirt.

Nolan, you don't need to do this, Elsa said. It doesn't have anything to do with—

It's this one, he said. This is Dad's shirt.

It is, Gwen said. That's it.

Elsa rubbed her face with her hands.

Nolan smelled the shirt once more. He wasn't sure what he hoped getting this right would make him feel, but it hadn't worked and he felt desperately sad imagining his father here. He looked around the tree house. He could imagine Ian crouched by the shore, observing ducks. He could even imagine Ian on Esther's porch with a pair of binoculars. But the idea of Ian helping Gwen map a uterus put him over the edge.

This doesn't have *anything* to do with Duck Twelve? he asked.

Your father's duck? Gwen said. No, of course not. She looked at Nolan strangely.

Below, the ducks were still going at it by the sound of things. The female was honking.

Why "of course not"? Nolan asked.

Gwen said, I'm trying to sound the alarm here. These ducks are slowing procreation. It's only a matter of time before that ripples up the food chain. Your father, on the other hand, thought Reversalism was going to save us all. She made a sweeping circular gesture with her pencil.

Wait, what? Elsa said.

Gwen put down her notebook and looked at them like they were idiots. Slowly, she repeated herself: Ian didn't think the Reversal was cause for alarm. He was using Duck Twelve to prove we should embrace the Reversal. He was obsessed with that duck. With one data point. She shook her head.

I thought the whole point of Reversalism was that we were fucked, Elsa said. Isn't that why everyone's even here? She knew she sounded panicky, but ever since Ian had moved to Leap's, she'd understood that her father had joined a doomsday cult.

It is. And we are, Gwen said. That's the whole point of Mitchell's Reversalism, anyway. Most of ours. But your father saw it differently.

But aren't the ducks getting worse? Nolan asked.

The ducks are going backward, Gwen said. Which in most people's books means worse, yes. But Ian didn't think backward was so bad.

Gwen lit another Virginia Slim. Elsa reached out and took it from her. The smell of Ian's shirt had lingered and she wanted to fill her mouth with smoke.

After she'd lit another cigarette, Gwen said: Your father thought it was possible for an organism to evolve too far. He liked to say that going forward didn't always mean progress, because sometimes taking a step back was the best thing.

Nolan had his hands in his hair. He believed what?

Of course, he was crazy, Gwen said.

Nolan grabbed Elsa, his thumb on the knob of her wrist, pressing it like a button. In Nolan's grasp, she felt his hopefulness. They had always understood each other in this way, telegraphing desires.

So you're saying he wasn't a Reversalist? Elsa said. She jiggled her legs, dragged on the cigarette.

He was a Reversalist, Gwen said. He just disagreed about what Reversalism meant. We don't agree on much, she admitted, but Ian really ran away from the pack.

Why did he tell you this? Elsa asked.

He told everyone at his first intellectual trust meeting, Gwen said. She held her elbow, let her cigarette burn away. He was so excited. He thought he was bringing us this good news and we'd all be so delighted to hear it. Let me tell you, that didn't fly at all. After that, Mitchell never wanted your father to publish anything. It would have undermined the credibility of our work.

Credibility? Nolan said.

Gwen nodded. The children looked at her.

Does Mitchell understand, Elsa said, that people ... She wasn't sure how to say it. Does he have a sense of how Reversalism is received—

On the mainland, Nolan helped.

Does he know that everyone thinks we're crazy? Of course he does, Gwen said. If he didn't, he really would be crazy.

They laughed awkwardly.

So why did he care if Dad published? Nolan asked. There's very little to ruin, reputation-wise.

Gwen shook her head. That doesn't matter. People talk about crazy. They fight about crazy. So long as everyone's saying the same thing. You know about Scientology, right? About creationism? New Earth theory? You think it's wrong, but you know what it is and that people believe in it. And that makes it legitimate, whether you like it or not. If people stop spinning the same story, that's when you go from crazy to invisible.

———

When the Greys returned to their shack, Jinx rushed out, pantingly eager, circling and staring past them toward the path, looking for Ian and finding, instead, the two of them. They stood on the rickety ramp over the tidewater. It was starting to get dark, bugs emerging in the dusk, and Elsa focused too hard on petting the dog.

Ian was joyful in his journals. Ian was beloved by boy geniuses and old ladies. Ian was looking for proof that the world was not going to shit after all.

But Ian was still dead.

Maybe if we found the duck, Nolan said.

Shut up. It doesn't matter. It's all crazy, Elsa said, even though she wasn't sure she believed this herself.

Nolan said, I'm sorry I got so worked up about the test. I just wanted to prove, I don't even know what.

Why do you care what these people think? Elsa said. It's just beyond me who you think you're trying to impress here.

Nolan wanted to say: The grown-ups.

It was what he did at work. It was what he'd done as a child. It was what he feared he was doing with Janine. He had always wanted to please the grown-ups. Because grown-ups were the ones who decided what was good and what was bad. If he didn't please them first, how would he ever know if he had the authority to be a grown-up himself?

Nolan wanted to say: It's you I am trying to impress.

Because Elsa had always seemed like a grown-up to him. Had been outspoken about how unremarkable she found him, articulating so precisely the ways he feared his father saw him, and so he could not help wanting her to see him better. To see him as someone who *knew* Ian. Was like him, even. But this was stupid. Pleasing her was an old trap and they weren't children anymore.

I'm sorry I made you come out here. Nolan grabbed the walkway railings, bouncing them a little. I just needed to know what he thought was so important.

I mean, I get it, Elsa said. She looked up from the dog. But I think being out here is just going to make you more confused and sad. These are not good people to go looking for answers from.

He laughed.

Elsa said, So let's just pack up his stuff and go, yeah? We've only got a few more days before the post boat comes.

———

The Greys gathered stacked folders of handwritten notes and tabulations. They put the many legal pads, the bags of feathers, the weatherproof notebooks away. They did this quietly. But as they thought about going home, to Park Rapids and to San Francisco, they wondered what this would mean for them. Ex-sister. Ex-brother. After all, Ian was the final thing they'd had in common, and now he was gone. Which meant, once they left the island, there was no reasonable reason for them to ever see each other again.

Eventually, it was late, it was dark, and everything was neatly in boxes.

Elsa was hunched over, reading Ian's field journal again.

Nolan walked a circle around the shack. He unstopped the vodka bottle and poured some into two cups. The pineapple juice had been sitting warm in its carton and was probably rancid, but Nolan poured a splash in each cup anyway. He handed one to Elsa.

What is this? she said.

We're mourning.

Elsa stared into her cup but did not drink. She looked up at Nolan.

You know, if Gwen is right about how Ian saw the Reversal, then maybe he didn't kill himself, she admitted.

Or maybe no one believed in him, so he did, Nolan said.

You mean *we* didn't believe him.

Either way, he's dead, Nolan said, and knocked his cup against Elsa's, a little too rough. The drink sloshed.

Even in light of what Gwen had said, even though Elsa's own certainty was slipping, Nolan was starting to understand what Elsa had been saying. Here, on the island, he was coming to think that there was no such thing as a person who would not, who would never, kill himself. Wasn't continuing to be evidence that a person believed he was owed space among the living? How long could a person possibly last if they didn't feel they deserved a piece of the world? Nolan felt entitled to precisely nothing. It was possible Ian had come to feel the same. Possible that the years of no one believing in his work had taken a toll.

Nolan drank his whole cup down and poured himself another. Elsa did the same.

She lay on Ian's bed. Just a mattress on the floor. Nolan lay next to her and held her hand. She didn't stop him.

I don't feel sad, Nolan said.

You might not.

Ever?

I might not, Elsa said.

That's not true.

It's because we don't know for sure. Whether it was an accident.

We know, Nolan said. You were right.

She turned toward him. New Baby—

Don't call me that.

Nolan—

Why do you think he did it? Really?

I'd rather not find out, Elsa said.

That's crazy.

I am totally sure that most of the time it's better to never find out anything at all.

Elsa.

Especially about Dad.

This is different, Nolan said.

But Elsa knew it wasn't.

It was when Elsa found out that Ian wasn't her biological father that their family had cracked.

It wasn't the first crack, but it was an irreparable one. Ian had known she wasn't his for years, since the separation, but had not told her. At the time, the lying had seemed like the biggest parental failing of all, but these days, Elsa sometimes thought that what they should have done a better job of was hiding it from her. Sometimes she thought that if they had protected her from the truth more thoroughly, everything wouldn't have gone so wrong. Elsa had made them wrong, yes, and pulled Nolan down with her, but *the knowing* was what had started it.

He loved you just the same after he found out, Nolan said. It didn't matter to him.

But he left, Elsa said. So it did. He left to start a new fucking family.

He left Ingrid. He still loved you. In spite of the biology, which was a really big deal for him, and you've never appreciated that. He only felt differently once you went and messed it all up later.

I messed it up?

Are you serious? Nolan sat up on the mattress.

I was hardly alone.

Nolan thumped the floor, and Jinx startled awake.

Yes, Elsa. You fucked things up.

The dog barked.

Elsa sat up and grabbed Jinx by the snout. She held her velvety muzzle as if to comfort her with her own silence. What a fucking child Nolan was. As if he had not been willing to come to bed with her. As if anyone ever did anything they didn't want to do. Elsa felt a quickening in her blood. A tingling in her knees. The vodka at work. All Elsa ever did was give people permission to be who they really were.

You helped, Elsa said. She prodded Nolan with her foot. If I remember, you were very good at helping. She laughed.

Shut up, shut the fuck up, Elsa. He slid away from her. Sat against the wall. You were the one who couldn't handle your shit and so you started with the sex stuff. And you only did it because you knew what it would do to him. And then after you'd properly fucked me over, you dropped me. Because I was never the point. Ian was the whole point.

It had nothing to do with the sex for him, Nolan.

Yes it did. Evolution, genetics, everything was about sex for him. It was about you.

It had remarkably, fucking insultingly little to do with me, and you know it.

It was that he didn't want you to be ruined.

Nolan threw his hands up. Well, you did it. Fucking congratulations.

Did what?

Ruin me. For him and anyone else.

You seem shipshape, Nolan, Elsa said. I think you've turned out just swell.

Are you insane? That's why we're here, Elsa. Because you did ruin me. You ruined all of us. You ruined Dad. And *if* he killed himself? Guess why.

These were her own worst fears in Nolan's mouth, and Elsa felt the blow in her spine, in her gut, behind her eyes.

We were just stupid teenagers, she tried. It wasn't that big a deal.

You weren't, Nolan said. It was your birthday weekend. You weren't a teenager.

That's not right, Elsa said. She got up, too fast, and the blood rushed from her head. For a moment she saw white.

You had just turned twenty, Nolan said.

Elsa felt as if she might be sick. She pressed her eyes with her fingers, hard.

Had her math really been wrong? She wasn't sure why it made any difference if she was twenty and not nineteen. And yet, it *did* matter that they weren't both teenagers. Nolan was right. She was going to be sick to her stomach. She looked around the shack, but there was nowhere to go. She was trapped. The post boat wouldn't come for days.

I'm going swimming, Elsa said.

What?

Elsa started stripping her clothes off.

It's past midnight.

I'm a big girl.

It could be dangerous, Nolan said. Dad—

Grow up, Nolan.

Elsa pulled on her bathing suit. Nolan saw that her flesh was damp and creased from her clothes; they had been cutting into her. Everything Elsa had ever done seemed to be a fight with her skin. A fight to get out of it or to find something beyond it that mattered to her half as much. Nolan had watched her struggle for years, and he could see it now—in the creases across her belly where her shorts buttoned, in the red welts where her bra straps had hung on her— all the ways she was still not free.

But Nolan loved Elsa's body. He loved it precisely because it was not like his own. The sameness of bodies was for real siblings and they were something different.

It was never the sameness of their bodies that made things monstrous between Elsa and Nolan. It was the sameness of their thinking. Their cultural Greyness. The way they snarled, worried, knew each other's thoughts as if they were their own.

Their bodies pulled together the same way other people's bodies did. And when it had all gone wrong, when they'd had sex, years ago, Nolan didn't really know why everyone had been so surprised. After all, he was half Ian, and Elsa was half Ingrid, and weren't those poles that had attracted before?

Elsa banged out the door, wearing only her swimsuit. Gone.

Elsa, Nolan called, but not very loudly.

Jinx came and sat her bony haunches in Nolan's lap. He pet her tentatively.

It's okay, Nolan said. Good girl.

A constellation of mute insects danced around the cup of vodka and pineapple juice Elsa had left on the floor. Nolan reached for his drink, and as he sipped, he thought that maybe Elsa was right that they would be happier knowing nothing. Maybe if they could forget that Ian had lost his mind for this research. Forget that he had slowly become someone unrecognizable to them. Forget that he had given up on either of them amounting to anything. Forget that he had stopped caring about his children. Forget that it was all maybe their fault. Maybe then, if they knew nothing, they could become something like happy.

Nolan ruffled the soft hairs behind Jinx's ears that would not lie straight. He thought of turning her loose. Just letting her run out the door.

You wouldn't last one day in these woods, he told the dog.

Lake Itasca

TEN YEARS BACK

Years before she swam in the silty Gulf where the Mississippi lets itself go, Elsa went to Itasca, the river's Minnesota headwaters. The Mississippi ran clear at the source, as yet unmuddied by its travels, and how Elsa loved its clean-pooling mouth.

It was Ian who took her. The first time she had seen him since the troubles.

Keiko had been sick, but she was fine, Ian said. A touch of cancer. She was being treated and they expected her to soon go into remission.

This story had come confusedly across the telephone line as Ingrid used a porous blue sponge to delicately soap away egg yolk and crumbs from fruit-patterned plates. Elsa sat at the kitchen table and watched Ingrid, the cordless nestled into her shoulder. People often called Ingrid when news of sickness came; a hospice nurse, they imagined, would know what to do. But this was different. Ingrid *hrmmm*ed at Ian, while she looked not at the plate she was redressing so tenderly, but out the window, at the shore of Potato Lake, where a plastic six-pack ring was being lapped at on the shore, a six-pack ring almost certainly left there by a lakeside boy who'd spent all night waiting for Elsa to come out and fuck and

144

when she hadn't, had found no consolation besides whatever those rings had contained.

Elsa thought Ingrid looked at those rings like she knew.

But Elsa had stopped going out to the lake.

Since she had driven to see Nolan and he had kissed her in the truck, she'd felt wobbly and frightened, like the past was going to explode in on her again at any moment. As a preventive measure, she had called the man named Dylan who had written his number on her arm that same night. The numbers were smudged when she'd arrived home after the long drive from Northfield, but they had worked. She and Dylan had been dating for a month now, and in spite of her reasons for calling him, Elsa found she actually liked Dylan: liked his worn jeans and sly humor, liked how he was the only thing that kept Elsa tethered to the present at all.

Still, when the phone rang, and it was Ian, Elsa felt sure that despite being twenty-five years old, she was about to get in trouble with her parents all over again.

Ingrid said, We'll see you soon, and hung up the phone, and tousled the little fruit plate dry with a clean towel, and placed it carefully back in the cabinet, while Elsa told herself she would not ask her mother who was coming. She could not make it so plain that she cared. Ingrid lifted the next dish from the breakfast table, jam smeared across it obscenely.

Who will we see soon? Elsa asked, even though she hated herself for it.

Life is too short, Ingrid said. It was something, as a hospice nurse, she was allowed to say. But it wasn't an apology. It was the kind of empty sweetness she'd tried to fatten Elsa on for years.

———

Apparently, because Keiko was sick, because life was short, Ian was reaching out to Elsa. He wanted to see her. After going silent for the five years since she and Nolan got in trouble. Despite moving out when she was six, the year he found out she was not his.

Elsa protested, but her mother refused to engage her.

Since Keiko's sickness, Ingrid had started to read *Anna Karenina*, a thing she had always meant to do and never found time for.

The women were sunk in the soft, low couches of the living room, waiting for Ian to arrive. It was cloudy and hot outside, threatening to rain, and Elsa was of the opinion that this whole outing should be cancelled. Because what was the point, really, of going to a park in the rain.

The point is to see your father in the rain, Ingrid said. The light in the room was weak and gray and the whole day made Elsa feel as if everything were intangible and sad and crushing her under its dogpile fatness.

He hates me, Elsa said.

Oh, he doesn't really, Ingrid said. Your father says he hates all sorts of things, but he never cares enough about the feeling to hang on to it for long.

You realize that makes him sound like an idiot, right?

Ingrid turned to page fifteen of *Anna Karenina*. Let's be kind, she said. He's a savant.

It's been five years.

You might consider the fact that you were the one who behaved so badly. It's him who should be in a bad mood about seeing you.

How can you say that? You're supposed to be on my side.

Because I love you, and no one else is brave enough to talk to you properly. You're a rather frightening young woman.

I'm twenty-five years old and I live with my mother. I teach second grade.

A suspicious cover story, Ingrid said.

There was knocking at the door. Elsa pressed herself deeper into the couch. She was afraid of seeing him, but more than that, she'd spent the past five years trying not to think about what she'd done and avoiding the thought that she might be a kind of monster person. A person who, in the face of her father and the knowledge he carried, it was impossible to deny she might be.

They went to the door. Ingrid opened it, Elsa standing behind her mother.

Ian was wet, but it wasn't raining. He held a dripping umbrella.

Caught in the neighbor's sprinkler. Hullo, Ingrid.

Hullo, Ian.

I won't keep her out too late, Ian said, as if Elsa were not grown.

Even though she had known for five years that Ian was not her biological father, Elsa could not quit the old habit of seeing her own face in his. Ian had always said she looked like her mother, Scandinavian genes running strong, but Elsa had only ever seen Ian.

Hullo, Elsa, Ian said.

He smiled. Such an effort to smile.

In that moment Elsa knew Ian was committed to pretending that everything was fine, just dandy, and that they would not talk about the past or Nolan or what had happened five years ago, after all. She hated him for that.

————

Ian had told Elsa the history of the place a hundred times. But on the car ride there, he told her again. She let him, because this was safer than talking about anything else.

Eight thousand years ago, nomadic tribes hunted bison and moose near the unnamed headwaters with flint-tipped spears. Eight hundred years ago, Woodland people created burial mounds near the shores. After that, there were the Dakota and the Ojibwe. After that, French fur traders.

It was only after all this that the headwaters were "discovered" by American geographer Henry Rowe Schoolcraft in 1832. Schoolcraft's wife was part Ojibwe, and he wanted to give the place an "Indian name." He spoke no Ojibwe, so he made one up. Schoolcraft combined the Latin words *veritas,* for "truth," and *caput,* for "head," and the lake and source of the river was named Itasca.

Elsa and Ian hiked the path to the headwaters, because while there were scattered ruins and other inlets, the little pool was the only true reason to come to Itasca.

There were very few people in the park. The threat of rain had kept them away. So they were alone on the trail, but once the history lesson had run dry, they did not speak. It seemed impossible that Elsa should speak. She needed to be forgiven to speak, and so she had to wait until that came. Ian was meant to start them off, she felt, but he wasn't making any signs of taking the lead.

They walked the path: crumbly pale sand, and rocks that got in shoes, and pine needles. Soon, Ian outpaced her, and she was lagging behind, which was embarrassing.

Elsa was out of shape, heavier than she'd ever been before in her life, and she wondered if Ian noticed and was disgusted by her, as she was disgusted by herself. She was fascinated and horrified by the new heaviness in her hips. The soft bulge of her belly and the way it formed a ridge above the waistband of her jeans. Even her fingers, Elsa swore, looked larger. The silver ring she wore on her thumb seemed tighter lately, her finger bursting around it, like tree flesh grown around an impediment. Elsa twisted the ring until it hurt. She suddenly needed Ian to speak to her so badly she could not stand it. She felt that she would die if she did not know, one way or another, if he still cared at all, and so she scurried farther ahead to catch up with him on the dusty slope, and she grabbed Ian's hand in hers and continued marching determinedly fast alongside him, keeping pace.

Ian stopped and looked down at their linked hands, searching for an explanation. He looked at his twenty-five-year-old daughter confusedly and did not understand what she needed at all.

Are you okay? he said.

It was mortifying. And she wasn't. Of course she wasn't. So Elsa snatched her hand away. Elsa ran.

It was exactly as she'd feared. That the moment she felt safe and expressed her love, however small, he'd pulled away and she'd seemed foolish. And this was how she knew she'd been right, he still thought of her as a monster, a thing no one could love. Elsa knew all this. Knew better. Knew this every day. She had just forgotten for a moment how thoroughly she had ruined things.

It was the third rail of Elsa's mind, and she had spent the past five years desperately training herself not to touch it.

She slipped up sometimes—thought of her father, which led to thinking about why she had not seen her father, which was because he was not her father at all, which led to thinking about Nolan—and just like that, Elsa might find herself crouching down on the school playground, unable to breathe, or shaking so hard in the quiet of her truck she had to pull over, or scratching at her own wrists so she left long marks along their pale undersides, clawing so she would feel anything other than the sickness of a remembering that chattered at her: Why had she done it why had she done it why had she done it?

She'd done it because they had lied to her, all three parents, for years. They were so intent on everyone getting along, on making things pleasant, that they had perpetrated this generational conspiracy to hide from Elsa who she really was. She'd only found out because she'd donated blood at a college drive, bragging to her friends how she didn't faint at the sight of the needle, but when they'd given her the donor sticker, NEGATIVE O HERO!, she'd been sick after all. Ingrid was A and Ian was AB, so how the fuck was Elsa O?

She'd driven straight home to Potato Lake, and when she came screaming into the house, she'd found Ingrid still in her scrubs, eating a tomato omelet. Ingrid sighed and told her the story, which had the nightmarish quality of being so strange it could only have been the truth. In this moment, everything Elsa had feared since Ian left them when she was six, the thing she'd exhausted herself worrying over for years, had arrived. It was finally true: she was losing her father.

He's still your father, everyone kept saying. I'm still your father.

She'd done it because Elsa didn't trust that. There was no more biological safety net. He would not stay with her no matter what, the way a real father would. There was no reason for him to love her at all unless she was very good, and Elsa knew she was not very good, so it was only a matter of time before she would lose him. The unconditional had been made conditional and she could not bear it.

How bad a thing could she do and still have him stay? If Elsa could stake out the outer limits of how wrong she could be, and still have Ian love her, maybe then she could stay safely within those boundaries. What were the conditions of Ian's love?

Maybe she'd done it because Nolan had grown so tall and had seemed, for a moment, like a stranger. Or because they hardly ever saw each other and so he *was* a stranger in all the ways except the one that mattered. Maybe she did it because he had baked her that stupid hopeful coconut cake.

Or maybe Elsa had sensed ruin coming for the Greys and wanted to get it over with quickly. If she was the one doing the ruining, yes, everyone would be angry and hurt, but at least Elsa would have chosen it. She hadn't chosen anything at all, it turned out, the whole twenty years they had been lying to her. This choice would be hers.

But she had gone too far.

Because even so many years later, Ian had looked at her hand in his like it was an impossible thing. So Elsa ran and ran until she reached the headwaters, and when she got there she was gasping, beyond out-of-breath. She tried to breathe more slowly. She could not be like this when Ian caught up with her.

Surely he was running, even now, about to catch up? She didn't see him.

Water flooded the plain of flat, tannish rocks in the bed. It pooled in places where the rocks were heaped up. The headwaters were absolutely clear. It looked like nothing. But it was something. And there was a message to remind you. A tree, hacked into a signpost. The trunk was carved and painted with yellow lettering that read:

HERE 1475 FT

ABOVE

THE OCEAN

THE MIGHTY

MISSISSIPPI

BEGINS

TO FLOW

ON ITS

WINDING WAY

2552 MILES

TO THE

GULF OF

MEXICO

Elsa leaned against the signpost and heaved, desperate for breath and hating herself totally.

When Ian appeared around the bend in the trail, Elsa saw that he was walking—ambling along in his green pants and stupid white sneakers—that he had not sped up at all to catch her.

Ian walked until he was standing next to her at the mouth. He did not look at Elsa's ugly red face. He bent down and started unlacing his shoes. He peeled off white sport socks, revealing his pale feet with the clean, rounded nails. He balled up his socks and put them into his shoes. Then he rolled up his pants. All the while, Elsa's chest heaved.

Ian rose and walked into the water. It must have been cold, but he didn't wince. He just looked around and nodded, as if satisfied by the arrangement of life available to them. The water coursed around his ankles. He held out his hand. He waited, Elsa on the bank.

(Sometimes Elsa thought of that day and how she did not let Ian pull her from the shore. Sometimes she told herself that if she had taken his hand again, if they had gone into the headwaters, maybe years later neither of them would have wound up choking on the Gulf.)

Leap's Island

Elsa stumbled over divots in the sand, the backs of her legs burning as she trekked across the beach. There was light coming through the waxy blur of the shack windows, she carried a Coleman lantern, and then there was the moon to see by. The strap of her bathing suit was tangled and she pulled at it, trying to make it lay straight.

Elsa stepped in a hole. Her foot came away wet. She had crushed a clutch of turtle eggs and a mucusy strand hung from her foot. She rubbed it clean with a handful of sand. There were turtles along the shore, flippering, making more divots, filling them with more slick ping-pong eggs. Elsa's chest felt tight. She wheezed.

She found it hard to breathe when she was made to think about things she'd done wrong. And she had done something wrong. He had been fourteen, and she had been twenty. It was awful, because twenty was so much older than fourteen. And it was awful, because twenty was still so young. Because, from the very first day, when she left him in that hole, she should have taken better care of Nolan, but also her fucking parents should have taken better care of her. It had happened the week Ingrid admitted that Ian was not Elsa's father. That they had lied to her for twenty years. Back then, Elsa could barely hold herself together. She'd been exploding and collapsing in on herself like a goddamn dying star.

Why hadn't anyone helped her?

Elsa approached the tide line. She set down her lantern and waded in.

The water was blood-warm. The fucking South. Everything ran hot and bodily. It wasn't good for her. She needed Potato Lake, which smelled green and reassured her of who she was. She needed the Minnesota freeze.

Elsa waded deeper into the warmth. How did a person drown himself? The water was black and reflected the lantern light from the shore in garbled spots. Elsa could not see her feet, and she thought maybe it was like disappearing yourself. A magic trick. She waded ahead. The small push and pull of the current urging her to go one way and then the other. You didn't swim to kill yourself, did you? Probably, you walked. Or carried something in your pockets. But Ian had been naked, only as heavy as his own self.

She imagined Ian carrying a great invisible something wide in his arms, rambling along the ocean bottom, walking through a forest of kelp, until he'd found a spot so deep he could put his burden down. She could do that.

Back then, what had wrecked her most was the fact that Ian had known she wasn't his since he'd left when she was six. That this was why he'd left, and that all that time afterward he'd only been pretending he was still her father, when he knew full well there was nothing of him in her at all.

The water came up to the small of Elsa's back. She slogged deeper. It came to between her shoulder blades.

When she'd first heard Ian was dead, she'd imagined violent southern riptides. Hot-weather storms. She had not imagined the Gulf. The water lapped quietly.

He would've had to swim through this bathwater until he'd exhausted himself. Elsa started to paddle. He must have worked to drown himself.

Elsa stroked. She swam a long time. She was a good swimmer. Was Ian? How long had he paddled before the water took him?

Back on land, the lights in the shack went out. Elsa treaded water. The moon was bright, but the new darkness Nolan had created spooked her. She was very far out now.

She paddled back a bit, too fast, and then had to stop to catch her breath. She was still very far away.

Why hadn't anyone helped her?

Elsa laughed, choked on water. Spat it up again.

Elsa had always told herself she'd lost Ian once he'd found out she wasn't biologically his. But she hadn't—Nolan was right. She hadn't even lost him yet when they'd walked in Itasca and he'd tried to pull her into the headwaters. Even after everything, Ian had held his love out to her again and again, and every time, she'd refused to take it. Because it wasn't perfect. Because she couldn't tell the difference between unconditional and infallible. Because she wanted back the illusion of her childhood, that era of certainty, and if she couldn't have that, she would take nothing.

It was too late now. She dunked and choked again.

She was too far away.

She had only wanted to know what it felt like. Not to do it, really. She was so sure Ian had drowned on purpose, but looking back at the distant shoreline, she supposed she'd now proved that it could have been an accident. Maybe he'd come out this far not really meaning to do it, just curious about what it would take. She laughed. She was so stupid. She floated on her back. This was what they told the children of Potato Lake to do if they got tired while swimming. The dead man's float. Elsa floated like Ian. She saw Orion and Cassiopeia. She saw the moon. She did not see Mars, but she knew it was there.

Then she smelled boat diesel. A waft of it over the water and the sound of a motor. Someone was coming toward her. Someone would save her.

She treaded water as the lights of the boat got nearer. Her legs grew rubbery. The engine got louder. She was alone and half naked off the coast of an island full of quacks. Whoever it was might do something horrible to her. Was that better or worse than being left to drown? The diesel was thick, and she coughed. Fine, she thought, let the boatman come.

But then there was music. As the boat neared, she heard the distinct beat of a dance song everyone was playing that summer.

Hello? Do you need help? came a voice from the boat. The song went away.

No! she shouted, suddenly afraid. Go away! She tried to swim, but her legs cramped and she dunked under. Came up again.

I don't need help, Elsa said again.

Elsa Grey? he said.

The boat drew near, and in the lantern light she could make out a case of beer on the bench. A radio. And Mitchell Townes.

Mitchell? Elsa said. She was out of breath. She dunked under again. She could not keep treading much longer.

He reached over and grabbed her elbow. I'm going to heave you up, alright? he asked. As if, without her permission, he would let her drown. Would be too polite to keep her from doing it.

Fucking help me, Elsa said.

She kicked as Mitchell grabbed her under the armpits and hoisted her into the boat.

She scrambled up and sat on the bench. She panted, dripping water into the boat. She pulled her bathing suit straight. Mitchell was close, and she could feel his breath, which smelled like beer. Could tell by the way he was looking at her that he was at least a little drunk.

Elsa hugged her arms across her chest. Suddenly she was cold. Mitchell took a blanket from beneath the bench and handed it to her.

What are you doing out here? he said.

I was drowning myself. Experimentally, she said. But I didn't factor in all the variables and I almost actually did it.

She'd tried to jettison her whole self into the sea, and the sea had taken her too seriously. Elsa could now see how distant the shore was. It seemed impossibly far, one girl's body across all that way, and it was just pure luck that Mitchell had come along.

You could be sad and also die the wrong way. You could be sad but not be dead because you were sad. Shivering in Mitchell's boat, she saw this. So maybe Ian's death *was* a kind of unforced error. Maybe thinking that she and Nolan had supplied Ian with the force to kill himself was straight-up millennial narcissism.

To think: she'd imagined the two of them together might be more powerful than the whole of the Gulf.

Mitchell lifted a can of Schlitz. Elsa took it. She was not dead and she was going to drink a Schlitz and this was good. It was warm but bubbly.

What are you doing out here? Elsa said.

Mitchell reached for the radio and turned it up. A baseball game was now playing. The Texas Rangers.

Rebroadcast. Signal's stronger out here, Mitchell said.

Mitchell looked older than she'd first thought. A little leathery. He sipped his beer and she hers. She pulled the blanket closer around her. Her hair was soaking it clean through.

How did *you* get to be a Rangers fan?

I spent a while on the mainland, Mitchell said, when I was eighteen. He pivoted to show her the back of his leg. His tan revealed the long, shocking white scars she'd noticed at the Lobby. They were crenulated and puffy and covered the soft underpart of his knee. There was also a piece missing from his calf, she saw now.

How'd you do that? she said, because she could tell he wanted her to ask. And because she liked it when people offered up their bodies in this way, as evidence.

———

It was stupid and it was his fault. He'd been moving too quickly. His father, David, had asked him to build new steps for his mother's shack; the old ones were rotted through, like every other soggy thing on the island. Why this was his job and not David's, he didn't know. Mitchell was eighteen and resented being bossed around, but his father bossed around everyone on the island, so he couldn't complain.

The saw had been balanced on the porch railing. He'd laid it there only for a minute while he drilled together the finished planks. When he'd put the drill down on the step, the saw had tipped. It was heavy, a crosscut saw, and so had its own momentum as it fell, teeth first, like a mouth, from the railing. Mitchell tried to move away, but he'd pivoted on his back leg and so the saw bit into him, wedged into his calf, right below the back of his knee, at the top where the muscle bulged out. It did not cut clean through. Instead it stuck there, the weight of the saw pressing farther and farther into his flesh.

He grabbed the saw. He should have cut everything first before he started assembling the steps. He should not have put the saw there. It was hasty. His brain told him this over and over now that the blade had sunk into his leg. His brain told him this with the urgency of a new thought each time, as if to understand this now could undo what had already happened. It was such a small slice of time that had passed. Surely he could cross back the way he'd come? Go back to just a moment before?

Mitchell yelled. The delay of feeling had expired. His body wanted him to run, as if it could get away from the pain. But Mitchell made himself be still. He held the saw steady as he slowly lowered himself to the ground. He twisted around to see the back of his leg. There was a flap, and it was dark, almost black near the edges; the blade had not been clean, and there were beads of blood emerging from the sides. Mitchell's back seized up with revulsion, and pain, and he shivered, but still he held the saw. He knew he needed to pull it out, that he would not be able to get to help if he had to hold the saw at the same time. But there was a hot white line of pain in his body that would resolve itself into a scream when he pulled the blade from his leg, and he didn't want to do it.

He pulled the saw carefully, a workman with his tool, and as the teeth retracted from his flesh, he yelled because there was nothing else to do. The flap gaped away from the leg it belonged to, and Mitchell dropped the wet blade onto the ground, and he pressed the flap to his leg and yelled again.

He knew the wound was dirty inside. He did not want to press it closed. He wanted to open it up and wash it. He wanted to look inside and see what was there. But if he did, the blood would come too fast, so he pressed. And he stood. And he went looking for help. And as he did, blood trickled from beneath the well of his knee and down his calf the way sweat does when it runs into a sock.

Mitchell found his way to his mother, who lay him in his bed while she tried to clean the wound. Get David, she told one of the women.

David came, but refused to take Mitchell to the hospital. He'd managed to raise his son on the island for eighteen years without exposing him to the poison of mainland life and he wasn't about to change that now. David left the room, knowing he would be unable to hold to the ideals he forced on everyone else if he had to stare his son in the face while he proclaimed them.

Mitchell's mother gave him someone's painkillers, and one of the men stitched his leg up with fishing line, and everyone said he would be fine, even though they all knew that this was what *they hoped* would happen, not what was likely. This was how every bad thing ever happened to the Leap-Backers: insisting on believing in the world they wanted in the face of the world that was.

And of course Mitchell wasn't fine. The wound was infected and only got worse.

He was sick for weeks, hallucinating with fever and infection. Time started to slip for him, and by the time Mitchell's mother got him off the island and to the hospital, the wound was septic and they had to cut away part of his leg.

In the hospital, Mitchell grew to love the morphine drip they gave him.

Time kept slipping.

Mitchell had elaborate morphine dreams spun from the stories his father used to tell him about the Darwin Walking Backward and the island reverse-spinning into a pure and uncorrupted state. He dreamt of Darwin's skull cane, tortoises, finches, the HMS *Beagle* cutting backward through its own wake.

At some point, his mother went back to the island. She just really hated hospitals, she explained, couldn't bear all those sick people and machines, the way the hospital smelled. Mitchell remembered his mother shoving money into his hospital pillow before she went. Mitchell had seen money only a few times before; they had little use for it on the island. The green bills sticking out of his pillowcase were so miraculous and strange that he kept staring at them, and perhaps it was because he was so distracted by the money that he could not remember what it was his mother had said about returning. Whether she had promised to return to him at all.

On the day they were meant to discharge him, it occurred to Mitchell that there was no one around to tell him what to do, which was terrifying and thrilling. It was the first time in his life this had ever happened.

He was on his own. He could choose.

So he ran away.

He had one pair of hospital pajamas and a bottle of OxyContin.

He crashed in shelters, he crashed in churches, he crashed in strangers' vans. He crashed with kids he sold Oxy to and he crashed with kids he bought heroin from when the Oxy got too expensive.

Mitchell spent two years running and crashing, and time slipped for him in new ways.

He told himself that anything was better than going back to the island.

But one morning he woke up with the Darwin tattoo. A black outline of the HMS fucking *Beagle* on his bicep that a friend had done for him the night before when he'd been out of his head. Seeing the *Beagle* there on his arm, it was hard to deny how much he missed the island. Some part of his brain, tired of being ignored, had made the evidence conspicuous on his body. And Mitchell couldn't ignore it, not when his arm throbbed all week. He was dope sick, and tired of crashing, and maybe the island felt like the only place he might be able to get clean. On the island, he would have no other choice.

Mitchell made it back to Leap's, almost nodding out on his way across the Gulf in a boat with an about-to-kick motor he'd traded the last of his stuff for, but when he arrived, he saw the wreckage of the commune on the shore and realized it was gone.

He was too late.

His father had been dead a year; his mother had run away. He would never see either of them again. This wreckage was his inheritance.

Mitchell got off the boat. A new man on an old shore.

———

Elsa reached over and pulled Mitchell's leg toward her. She touched the scar. She cupped his calf in her hand. Mitchell leaned into her grip.

He piloted the boat back home.

Mitchell took her to the Lobby. It was dark, and from the pool, the popping sound of the fish mouths breaching the surface came in intervals. There were several ducks sleeping beneath the stairwells, and Elsa left wet footprints on the wood steps as she followed Mitchell upward. He carried a lantern.

You live up here? she asked.

For a long time now, he said.

Upstairs, the walls had once been papered in a pattern of ferns, but large strips had fallen away, and beneath the paper the walls were a mottled reddish color, paint or mold. There were alcoves along the hallway with dead sconces in them, their frosted glass grown over with moss. The floor alone looked unaged, as if Mitchell himself had scuffed it to a good polish over the course of many years.

Almost his whole life had been lived on this island. Elsa wanted to learn how to be alone and to need nothing like Mitchell. She would need to, if she was ever going to survive on Mars.

She knew that fucking people who seemed as if they had all the answers wouldn't get her any closer to her own. Would not change who Elsa was in any permanent kind of way. And yet.

The enormous bedroom he led Elsa to held the skeleton of a canopy bed with a made-up mattress and pillows on it, clean and printed in colorful chevrons. There were three jugs of water on the floor. Expensive-looking, bulbous light fixtures hung like clustered grapes above an empty fireplace, and when Mitchell toggled a junction box on the floor, they lit up, buzzing slightly. The room smelled of lemongrass oil.

Mitchell did not lead her to the bed.

Because in the corner was something like a yurt. It was a geodesic dome, the size of a four-man tent, built with well-sanded two-by-fours. Bright canvas had been stapled to its honeycombed rungs. It looked like nothing so much as a man-sized pupa, a larval cage, and it glowed softly, a Coleman lantern running inside.

Did the boys build that? Elsa asked.

They want to build them for the buffles, Mitchell said. They think it will fix them.

That doesn't seem right, Elsa said.

We can't be sure, said Mitchell. He disappeared inside the tent, and Elsa could hear him taking off his belt.

She knew this wouldn't solve anything, and yet, here she was outside of this damn pupa.

She'd sworn she would change, again, or for the last time. She'd promised to never again be the way she was with that bartender outside the cowboy dive, half-feral and buckle-fucking him on the porch. Would she ever be allowed to make different mistakes in her life?

Elsa untied the knot in her suit behind her neck. No, it wouldn't solve anything, but she felt desperate to let someone rush in and fill her with new feelings and new questions and new fucking and new regret, because even all that was less painful than being her own actual self.

Elsa fell into the same traps over and over again because she knew that inside she was wrong, so why not let Mitchell, or anyone, rewrite the space inside her. Why not let them annihilate her completely? There was a kind of pleasure in being relieved of her own self. She pulled down her bathing suit and it was cold and wet around her ankles as she kicked it away.

San Francisco

He'd made her a cake. Lemon coconut. Keiko had said it would be nice if he did something for Elsa, for her birthday, because she'd been having such a hard time lately. With what? Nolan asked, but Keiko didn't offer particulars. There had been a week's worth of hushed phone calls, and now Keiko said that Elsa and her mother were in San Francisco for a special birthday shopping trip. It seemed insane that they would come all the way from Minnesota, but what did Nolan know about girls and shopping?

Nolan strained seeds from lemon juice. Nolan whipped frosting. He layered the thick cream between the sections of the cake, put them together, and patted the top, supple and spongy. He frosted the cake, careful to do a crumb layer first, and sprinkled an even, fragrant layer of flaked coconut onto the frosting.

Nolan had taken Home Ec as an elective instead of Metal Shop, because he noticed that only girls took Home Ec, and he figured if he were the only boy in class, something good would happen. It was his freshman year of high school, and Nolan was fourteen. He was interested in girls, but he could never figure out how to act around them. Home Ec was good for this. He was told exactly what to do, and Nolan found that if most of his brain was busy trying to chiffonade basil or macerate strawberries when one of the girls spoke to him, he'd answer back no problem. I love your hair, the girls said. Nolan wore his hair in a ponytail tied with a leather thong. He was going for Keanu Reeves. He was pretty sure girls loved Keanu Reeves.

So when his mother said that Elsa was coming to town for her twentieth birthday, he made a cake. He was doing it because he was good at it. He was doing it because his mother had asked him. He was not doing it for Elsa. Elsa had tried to kill him when he was small. He'd seen her only once or twice a year for the past decade, and she'd always made it clear that seeing him was a terrible chore.

As Nolan wiped the rim of the cake plate clean, his parents buzzed around the kitchen unloading groceries and setting the table. They were edgy, whispering to each other hoarsely. For the first time, it occurred to Nolan that these family reunions might be a chore for them, too. Were grown-ups really still on the hook for doing things they didn't want to? Nolan would be fourteen forever. Or at least, he would make sure to still be cool later, like he was now. He'd like to be eighteen. Or twenty-one, in case it turned out he liked beer. Twenty-one was the absolute maximum. Being any older than that looked to Nolan like too much work.

———

Elsa arrived at their apartment complex raging. She burst in the door, leaving her mother in the car yelling after her to please put on a jacket. Elsa would not put on a jacket. She was wearing a black sateen tank top. She was wearing a bra with green straps and a lot of pushup padding going on, unless those were just Elsa's boobs now. She was heavier than Nolan remembered. Heavy was bad; he knew this from the girls in Home Ec. They stole spoonfuls of the buttercream frosting Nolan made because they said it tasted better than theirs. They clicked spoons against their teeth and said they really shouldn't be eating frosting because it would make them so fat. They clutched at their stick thighs as they said this.

Anyway, Elsa was not fat. There was just more of her than there was of the freshman girls. Her legs and hips were thick, and her waist nipped in alarmingly. She was so pale, so blonde, and Nolan thought she looked strong, like she was meant to be working a farm, sweating joyfully outdoors, not dressing like an anemic punk.

Nolan noticed Elsa appraising him too. He unhitched his slouching back so she could inspect him properly. He was five foot eleven now. He was getting grown up. Keiko told him all the time: Too big! I wish I could keep you little. I would keep you in my pocket. Right here, she would say, and pat her breast pocket.

You got tall, New Baby, Elsa said.

Nolan said, I made you a cake.

———

At dinner, Elsa did not look at their father. Elsa was at Macalester, studying education, and Ian asked her questions about her classes. But instead of answering, she made elaborate forkfuls of food and then ate off the tines in a nibbling way that Nolan found disgusting but kind of sexy.

Elsa, Ingrid said.

Ian and Keiko exchanged looks but did not know what to do.

She's really loving it, Ingrid said, answering for Elsa. Elsa snorted.

Nolan had never considered being rude to his parents, and the way Elsa disobeyed them so fluently thrilled him.

After dinner, he brought out the cake with twenty blue candles in it. All the parents complimented him on how beautiful it was, and as they sang to Elsa, it was almost a nice moment. But Elsa's face hovering in the glow above her coconut birthday cake was so intense that the adults' singing quavered. When she blew out the flames, they were too afraid to ask what she had wished for.

They ate their cake in silence.

Ian suggested that the children give the adults some time to talk. We have things to discuss, he said, and looked at Elsa meaningfully.

I'm here, Elsa said. I'd like to talk.

Keiko suggested the children go for a swim in the complex pool.

Night swimming! How exciting, Ingrid said. And we just bought you that new swimsuit, isn't that lucky, Elsa?

Why can't we talk now? Elsa said.

Nolan, go change into your suit, Keiko said.

Nolan shrugged and went upstairs to change into his suit, knowing it was his job to take Elsa off the parents' hands. So they would have a moment alone to talk about whatever it was grown-ups needed to talk about.

———

At the heart of Nolan's apartment complex, there was a small indoor pool. The lights were always orange and wavery inside and the air was warm and steamy with chlorine and cleaning bleach. There was Astroturf around the perimeter. Chaise longues. A number of enormous potted plants, waxy jungle leaves and ferns. The deep end was only eight feet, and there was something hospital-like about the ladders and steps with their handicap-accessible railings, as if the average user of the pool was assumed to be infirm.

Nolan threw his towel down on a chaise and jumped in. He loved to swim. He wished the pool were bigger and outside. He swam laps at the high school sometimes. Vaulting between the beaded lane markers made him feel strong.

Elsa's bathing suit was navy blue with bright yellow trim. As Nolan swam, she apathetically waded in, then got bored and walked around the perimeter, pulling up the plastic tops of the pool filters, which made suction-y popping sounds.

What are you doing? he asked.

Looking for frogs, she said.

Nolan could see now that it was not a padded bra but Elsa's breasts he had witnessed before. And her butt was enormously round, nothing like the girls in school. They would call her fat, he knew, but it wasn't that. He felt a flicker of shame over considering Elsa's body in this way, but it was hard to stop and make exceptions just because she was his sister. She was also strange to him. Basically a stranger. Her body was a new and unknown thing.

Nolan swam the length of the small pool underwater, in one breath, pushing off the wall. He emerged breathing heavily, stretching his long arms above his head. He climbed out of the pool and toweled himself. He sat on a chaise next to Elsa.

It's weird here, Elsa said. Apartments. Weird you have this pool.

It's the complex's. No one's ever in here.

Your hair is so long, Elsa said.

Nolan shrugged.

It's wet, Elsa said. She took Nolan's towel from him and stood over his chaise. Bending down, she rubbed his head, drying his hair. The towel was nubby and smelled of Tide, and he liked the way it felt, her touching him like this. Ever since he had grown tall, Ian and Keiko had stopped touching him the way they had when he was a child, when he was still allowed to climb into their bed or spoon them on the couch. They used to squeeze him every day before school. His father would ask for kisses on his rough cheek, and Keiko would swat his butt if he misbehaved. Then, as if overnight, they stopped touching him. It was as if no longer being a child rendered him untouchable. As if his parents were telling him that this grown body was his alone. He understood, but as Elsa toweled his hair, rubbing his ears and neck, he wished they had not stopped. He ached for touching, had not realized how long it had been. Elsa lifted the towel and shook it out.

There, she said.

He wanted to ask her to do it again. Just to keep tousling his hair, but he was afraid that would sound babyish, so he didn't.

Instead he held his hands out to receive his towel, as if it were something he had lost.

Are you okay? Elsa asked.

I just want my towel, Nolan said, and he found that he was maybe about to cry, though he wasn't sure why.

Elsa stooped and handed him the towel, and as she did, she kissed him on the cheek.

Nolan squeezed the humped towel tightly. Elsa drew back and studied his face. She cocked her head, and then leaned in and kissed him again, on the mouth.

Nolan had kissed one of the Home Ec girls, once, quickly, on his way to the bus. But he had never *truly* kissed anyone. He pursed his lips tight against Elsa's, but she laid a hand on his shoulder, pushing him back a little, and her tongue parted his lips. He suddenly understood why people kissed. It wasn't like he'd thought it'd be: sweet like a valentine-heart kind of love. Her tongue was a muscle, pushing. Elsa tasted of the lemon curd, slick tartness, coconut, milky frosting tang.

Nolan stiffened immediately. Which was embarrassing, but then he thought that maybe it was good that this was happening with Elsa. As though it was less embarrassing with her than it would have been with the Home Ec girls. Maybe because she was older, or because they barely knew each other, or because she had tried to kill him when they were small, Nolan felt Elsa was the sort of person around whom he could say anything. Do anything. With Elsa, it would not be the end of the world if he was embarrassing or made a mistake and this was a kind of comfort, of rare ease—there was no other person in Nolan's life who made him feel this way.

Elsa pressed her hand to the bulge of his tented shorts and worked her thumb in circles, and Nolan thought he would die. Her other hand, she moved beneath her own swimsuit. Nolan watched.

Do you want to see it? she asked.

Nolan did. He stood and Elsa lay back on the chaise, tilting her legs open. She left her swimsuit on.

You're not going to take it off? Nolan asked.

You take it off. She rocked her legs. There were fine blonde hairs on her knees.

Nolan wasn't sure. Pulling off her bathing-suit bottom seemed too much. What if someone came to the pool and she couldn't get it back on in time?

Nolan knelt on the Astroturf, which pricked his knees, hooked a finger through the bottom of Elsa's suit, and pulled it to the side, so he could look. It was like what he'd seen in the porn he'd watched, but gentler. There was corn-silk hair, which he had not expected, because the women in porn did not have hair. His hand shook holding the suit taut.

He had not anticipated this, but Nolan found he wanted to lick Elsa there. An animal urge. And he knew this was a thing that people did.

He pressed his face into Elsa's crotch, and she made a small noise, surprised. She smelled like chlorine from the pool, but he tongued her all the same. There was a yeasty humidity to her body. He lapped at her, and she gasped and sat up, breathing hard, pushing his shoulders away.

I said look, not touch, Elsa said. Her face was serious and alarmed, and Nolan apologized profusely. He was so sorry. So—

But then Elsa started laughing, she was laughing at him, and this made Nolan want to die, so he scrambled up, shaking out his towel, pulling it around himself, angry and ashamed.

We should go back up, Elsa said. She straightened her suit and squinted at the stairwell beyond the glass door as if she could imagine nothing more horrifying. When she stood, her legs crossed at the ankles, her thighs pressed together, and Nolan wondered what it felt like to be a girl.

Nolan felt the sick guilt that came whenever he did anything that would disappoint his parents. He knew they were not supposed to be doing what they were doing. His parents would be mad if she were any girl, and she was not. She was Elsa. He was still hard in his trunks and the whole thing was so confusing that Nolan threw down his towel and jumped into the pool and furiously paddled.

I'm going to swim a few more laps, he said.

Elsa shrugged and left. Once the glass door had squeaked shut behind her, Nolan breast-stroked slowly from one end of the pool to the other, his eyes just above the surface of the water, blowing bubbles, only coming up for air as often as he absolutely needed to.

———

The adults had been drinking and were having a grand time. Their mood had improved with the absence of their children. Keiko and Ingrid were holding each other by the shoulders, and it was decided that Elsa and Ingrid would stay the night, Ingrid being in no condition to drive back to their hotel.

Ian was a little flushed in the face, merry in the company of the two women he loved. He was in a charming mood, charming being a thing Ian could be but seldom was, because it seemed a waste of energy. But the tension of the meal, the worrying over Elsa, the desperate way Ingrid had pleaded for his help, the way Keiko had reminded Ian that she had always said they should have told Elsa the truth but hadn't wanted to overstep her bounds by insisting... yes they all remembered ... yes, Keiko had perhaps been right ... it was all too much. Elsa was furious, wanting to talk, the parents knew, but they were cowardly, fearing the fight they knew would come but which they wanted to delay. They were afraid how Nolan would take the news too; one furious child was enough, too much, really—they couldn't bear the thought of two. And wouldn't it all be easier in the morning? They'd had a hard week and would cut themselves this slack. Give themselves one more night before they had to face up to the effect that their lie, *their lie of omission,* had had on Elsa's life.

After the children went down to swim, and they had finished the first bottle of wine, they opened a second. And when they had drunk that, they had started to feel better about the whole thing, so they opened a third. And suddenly, everything did not seem so bad. They were good parents! They were muddling through the best they could. Keiko and Ingrid and Ian felt safe and in control, like they were outnumbering the children with the three of them there together. Three parents! What could three parents not do against one surly teenager? Twenty years old today, Ingrid reminded them. Of course, of course, but with Elsa out of the room, they were able to say to themselves: She's just barely beyond a teenager. She's a sophomore in college. Remember yourself at that age. Of course she's taking it badly. But she'll be fine. She'll get better. This too shall pass. They would talk to the children tomorrow. They would explain things to Nolan. They would assure Elsa that nothing would change, that Ian was still her father, even though he was not strictly, biologically, her father. They would propose a family vacation. They would propose family therapy. They would propose joint Thanksgiving. They congratulated themselves for waiting to make these decisions as a triad, for co-parenting so effectively by prudently delaying the conversation one more night.

In the warmth of the third bottle of wine, a Pinot Grigio that they all agreed tasted like green tomato stalks, like narcissus flower, like steel, just as it said on the label, the parents truly felt that everything would be fine.

Ian was a little drunk when the children returned from the pool. Elsa, then Nolan, bolted upstairs, hair mussed from the water.

We're staying the night! Ingrid shouted after Elsa.

Ian prepared the pullout couch in the living room with panache. He made a big show of flipping out the sheets, white with little red flowers, like a toreador. Letting the sheet billow and then fall neatly, perfectly smooth. He was a man who appreciated seeing any small task well done.

You're showing off, said Keiko, who came bearing an armful of pillows, and who knew it was terrible to resent a child, but who sometimes resented Elsa for bringing this drama into their lives. She wasn't even *her* child *or* Ian's. Keiko caught herself. She didn't mean that. Elsa was still theirs. She dropped the pillows and retreated upstairs. It was only for the weekend.

Tucking the corners in tightly, Ian turned to Elsa, who, in her pajamas, a t-shirt and pair of cotton shorts with clovers printed on them, was now leaning against the doorframe sulkily, arms crossed. He saw they were alone.

Come here, Elsa, Ian said. I'll tuck you in.

I'm twenty, she said, not moving.

She waited for Ian to say something else, but he didn't. He pulled the sheets taut across the bed.

You're not going to apologize? Elsa asked. Or explain?

We'll talk about it in the morning, Ian said. He could not look at her.

It's decided, he said.

He made a show of whistling as he continued to make the bed. He was drunk and he knew he was being cowardly. He wanted to pull Elsa to him and tell her that it didn't matter, he was still her father, but how did one go about proving such a thing? Had he not been there, all this time? What could he possibly say to convince her if the past twenty years of their lives had not done the job? He could tell her that it had been shocking, had been hard, at first, but that had been *years* ago. This was all ancient history for Ian. But of course, the wound, the news, was still fresh for Elsa, and the way she held herself, tense and curled, made him wary, as if she might spring at him if he tried to comfort her or explain.

It was absurd, but frankly, Ian was afraid of her.

So Ian said nothing. Ian fussed with the sheets. He made the bed, because it seemed the sort of thing a father would do for his daughter, and he hoped it would be enough.

You're really not going to even talk to me until the morning? Elsa asked. Why can't you—

Ingrid walked into the room, and he was saved. Ian patted Elsa on the shoulder. As he left, he kissed Ingrid on the forehead, holding her face in his hands, as if bestowing a benediction.

Good night, girls, Ian said, and he left. He went to bed. All the parents did.

———

Nolan could not sleep. He had faked brushing his teeth because the taste of Elsa was too strange and new for him to wash away. He lay on his back beneath a green quilted down comforter with a flannel underside. He ran through the memory of what had happened again and again, as if there was some necessary essence he could glean from it. Eventually he pulled down his boxers and took himself in his hand. He couldn't not think about it. He knew it shouldn't have happened. And now that it had, the best thing was to forget about it. But he kept thinking of Elsa's hand on his dick, of his tongue inside her, and the smell of chlorine. He thought of how it felt when she was toweling his hair. He stroked himself under the covers and it got uncomfortably warm, but Nolan didn't throw off the blanket because he was too embarrassed to even see what he was doing. The door creaked and his hands flew up over the covers.

Nolan.

He didn't say anything.

New Baby.

What?

It was Elsa in the doorway. Her hair was long and loose around her head, and she was backlit by the nightlight green of the hallway. She glowed like an alien or the swamp thing in silhouette. She eased the door closed behind her.

What are you doing?

I couldn't sleep.

Where's your mom?

Passed out.

You have to go back.

Just let me lie here with you for a moment.

She pulled some of the covers to the side and got in. They stared at the ceiling.

Why couldn't you sleep? Nolan asked. His boxers were somewhere around his ankles.

Isn't it weird how they all get along so well? Elsa said. I fucking hate them.

This was not what Nolan had expected. He did not want to be reminded of their parents now.

Why is it weird? he asked. He drew his knees up.

That's just not normally how things work.

I think it's nice.

It's creepy. I hate it.

You'd rather they screamed at each other?

Sometimes you should scream, Elsa said.

Do you want to scream?

All the time.

Me too.

Liar.

I want to scream right now. You don't know about me.

I think I do, Elsa said.

We never even see each other, Nolan said. You're only my half sister.

A look passed over Elsa's face, of pain or worry. Nolan could not place it. She rested her head on his chest.

They were quiet. And in the quiet, really, anything seemed possible. Maybe no one would notice. Maybe even they would not notice. Right now, strands of Elsa's wet hair plastered across his chest, hard under the blankets, Nolan was focused on keeping his breathing deep and even, but there was something catching at the base of it which he knew revealed too much. If he didn't focus on breathing, he would groan like an animal. The girls in Home Ec would be repulsed by this, Nolan decided, but Elsa did not seem to think his wanting was embarrassing, and he felt again that every part of himself might be allowed by her. That she would not judge him.

Elsa took Nolan in her hand and then he did groan, pressing his face into the comforter his mother had bought him for Christmas, because the old one had animals printed on it and he was too grown up for that.

He should stop this, should just wait until the Home Ec girls were older and he could figure out how to be with them. But what if he felt this turned-on and lame forever, and it never got any easier? What if he never figured out how to ask them out? Or to speak the things he wanted?

What if he didn't want to have to be the one in charge?

Elsa seemed so certain of what they were doing, and when he thought of giving in to her certainty, letting her run this experience, he felt a pleasure so intense that he rolled his shoulders as the feeling traveled down his spine.

Elsa twisted and slid under him and then she took him by the hips and canted him toward her, tipping him toward the inevitability of it all. Elsa stroked him again and she was only using one hand, the other gone, doing something to herself that Nolan could not quite fathom, but when she took his hand and pressed it to her he felt that she was wet, and Nolan knew what to do, but—

Elsa, he said.

Put it in, she said.

Elsa, I—

I want it, she said.

She helped and he sank into her and he grabbed her shoulders and squeezed as hard as he could because suddenly he wanted a hundred new things he'd not even imagined before.

Elsa rocked her hips to meet him, and Nolan shut his eyes, and as they moved he was afraid and also he could not stop. The feeling was everything and the feeling was almost too much.

But then he opened his eyes, and when Nolan saw the way Elsa looked at him, it was wrong.

She looked determined. They were still fucking and it still felt good, but it was like she was thinking about something else too, like she wasn't really there, and this made Nolan feel incredibly lonely.

In the privacy of that awful moment, realizing that Elsa had left him rocking inside of her alone, he came. He gave a small wail. Elsa clamped his mouth, but the noise was enough.

Ingrid woke to find Elsa out of bed. She hunted for her, wine drunk and sleepy. She had been dreaming of trees, of a forest, of home. Ingrid pressed the flats of her hands against the hallway walls of the apartment the way she had gripped the trunks in the dream, and she feared Elsa had perhaps run away. She'd been so angry. Had so clearly wanted to have it out with Ian. With all of them. And maybe Ingrid should have let her. Should have sided with her daughter instead of the adults. But it had seemed too big a decision to make on her own. Had seemed so much easier to ally herself with the parents and to push off the hard conversation until morning.

Ingrid opened the door to the bathroom. She opened a linen closet. Where was her daughter?

She heard a sound like a cry and without thinking opened the door to Nolan's room, where it had come from. In the bed, she saw the forms beneath the covers clutch into one ball, like a startled beetle.

What— Ingrid said. She still felt the happiness of the wine and the evening and the trees of her dream sounding within her, so this cold, new feeling took a moment to trickle in. The children's faces appeared above the comforter, unfurling.

What— Ingrid said, and she understood.

Elsa said, Mom, don't—

But Ingrid held up her hand. She could not handle this alone. There were three parents. They outnumbered the children. She could handle this so long as there were three parents. She turned and stumbled down the hall to find Ian and Keiko.

Ingrid left, and the sound of voices from the other bedroom murmured and then there was shouting, then hushing. Nolan began to cry. He felt so small and wrong. Soon, they would come down the hall. Soon, trouble was coming. Or something worse than trouble. Something new.

Elsa whispered in his ear: Stop crying, New Baby.

Don't call me that, Nolan said.

It's okay, Elsa said. Ian's not my real dad.

Just stop, Nolan said.

It's true. I found out this week. You and I aren't actually related at all.

No, Nolan said.

He cried harder. Nolan was relieved and horrified. But the invisible genes that did not link him and Elsa did not matter so much as the words that did. And he understood then that he could have kept Elsa as a sister *or* slept with her. It was a choice, and what he'd just done was to have given her up. Nolan had not meant to choose, but he had, and he had chosen wrong. It was a thing that could not be undone.

The parents were still talking in the next room. Nolan pulled at the flannel comforter. Why did no one come for them?

If we're not related, it's not wrong, Elsa insisted. I'm not your sister.

Nolan felt a new rush of sickness as he considered that the feeling of unconditional acceptance he had felt with Elsa by the pool was *tied* to her being his sister. That it was the comfort of siblings he had wanted, wanted more than the sex, but now, by sleeping with Elsa, he'd ensured that he would never get to feel that way again.

He had traded something rare for something cheap, and he had lost her. They had lost each other.

II

Darwin Walking Backward

A touch of the hand and this burning would, on the instant, beautifully reverse itself . . . out of dust and coals, like golden salamanders, the old years, the green years, might leap . . . all, everything fly back to seed, flee death, rush down to their beginnings . . . moons eat themselves opposite to the custom, all and everything cupping one in another like Chinese boxes, rabbits into hats, all and everything returning to the fresh death, the seed death, the green death, to the time before the beginning. A touch of a hand might do it, the merest touch of a hand.

"A Sound of Thunder"
Ray Bradbury

10

You are in a town but you are always on an island.

You can crawl over an island's surface, small moth on a hot glass bulb.

You can fling yourself against it, try to immolate yourself in understanding.

But you will crack yourself open before an island lets you in.

9

Back in time, that second night on the island, when the night birds had been calling. When Elsa returned to bed and Nolan was asleep, his hair looped in a bun. When Elsa had raked her fingers along his skull, pulling his hair free. When it had spilled across the pillow.

Nolan woke.

It was hot, so he sat up and pulled off his shirt. The bed smelled like a body. He had sweat into these sheets, and now here was Elsa's smell, something elemental. The green humus of a riverbed.

Nolan gathered his hair at the nape of his neck. Elsa ran her fingers through, pulling it free again.

They turned to each other.

Her ample form. His long, slender one. It was dark and there was nothing to say.

They shouldn't be so close. But the island didn't care. Leap's was out of time, the twenty-ninth of February, and their ears still hummed from the whirring of the generator—or was it the legions of bugs, or was it was the moon's neon-sign drone, or was it the water that looked still at night but was always moving?

Maybe it was the sound of their two charged bodies, so long kept apart, which now clung to each other for comfort. They went no further. They went this far.

And who was there to care that they lay like this?

On this island?

The ghost of Ian Grey.

Wasn't this the surest way to make him reappear?

If there was any way to conjure their father, to force a resurrection, this was it. Elsa pressed back into Nolan, and he curved around her, jutting his knees up behind her legs, snaking his arms around her. She bit his arm. He smacked the flat of her thigh. She bit him harder.

It was a game. A dare. What could they make happen?

Ian?

Olly olly oxen free.

8

Farther back:

Every wave of tenants had sought to escape their mainland lives on the island. The Reversalists were only the most recent inheritors of its wildness.

In a muddy inlet, a frog *braapp*ed a call, his gullet pulsing full and ripe as he summoned partners from the forest.

The ducks were molting. Earlier this year than last. A family huddled together on the stream bank, and their down was swept away in the current.

The woods at the center of the island were dense with trees and fast-sprawling shrubs. The canopy made the darkness in the lower layers absolute, except for the moonlight on the skins of berries on bushes, plump and full of poison.

Walking paths had been trampled through the brush by Reversalists moving from shacks to the Lobby. Some Reversalists spray-painted personal blazes. Orange to Gwen Manx's house. Blue to Esther's and Gates's. Metallic silver to St. Gilles's. The miniature deer who lived on the island, blunt-faced with stubby horns, abandoned their tunnels through the greenway and gleefully trotted along the humans' trails. They frisked in the cleared space. Rutted in the soil. Rubbed the velvet off their antlers against the trees, sometimes erasing the spray-painted blazes the scientists had put there.

It rained and everyone on the island heard the sound against the metal roofs of their shacks. They listened to the heavy rustle of fat raindrops crashing through the canopy leaves, pinging off the roofs, and the sound was like the ticking of a giant, erroneous clock that could not keep the time.

7

Ian Grey is stumbling, naked, on the beach. He has gleefully flung off his clothes; he will not need them now. His long white thighs glow in the moonlight. He has realized what he must do. He is wearing his glasses and he looks up at the moon. He does not need glasses to see the moon, so he tosses these away as well. Ian looks behind him at the wood. He looks in front of him at the ocean. The Gulf is green and frothing. He takes a step forward. Yes, this is correct.

Ian Grey steps into the tide so it laps at his ankles. The sand caves in a little, and soon it is gathering around his feet, a reclamation. Ian Grey in the water, the primordial soup! Ian Grey going back going back going back. Like every generation before him, he'd risen, and now his turn was up. And why not. Let him recede. How much good had they done anyway?

The smell off the Gulf is brackish and fertile, and it really is a perfect night to be like a duck in the sea. He wades deeper into the water and it closes warmly over his thighs his balls his belly the small curve of his back his nipples his chin. Such a perfect night! Don't ruin it.

He paddles in the water, heading away from shore.

Ian gets tired. He goes under. He thinks that perhaps this is like a dream where he does not think he can breathe underwater but if he takes just one mouthful, lets it cycle through his lungs, yes, then he will adapt and he will breathe the water just as easily as he'd ever breathed the air. He gulps a little and the heaviness and burning panics him. He struggles to the surface and coughs. He goes under and comes up. Under and up. He is so tired. But he chose this, didn't he? He is almost asleep, and then there is a noise.

A boat with a group of laughing young people in bright swimsuits playing cheerful music motors near him. Ian tries to say something but cannot. He beats his arms, but they give out and he goes under again.

In spite of himself, he thinks:

Maybe the children will save him.

The boaters in colorful shorts chortle and sing, and they do not hear Ian.

Of course they don't. It is only natural that they should leave him behind. Only natural that he should give himself up and let these young people have a go. Make room, make way for what comes next.

Ian cries out in delight: Children!

The noise of their thumping music drowns him out as they steer the boat away and back to the far shore.

6

It was a year between when the Reversalists came and when Mitchell first returned to the ruins of the Leap-Backer's commune, dope sick and in search of anything like a home.

(Later, the old commune postman would come in his boat with the letter from the lawyer turning over the Townes inheritance to him. Later, the first scientists would respond to the letters Mitchell sent promising them free housing and resources for research. But before that, it was a long year.)

Mitchell spent his first weeks back detoxing, dreaming and puking, in his parents' old shack, and during that time he turned furious. Furious with them for abandoning him at the hospital. Furious with them for not being here now, when he'd finally got back.

In his fury, Mitchell wanted to erase every trace of them, and all the Leap-Backers, from the island.

He forced himself to work sooner than he was ready—tearing down the old shacks. Rehabilitating the ruined gardens to feed himself. He worked in the sun in his shorts, and he turned a shade of brown that always seemed to have an angry redness underneath. He collected everything the Leap-Backers had left behind, and he burned it in giant fires on the beach at night.

He burned dreamcatchers and bassinets and sarongs. He burned the *I Ching* and the Bible and *The Prophet* and *Walden* and *Self-Reliance* and *Zen and the Art of Motorcycle Maintenance*. He shouted at the blaze. He burned everything in his father's office. All the minutes of community meetings, all the declarations of reconciliation and proposals for peace, all the children's poems about Darwin, all the official correspondence on letterhead that bore the Leap-Backers' symbol: a silhouetted man, tall, slump-shouldered, with a beard and a walking stick, one leg stuck out behind him impossibly. The Darwin Walking Backward, symbol of hope, stepping into the more innocent preindustrial past.

(Later, Mitchell would decide to keep the Darwin Walking

Backward as the logo for the Reversalists' movement by reversing its meaning, like an upside-down tarot card. He would take his father's symbol of hope and make of it the opposite. It was a petty revenge, but it pleased him. He would make the Darwin a signifier of doom.)

Mitchell didn't want his father's metaphors. He wanted science. Yes, Mitchell had seen life on the mainland and hated it as much as his father had, but the hospital had saved him when the Leap-Backers refused to. The nurses had cared for him when his own mother fled. And despite having no education beyond what the commune had taught him, Mitchell, in his fervency of newly sober belief, saw himself as a man of science. He had got himself clean, after all. Clean from dope and clean from the lies the commune had fed him for years. So he would stay on the island, and he would bring others. Instead of his father's farmers and peaceniks, let him bring science. Bring scientists.

His father was dead. Let him speak back to his dead father.

5

The Leap-Backers believed in Darwin the way people who have not read Darwin do, and they made of him what they would. They believed that the influences of the mainland, of 1968, were poisonous, and that humans were adapting into the wrong kind of creatures. They believed that living on the island, away from those influences, would allow their children to adapt into more natural beings. That they could restore human experience back to the good old days.

And what days were these? Anytime the Leap-Backers tried to pinpoint when things had started to go wrong and what time period it was they were wishing to return to, they were inconveniently faced with the past. And the past was ignorance and squalor, was oppression and slavery, was genocide and theft and war and struggles that made their own feel small. It was important not to be too specific, the Leap-Backers realized, and eventually "preindustrial days" became the consensus.

The Leap-Backers' children knew only what they were told, and it was David Townes who told them about living according to the Darwin Walking Backward and how lucky they were that the island protected them from the evils of the mainland.

At night, these children, Mitchell among them, snuck out of their homes. They crept past the sleeping parents in shacks, past the ruins of the Lobby, where, in the kitchen, pots of rice were being cooked for the next day's meals and everything smelled of grain broken open. The children snuck to the beach, where the water lapped gently, and they could see the shadowy bulk of the Landing, miles away, and wonder about the flickering lights on the other side.

One night: something new. An explosion of sound. One child screamed. Another peed himself. There were great bursts of shrieking fire in the sky. Twisting bands of light rocketing up, then fizzling. Purple trails popped and expanded into chrysanthemums and violet sparks showered the night. This happened again and again and from the far shore came the sounds of shouting and screaming.

It was just like David said would happen. The people who lived on the shore were destroying themselves. The smell of gunpowder and smoke that rolled over the water confirmed this for the children.

They were all dead, the people on the shore, and the children felt sorry for them.

They went home gravely, adult, knowing what they knew. The Leap-Backers, they were sure, were the only ones left, the true inheritors of the Earth.

The children slept well that night, snug against their fathers' furred backs, their mothers' warm and slumping breasts, which they butted their heads against for luxury and comfort. They were still alive and they were safe and they were lucky.

4

In 1963, Teddy Townes suffered a heart attack in the main lobby of Leap's Retreat—Grand Hotel and Paradise Spa. The project was not anywhere near complete, but the lobby and facilities complex had been finished and several key investors and VIPs were there for an inaugural weekend stay.

Teddy wore a yellow tie, tight around his neck. His son David was beside him. Heir to Townes enterprises. Teddy had asked David to just please wear a suit and cut his hair. But here was David, hair to his shoulders, wearing some horrible patterned shirt.

The investors had spent their first day on the island drinking cocktails at the tiki bar and they were all now good and soused on Moscow Mules and Gin Rickeys. The investors' wives had gone swimming in the heated indoor pool, a flock of pastel suits, paddling with their heads above the water so they would not muss their hair and makeup. They swam to the tiled edges, grabbing their husbands' shiny shoes with damp hands, saying: Just come in, you won't believe how warm it is.

In honor of the event, Teddy had imported a dozen bufflehead ducks, picked for the males' beautiful feathers, and released them in the pool atrium. They clustered beneath ferns and a few swam in the turquoise water, the wives shrieking delightedly when the ducks paddled near them.

His guests were relaxed and as giddy as children. Teddy was delighted. His hotel would be a kind of paradise for those who could afford the luxury of forgetting the mainland.

And 1963 was a good year for forgetting. The guests of Leap's Retreat swam and drank and willed themselves to forget the grassy knoll in Dallas, to forget the fire hoses in Birmingham, to forget the helicopters over Vietnam, to forget the tape over Cassius Clay's mouth, and to forget forget forget Valentina Tereshkova, who got there first.

That night, Teddy led the guests in a toast: To the original guests of Leap's Retreat—Grand Hotel and Paradise Spa! There was applause and a clinking of cocktails. It was perhaps because David was the only one unenthused by the toast that he was the first to notice that his father was red in the face, his eyes quite bulgy. Teddy buckled, and over the din of the cheering guests, David shouted for an ambulance even though they were on an island.

You'll finish it, won't you? his father gargled.

David did not finish it.

David put all construction work on hold and began camping in the Lobby amid the remnants of the party: spilled cocktails, paper drink parasols, a lost bathing suit, one of his father's loafers.

This was David's inheritance, but he did not want it. He lived in the Lobby for six months of grief and confusion as he watched his father's work, so recently constructed, crumble and be reclaimed by the island.

And as it did, David found he felt better.

David soaked in the presidential suite's enormous bathtub. He submerged himself and chain-smoked and studied the lichen spreading greenly across the wallpaper his father had imported from Japan, a pattern of ferns. Ants had the audacity to build great, tumbling heaps of homes inside the grand corridor. The cones reached high, two and three feet, red friends marching in and out of the entryways, conducting business, enterprise, progress.

All the ducks but two had waddled away from the Lobby soon after the initial debacle, realizing that inside living was not for them. The two that stayed circled the green, chlorine-depleted water of the swimming pool. David liked to stand at the pool's edge, smoking a joint and feeding them. David fed them bread. He fed them rice. They ate whatever he gave them. If he sat on the ground, they would even sit in his lap and let him pet their feathers. Stupid birds. But sweet. Pets. He dragged on his joint. It was not their fault that they had adapted to this tame life. That the world they were trying to be good at living in was really just a chemical puddle and a series of handouts.

He was high, but something clicked for David. Or perhaps something clicked for David because he was high. He went to the doorway of Leap's Retreat—Grand Hotel and Paradise Spa and looked out at the island. He was naked except for his shorts as he squinted into the swampy forest. He didn't want to go back to the mainland. And perhaps he didn't have to. Maybe there was a better way of living, here.

That week, he started using the stacks of abandoned building supplies to construct seven shacks. When they were done, he called his friends. He said, Let's start something here.

3

There were other years, and other Towneses, but spinning backward rapidly enough, we find the original. Albert Townes discovered and founded Leap's Island in a leap year, February 29, 1919.

He and his men were hauling steel and pig iron but having a terrible time of it; every day Townes woke up hoping US Steel might buy them out and make them all as rich as Carnegie. He was looking for an exit strategy—and then they found the island.

Townes and his men anchored and took smaller boats to shore.

They delighted in the discovery.

We say discover, but of course, the island had existed before Albert Townes had ever set foot on it. An island has nothing to do with the men who ride its back. Who drink from its streams. Who drown on its shores.

Townes and his men crept into the home of a family of Choctaw Indians who lived on the island and slit their throats in the middle of the night. They left their bodies out of doors, and as they built their settlement, they watched the family's flesh turn to jerky and saw flies crawl over their eyes and saw birds, carrion hunters, pick at them, and Townes and his men told themselves that but for the grace of god this would be them. Those Choctaw would have murdered us in our sleep if we had not killed them first, they said, and because we did, here we are on our island. We are so lucky. So blessed. By the grace of god we are here.

2

When the mother of the Choctaw family who were murdered on the island was a girl, she had a favorite story. Her name was Nita, and the story was about a turtle and the movement of the world.

On that same island, her own mother had told it to her.

In the story, a girl was crying, and a turtle made fun of her for being sad, so the girl hit the turtle, and she cracked his shell into pieces. The girl ran away, and the turtle cried over his broken shell, but then red ants came and stitched it together in a patchwork so the turtle's shell was whole again.

Nita's mother told her that their island was just one of the turtle's many shell pieces and that sometimes the world moved when the pieces bumped up against each other because the world was being restitched. Made into a better arrangement of itself.

Even when she was grown, Nita would lie still at night and wonder if she could feel the island moving beneath her. The world becoming something better. Sometimes she thought she did, but other times Nita wondered if she only *thought* she felt the world moving *because* of the stories her mother had told her about it.

Maybe all stories are a trick.

Still, at night, Nita waited, thinking of her children and hoping to feel the kind of movement that would allow her to believe in the stories she needed.

1

The island is an island. No men live here. There are no stories about it. No one has named it. No one has declared its purpose.

The animals who live here have always lived here or have come by chance.

New plants spring up when bird droppings full of seeds plop down. The first of the poisonous berries will arrive this way and the island's many moronic opossums will eat them, their oily black eyes dimming, their pink toes curling tight, because they cannot resist the sweet poison. Other craftier rodents, muskrats, learn quickly not to eat the berries. The muskrats build immense networks of burrows beneath the soil and stuff their nests with the molted feathers of migrating geese, because they are the softest, and in the southern winters, they curl into these feathers at night, fat with grasses and lilies and snails, as they weather these mildest of hard times.

The pill bugs are pilling. They roll, flexing their armor, their translucent legs splayed. They dig enthusiastically into the ground, their whole lives focused on one purpose, driven forward, through the soil.

This is the island alone. Still without man. And in stillness, there is happiness. In the absence of story, only fluid circling joy.

0

Everyone here is insane, Elsa said.

They have their reasons, said Nolan.

They have stories, not reasons.

What if you're my story? What if the story of why I'm on this island is you?

What's my story?

Your story is Dad.

Go to sleep.

Tell me a story.

III

The Paradise Duck

It was easy enough to despise the world,
    but decidedly difficult to find any other habitable region.

The House of Mirth
Edith Wharton

San Francisco

Elsa rolled the rental car window up and down on the highway so the whole car rattled and grew cold. Ingrid remained uselessly calm, letting Elsa do it. They were on their way to Elsa's ex-father's house for her "birthday." It was a farce that made Elsa want to scream.

And this was the week for screaming. The week Elsa had come home demanding to know why her blood said that at least one of her parents was not her parent.

The week Ingrid told Elsa that Ian was not her father and that she had hidden this information from her for twenty years. Elsa screamed and broke two ceramic bowls once she understood that Ian *knew*. Had known for years. That even Keiko knew.

Ingrid did not scream. She had always been hopelessly serene, had a nurse's patience, even at home, and it drove Elsa crazy. When she was small, Elsa came home from school with end-of-the-world problems. The mug she had made in art class had shrunk so small in the kiln that only a doll's portion of liquid could be drunk from it. The boy who sat next to her had been stung by a wasp right next to his eye. No matter how awful anything seemed to Elsa, Ingrid would understand, find the sunny side, trust in the universe, and try to calm Elsa down. Even when Ian left, Ingrid never once seemed distressed that their family was dissolving.

Perhaps, Elsa thought, Ingrid was this way because she had spent the past thirty-five years of her life as a hospice nurse. Ingrid's job, every day, was to interact with the dead and dying and while she was sad when she came home sometimes, mostly she was calm. It was as if her shifts drained her capacity to care about anything smaller than a typhoon, a bomb, anything smaller than literal, actual, immediate death.

This was the week Elsa learned that her biological father had been one of Ingrid's patients.

Elsa's father had been in hospice, but he was not old. He was twenty-five, and he had cancer in his lungs and in his blood, and he was a Quaker and a virgin because he'd been waiting for marriage. He was full of regrets.

He told Ingrid he was afraid of his life flashing before his eyes when he died like people said it did. Wouldn't it be so ugly to have to watch a thing like that? It would make you cry. He imagined people shouting: Don't go in that room! Kiss this girl, not that one! Why aren't you paying attention to that car? Why are you smoking those cigarettes? Don't you know you're running out of time?

It would be better, he said, if your life flashed backward. Time and possibilities would be given back, unspent. You would see yourself stripped clean of experience and pain. Watch each refired memory safe in the knowledge that it would soon be over. Or better yet, *undone.* To see your life run backward would be a kind of unknowing. Of forgetting. And imagine the peace of seeing yourself grow clean and refurl into a moist bud of a thing. Yes. That was what Elsa's biological father wanted.

That and to have sex before he died.

He wanted so little from the end of his time on the planet. So of course Ingrid slept with him.

He was not strong enough for most things, and so Ingrid lowered herself onto him gently and rocked there. She lifted herself and pushed against him, and he came almost immediately. It was his first time and his last time all at once and that was how Elsa was conceived, in that confused moment of coming and going. Of living and dying. Of moving forward and backward all at once.

Of course, Ingrid did not tell Elsa any of this. What she told her was: He was very beautiful, and very sick, and a Quaker. He was laughing all the time even though he was dying. He had been saving himself for marriage and then, instead of marriage, he had a hospital bed. That he had asked Ingrid whether she would take him out for chocolate ice cream (Elsa knew how Ingrid loved ice cream), and so she'd taken him out, and then one thing led to another and now here was Elsa. The ice cream had been strawberry because they were out of chocolate and Ingrid regretted that. That on the third to last day of his life, Elsa's father had had to settle for his second-favorite ice cream flavor. Other than that, Ingrid regretted nothing.

Elsa hated this story. It was such an Ingrid story. It was charming. It was sappy. Her father was a Quaker, for fuck's sake. It was exactly the sort of magical moment that Ingrid thought made the world wonderful, and exactly the sort of thing Elsa had spent years trying to show Ingrid made her naïve and dreamy and maybe even a little bit dumb.

They were getting close to San Francisco, to Ian's house, and Elsa rolled up the window of the rental car. She asked, Why didn't you just tell me?

Because I wanted you to have a father, Ingrid said. And I was married to Ian, and I knew he'd be a good one.

Do you ever feel just sick over how wrong you were?

I wasn't wrong, Ingrid said. Ian was a great father. It was unfair of me not to tell him. To let him love you so much for six years and then for him to find out like that. But, of course, it was too late for him to stop loving you.

And to Elsa, this was the worst part: Ian had found out about Elsa's origins around her sixth birthday. It was the explanation for her parents' divorce, for Ian's departure from her life, the thing Elsa had been choking on, trying to understand for years. The answer had been sitting there, the whole time, but he had hidden it from her. That Ian had denied her this explanation was a betrayal almost as bad as all the rest.

But he did leave, Elsa said. He left.

He left me, Ingrid said. I did an unforgivable thing. But he's never left you.

What if he does? Elsa said. What if I do something wrong or behave in a way he doesn't like, and then he just leaves because hey, not really his kid?

But you are his kid, Ingrid said. You're so totally his kid that you think biology is the only way you *can* be his kid. When really, what matters is that he talked to you in my stomach and he saw you being born and for the first six years of your life he was your father completely. He could never leave you.

But what if he does? Elsa said.

She had hated losing Ian from her house, but it was true he had not stopped calling or visiting or being Ian. He had not stopped teaching her about animals and making the face he did when she asked him a question the answer to which he didn't think she'd understand and was formulating the best way to tell her where baby whales came from or where crickets went when they died or how a snake knew when it had eaten its fill. But that was not enough now. She'd felt a tenuousness to their relationship after he'd left and had banked on their genetic filament—reassured herself that she could yank on that cord at any time, and he would come, because she was his.

Elsa toggled the rental car window again, and when the cold air rushed through the car like a wind tunnel, Ingrid only lowered her sunglasses to protect her eyes.

———

Dinner had been a disaster. Elsa had seen to that. And now the parents had gotten rid of her by sending her off with Nolan. Elsa shuffled along the perimeter of the pool, pulling up filters, furious and bored. How dare they try to pretend to be happy and fine and force her to go through that spectacle of a dinner like everything was normal? How dare they talk to each other, but not to her, when it was her they were discussing? How dare they force her to squish every terrible feeling she was having down inside her? And how dare they not tell Nolan what was happening, make him wait to find out in the morning, until they were "ready to discuss it"? How dare they do to him the very same thing they'd done to her—lie, and say it was for their own good? Lie, and pretend the world was fine, so you trotted out into it like an idiot who doesn't see the storm coming. Nolan wasn't a baby. He was in high school, for fuck's sake.

She watched Nolan swimming in the pool, the muscles of his shoulders and chest propelling him neatly through the lanes, his hair streaming behind him, and for an idle moment, Elsa considered seducing him like she'd been doing the boys at college. She was on the pill, and the boys she fucked at school, she fucked for sport and for pleasure. To forget herself a little while. It was easy. Still, the swiftness with which she turned this gaze on Nolan surprised her.

Ugh, Elsa thought, as the idea materialized. He's your brother, gross.

But then Elsa remembered: he wasn't. Not even a little bit.

Elsa was Ingrid and the Quaker, and Nolan was Ian and Keiko. They had nothing between them but a dozen weekends of shared parenting. Nolan was no longer her brother. He was no longer anything at all.

It was still gross, Elsa thought, as she pulled the caps from the pool filters and stared into their hidden wells for secrets, or something small and dead. The parents were having their stupid summit, trying to figure out how to most healthily assert that Ian was still her father. Keeping Nolan in the dark for one more night and making her wait. But what would Ian say if she did seduce Nolan? Kiss him, maybe. More. She could show them how wrong they were. That there *was* harm in waiting. She could show them he wasn't so young.

And as Elsa sulked around the pool and considered how she

could make her parents as miserable as she was and punish them for what they'd done, a kind of logic equation came to her. One that pitted biological truth, her father's favorite kind, against emotional truth. The logic ran like this:

If I am his daughter, it is not okay for me to sleep with Nolan.

If I am not his daughter, it is acceptable for me to sleep with Nolan.

And so she would see, wouldn't she? She could force an error, and Ian would have to choose between accepting a monstrous daughter whom he loved in the face of any vile thing she might do, or accepting the biological truth of the matter. That she was not his. That she was an unrelated girl who'd slept with his biological son and nothing more. Was Ian's love conditional?

The parents, all three of them, thought they were handling this so beautifully. But they had lied to her, for years, and now they had dropped this dead Quaker on her just when she'd thought she'd figured herself out.

They'd taken her certainty away, and she would ruin them for it.

Nolan climbed from the pool. Water coursed off his body. He was a beautiful boy. His perfect hair falling in his perfect face. Elsa held out a towel. Here, she said, Let me, and then toweled dry his damp head.

Leap's Island

Elsa woke up alone in the pupa. Morning light illuminated the canvas honeycombs. She should not be here. Maybe she could stay here forever.

Just outside the tent flap, she found a neatly folded set of t-shirt and shorts. Mitchell's. She smelled the shirt. It was not an especially intense, pleasant, or sexy smelling shirt, but she put it on anyway. She felt dehydrated and dirty. Her hair was salt-stiff and her legs were rubbery as she descended the stairs.

She crossed the Lobby. She would find Mitchell. They would eat breakfast. She needed to spend one more hour with someone who didn't think she was a monster. Then she would go find Nolan and they would make up. Or they wouldn't.

As Elsa passed the dining room, she heard voices. She peered around the door and saw Mitchell and Esther Stein.

They were eating breakfast, having what looked like a meeting. There were stacks of papers between them on the pink linen cloths. Mitchell was annotating something with a felt pen and drinking coffee, every so often passing a page across to Esther. Esther had a large plastic calculator out and was punching at it. She had her glasses on and hadn't touched the bowl of yogurt at her elbow.

Elsa could go in and join them. She could ask if they were working on the *Nature* article. But seeing the two of them like this, Elsa knew she would sneak away from the Lobby and not do anything of the sort, because she was ashamed.

Elsa and Nolan had told themselves the Reversalists were crazy, but Mitchell and Esther, sat down to breakfast, with their quiet understanding and their work, didn't look crazy, whereas Elsa, hiding, peeking around the dining room wall, wearing someone else's clothes, hair dirty after having thrown a fit and nearly drowned herself, did.

In the moment before Elsa ducked her head back through the door and left them to their meeting, she felt like a fool.

Yes, because she'd fucked Mitchell, and it was the same old thing. Hoping other people's certainty would bring her closer to her own. Other people telling her when she was and wasn't allowed to be loved. When she was or wasn't good enough. When had she consented to the rules by which she seemed to be playing this infinite game? Maybe the sooner Elsa stopped trying to hunt down some class of people who had all the answers—adults, scientists, Mars missions, Ian—the sooner she could stop the cycle of trying to win. Could look around and decide what kind of game might actually be worth playing.

And it wasn't just that she'd fucked Mitchell. It was also that she and Nolan had told themselves they'd come to Leap's Island for their own reasons and that Reversalism had nothing to do with them. But they'd been ridiculous since they'd arrived, acting like the children they once were—performing a dumb show of their past as they looked for answers about their father and how everything had gone so wrong. And maybe that was exactly what Reversalism was. Getting so wrapped up in the story of how your life went wrong that you acted that wrongness out, over and over again, and forgot to keep on living.

Elsa slowly backed away and returned to the Lobby. A pair of buffleheads waddled across the floor, brisk as businessmen. She went to the bank of telephones and stroked a smooth, black receiver before picking it up.

Elsa stood defensively, the receiver in the crook of her neck and the long cord wound around herself. She looked down at her feet, filthy and crabbed at the edges. She dialed.

Hello?

Hi, Mama, Elsa said.

How is it going out there?

We're almost all packed up.

How are you doing out there?

Fine.

How is Nolan?

Do I have any mail?

You have mail from Mars.

It's from Holland.

I opened it.

Of course you did.

It's details about your interview.

Save that for me.

There was a soft honking and four more damp undowny buffleheads marched out of the pool, shaking themselves and leaving a trail of wet behind them.

He's really gone? Ingrid said.

Yes. These people, Mama. I can't even tell you.

Just come home. Leave them to themselves.

Dad had a bunch of research going on here—

The algae bloom just started on the lake, her mother interrupted.

And just like that, Elsa could smell it. She could imagine the deep mineral stink of the blooms in the water. They floated like Japanese paper flowers, undulating in the shore pool, collapsing to nothing when you pulled them up.

What are you doing right now? Elsa said.

Talking to you.

But what else.

I'm drinking a cup of coffee in my lavender bathrobe on the deck, deadheading petunias. I hate them. I only planted petunias because you like them. But they only bloom a little while and then they turn slimy, and they're sticky and bristly when you deadhead.

They look like little trumpets, Elsa said.

Come home, Ingrid said.

Soon.

They hung up. The Lobby was empty except for the ducks.

Elsa took the path back past the marina. She told herself that maybe Nolan would be gone when she got to the shack. Maybe he had found a ride to the mainland, and they would never have to look at each other and try to apologize or fight again, and that would be easier.

There were buoys not far off, bobbing back and forth like drunks. Sitting on the buoys were pelicans. Four of them. With their dark-rimmed eyes, they watched her sadly, like so many Charlie Chaplins in a silent movie. One flexed his throat. He barely seemed real.

She told herself: none of this matters. These pathetic people. Her father's research. The ducks. The island had tricked her into believing its reality because the Reversalists were contagious. But this wasn't the real world.

She could see her mother so clearly: in her bathrobe, making a face at the petunia flesh stuck purply to her fingers. Potato Lake was the real world. Nolan was real, but maybe gone too. A pelican gurgled. Elsa clapped her thigh and spooked the birds away.

———

Elsa found the shack empty. Nolan and the dog were gone.

She'd wished for this, hadn't she? Instead, she found she could not bear the thought that Ian's death had vanished the last cord between her and Nolan and that there was no reasonable reason for them to ever see each other again. Could they be trusted to be reasonable together? Could she?

She wanted to know she would see him again. Nolan carried so much of Ian with him. And this was part of it. But it was also Nolan himself. Nolan qua Nolan.

She didn't know what to do with that.

The green field journal was on the table, and Ian's old iPod was still sitting there. She grabbed both and went to the deck. It was warm and she lay on a towel, her head on the pink plastic tiger.

Elsa hoped he'd taken the dog. That Jinx was not lost. Though that seemed unlikely.

Weak morning light cut in slats across her belly. She clicked Ian's iPod on and snugged the headphones into her ears. There was Satie. The first of the *Gnossiennes*. She let it play, slid her sunglasses down her nose, and opened the journal.

PERSONAL FIELD JOURNAL OF DR. IAN GREY

Watched the Paradise Duck cavort for one (1) hour today in the western inlet. Sustained joy for the whole period of cavorting. Activities included self-dunking, self-splashing, self-bathing. Each act seemed to generate new and equally fresh delight on the part of Duck Twelve. Renewed activity greeted as new activity. Feedback loop of self-amplified pleasure. Reached a state of pleasure and entertainment almost violent. Unsustainable levels of glee. Thrashed in delight; thusly reeds entangled feet. Immediate panic and despair. An extremity of honking and thrashing. Abnormally intense. But resolved quickly. Abnormally quickly? Seemed to forget incident as soon as it was past. Then resumed cavorting. Regarded water droplets permeating feathers. Their disappearance a mystery? The sensation pleasurable? Playfully snapped at said water droplets attempting to catch them before they...

DROPLETS!!! Sample to be taken for comparative permeability but very hopeful. Duck much easier to catch than others, and less intensely unhappy to be caught and have samples removed. Waders full of mud. Possibly some insect life. Perhaps need new waders.

Elsa felt Nolan's footsteps vibrating the floorboards. She pulled the headphones out. He stood in the doorway, stooped to fit himself within it.

She squinted up at Nolan through her plastic sunglasses. Where's Jinx? Elsa asked. At the sound of her name, the dog came trotting through the door, circling Elsa. Her fur was hot from the sun.

Where have you been? she asked.

I stayed up all night reading that, he said, pointing to the journal. And now?

Out walking the beach, he said. Thinking. Where were you?

I slept at the Lobby, Elsa said. She saw Nolan take in the man's shirt she wore, but he couldn't be bothered with her bad behavior.

I thought you left, Elsa said.

I want to find Duck Number Twelve, Nolan said, pointing at the journal again.

Elsa sighed. Nolan, we don't even know how to find it.

Yes, we do, Nolan said. He lists the places he's seen it in the journal. We can hike out to the sites. There are only three of them.

What if we get lost and miss the boat, she said.

Elsa, I think it's important, Nolan said.

I think Dad thought it was important.

I'm not ready to accept those aren't the same thing. I just want to see this amazingly special fucking duck he loved so much, Nolan said. After that we'll leave. But I need to see it.

And of course Elsa wanted to see the duck too. Of course Nolan could admit to wanting this and Elsa couldn't. The problem was that Nolan wanted answers, and Elsa wasn't sure what she would do with answers if she found them.

What if we don't find it, Elsa said.

Nolan sank down and rested in a deep squat so he was on the same level as Elsa. We just try, Nolan said.

Elsa stroked Jinx. She and Nolan couldn't fight. She had almost lost him. Maybe they could avoid being like they were before. Maybe they could be something different. To make that happen, she needed to apologize, but she couldn't quite bring herself to do it.

She said, I'm afraid the duck is real.

It's obviously real, Nolan said.

I mean I'm afraid he was right, Elsa said. What if we find this duck and all of a sudden it looks like Dad wasn't crazy? That he was actually onto something the whole time—

Then we're assholes.

Elsa nodded. It's probably just a duck, Elsa said. Nothing special.

Even if it's not, I just want to know what he was seeing, Nolan said.

Elsa nodded. Okay, she said.

The Greys understood that it didn't matter whether or not the duck was actually special. What mattered was that Ian had thought it was special. Thought it was happy. What did happiness look like to Ian? They knew it didn't look like Elsa, who had broken his heart twice, once on purpose. They knew it didn't look like Nolan, who had never managed to be enough like him or Keiko to make Ian marvel. Ingrid had betrayed him, and even Keiko had not been enough in the end.

What was enough to warrant Ian's attention? What did Ian love enough to stalk in the woods and the mud and the salt?

The Paradise Duck. Jesus H. Christ.

———

They packed their bags. They took the twin field journal and logbook. They took Ian's sleeping roll and tent. They took a small bag of feathers for sentimental reasons. Nolan packed two sets of Ian's clothes. Elsa took his Beethoven t-shirt. Jinx worried as they shoved things in bags, whining as her home disappeared. They packed their last stale bagels and a jar of peanut butter they'd bought on the mainland. They packed pouches of dried fruit. They filled their water bottles. Elsa took Ian's iPod.

Nolan sat on Elsa's tiger float, deflating it to a shriveled husk. He toweled off the crumpled plastic and came over to shove the bundle into Elsa's pack, which she wore. She stood straight, holding Ian's journal, as he forced the bundle down, the weight of his shove pulling on Elsa's shoulders.

They were ready to head out.

Nolan stood back and clapped his hands together. There, he said, satisfied.

You really are so much like him, Elsa said.

Nolan felt as if he might weep. He felt as if he might kiss her. It was such a stupid little thing to remind her of him. The satisfied clap of a job well done. But he knew she was right. He wanted to be better parts of his father. But if Elsa could see him in the clap, it was enough. It was so much.

Should we keep his blanket? Nolan asked, pointing to the unmade bed. It smelled like Ian, Nolan said.

Elsa didn't know. They had proved this once already.

Elsa said: I have no idea what our father smelled like. And began to cry.

They put down their packs and lay on the bed, smelling the smell that was mostly theirs but was also, maybe, their father's. Nolan grabbed a fistful of the knitted cover, balled it up, and pressed it to Elsa's nose.

Smell, he said, pressing the fist of fabric harder against her face.

Elsa smelled.

Nolan, I think that maybe you were right. I want you to know—

Hey, read to me, Nolan said. He retrieved Ian's journal.

Nolan, Elsa said. Listen, I'm sorry. I'm saying I'm sorry, about everything. Last night—

But he couldn't bear for her to say it. He'd thought it was an apology he wanted from her, but now he knew an apology was irrelevant. What he wanted from her was Ian. No one else could do it, use X-ray vision to look past his own mediocrity and weakness and general not-enough-ness and see the shape of his father. His mother too. His parents were gone, but Elsa could show him the parts of himself that were worthy of them. If she apologized, it would ruin everything.

You'll feel better in a minute, Nolan said. Just read to me.

PERSONAL FIELD JOURNAL OF DR. IAN GREY

It frisks in a moment of stolen time! Observing Paradise Duck interacting with Female Duck Seven. Seven normal relative to other UBH. Perches on railing to dry. Daily activities purposeful and frenetic. Paradise Duck enjoying leisure time. Paradise Duck attempts to initiate play with Seven. Seven resists, honks aggressively, continues feeding. Second attempt. Seven capitulates, cavorts briefly, goes back to feeding. Third attempt leads to mating. Duck Seven mounted twice by gleeful Paradise Duck. Will any existing mutations be passed on? It's a mutation, almost certainly. Lab results will show which pair. One sample from Twelve in already. Must send samples of Seven in case of any offspring. Use Georgia lab. M working out of Louisiana. Will visit Site Two tomorrow.

There are three sites where he saw the duck, Nolan said. One is at the cove. The second is at a sinkhole in the middle of the island, and the last one is somewhere out by Gates's and Esther's houses. If we head out now, we have enough time to visit all three before the post boat comes.

Not so long ago, Elsa had been wishing for the post boat to come and save her from Nolan. To take her away from this place. Now all she wanted was for Nolan to let her apologize, before it was too late. Now the post boat was coming, and it felt as if they were racing the clock.

Let's go, Nolan said.

Nolan, wait a minute, listen, you were right about back then. I—

Nolan stood up and whistled. Jinx trotted to the doorway.

———

They went into the woods. Through the paths that led to the first of the three sites where Ian had seen the Paradise Duck. It took them thirty minutes to reach Site One, the cove.

It was a long rocky beach of boulders and black stones. Only a ribbon of sand slipped between the overhanging trees and the shore. One tree had fallen and hung its head over the bay, trailing moss. Its trunk had been smoothed by the waves, and swimming and feeding beneath it were half a dozen undowny buffleheads.

They tied Jinx's lead to a tree from which she could not see the ducks. The children crouched on the largest of the boulders. Elsa slid out of her pack. Nolan pulled off his sweaty shirt and traded it for one of Ian's: faded gray with a monarch caterpillar on the front, curled into a question mark, dotted with a green chrysalis. He pulled it over his head.

Elsa slipped the field glasses around her neck. Twisted the dial to bring the cove into focus. The ducks were squat and round as loaves of bread upon the water. They traveled in orderly circles as they snapped at the grasses beneath the fallen tree. The males' green necks ruffled slightly in the wind and all of their bellies were damp and disheveled at the waterline.

How will we know? Elsa whispered. We can't catch it.

Nolan passed her the field journal.

PERSONAL FIELD JOURNAL OF DR. IAN GREY

As other UBH dive for weeds and snap at bugs, Duck Twelve drifts for fifteen minutes, watching the horizon line. Appears deeply content. Does not eat. Occasionally cocks head in breeze to get better angle on feather ruffling around face. Squints eyes/ bleats softly. Listening to Bach's Arioso (Adagio in G) through one ear while observing so perhaps am projecting mood of deep tranquility onto duck, but don't think so. Duck Twelve appears to be in an almost meditative state. Other ducks ignore Duck Twelve and continue feeding. Must stop listening to Bach, but cannot stand drone of mosquitos otherwise apparent. Samples sent to Georgia last week.

Be the bird, Elsa thought.

The ducks drifted and dove. They surfaced with strands of kelp in their beaks. They ate clusters of larvae and kept up a constant banter of quacking as they drifted and fed. They chased the Jesus beetles skittering across the surface and ate them. They snapped at clouds of hovering gnats and motes of pollen. To the children they seemed cross, a score of bustling no-time-to-waste mothers. Not one of them seemed meditative. Perhaps Ian had been right about the Bach.

The children's backs grew stiff.

Elsa set down the field glasses. She had gone to bed with sweaty hair and today it was turned in thick, salty twists. She shook it out.

Nolan pulled a strand. You're going islander, he said. You thinking of staying?

Elsa rolled her eyes and twisted her hair up and off her neck. I'm thinking I'm going to the Netherlands in a month, she said. And after that, I'm going to Mars.

Oh my god, enough, Nolan said. He put down his own binoculars. What? Elsa said.

You're not going to Mars. Will you just stop?

I'm going if they pick me.

You're being ridiculous. Even for you.

Just because you can't wrap your head around the fact that the planet is dying doesn't mean it's not happening. This is a real exit strategy.

Nolan snorted.

He couldn't understand, Elsa thought, because his life was too bound up in bougie San Francisco minutiae. But soon it wouldn't matter who believed them, because Elsa would be gone.

If she could just get to Mars, Elsa thought, she would know what was her responsibility and what was not. Elsa would not need to worry about elections, or the prison-industrial complex, or the dye in pink birthday cupcakes, or pornography that made women want to whimper instead of moan, or the disappearing bees, or celebrities whose names wormed their way into Elsa's brain, she did not know how. She felt like wiping the clutter of her whole life clean and beginning over. Maybe everyone did. Maybe humanity needed a mulligan.

You're just jealous, because you think they might actually pick me, Elsa said. And Dad would have loved that. You know that you would never get picked.

Nolan shook his head. Listen, I know you're so tough. Such a badass. But you're not a fucking astronaut, Elsa. You really think that when colonization happens, they're going to recruit a team of random civilians to remake society? You're a second-grade teacher, not to mention a drinker, and you haven't done anything in the way of serious exercise in twenty years and—

I hike all the—

It's a scam, Elsa. A publicity stunt to get people excited about the space program. Maybe put their company's name on the map. Best-case scenario? It's to get people used to the idea that people like you and me *could* live on Mars someday. But I'll tell you right now—it doesn't matter whether you get picked or not. No one on that list is hopping a spaceship anytime in the next fifty years.

Elsa stood up. The laces of her hiking boots were muddy and spotted with dead leaves. She felt like running. Leaving. But she'd promised herself she wouldn't do that again. She would stick with Nolan this time. She pulled at the straps of her sports bra where her shoulders had started to ache.

Nolan was staring, as if waiting for her to come clean.

But Elsa wasn't lying. She felt like her insides were being crumpled.

She was an idiot. Of course she wasn't going to Mars.

The real surprise was that it had taken Nolan, of all people, to make her see this.

The era of certainty Elsa had hoped to bring back with Mars was impossible. It had never existed in the first place.

Elsa had trusted in the realness of the mission so blindly. She had considered that she wouldn't be picked. But she had not considered that the entire mission was not real. Would not happen. She'd trusted the people who ran the program because they claimed to be scientists. And Elsa believed in scientists.

But scientists, Elsa was realizing, were humans. Were sometimes also sad and wrong and desperate for any credible evidence of something to believe in. Sometimes, they were just as in the dark as the rest of us. Or maybe more, because the good ones knew better than anyone all the things we do not know. How important it was not to be ignorant, but to fully comprehend what was not yet known or knowable. To sit with this kind of necessary uncertainty struck Elsa as a harder task than her current burden of feeling she knew too much. A worthier one.

I mean, you knew that, didn't you? Nolan said. I can't be the first person to tell you this.

But you are, Elsa said.

Elsa was living on an island of crazies, and she hated home, and now she didn't even have Mars to escape to. All that was waiting for her when she returned was a new class of doomed second graders in the fall.

I'm sorry, Nolan said. I guess I thought you knew. I thought you were lording it over me because you thought I was too dumb to know it wasn't real.

In the bay, the ducks swam around each other in choreographed semicircles. Their wakes spun in concentric ripples, then disappeared into the larger current.

I really wanted to tell him I'd made the final interviews, Elsa said. She sat down on a rock. Even if he'd gone crazy, I thought Dad would think it was really cool.

He would have, Nolan said.

Elsa shook her head. He would of seen through it faster than you. It would have been so embarrassing. Him realizing how easily I was duped would have been even worse than this.

Worse than what?

Than New Baby telling me I'm a fool.

Nolan exhaled. You can't keep calling me that, he said. I'm a grown man with a job and a girlfriend and an apartment, no fucking parents to speak of, and about two decades' worth of shit from you. So please just stop.

Elsa considered Nolan. He was sweaty, his mane of hair tousled wildly, and he was wearing Ian's caterpillar t-shirt. He looked totally serious. He looked a lot like Ian. He looked a lot like Keiko. It was true that he was grown. His face was still beautiful, but his jaw had hard angles to it, and he had a fierce certainty about him that Elsa coveted.

She squeezed his shoulder. You are, she said. I'll stop.

Nolan nodded.

The buffleheads were finished feeding. They flew up in bursts of flapping and then perched, all in a line, on the branches of the fallen tree. They shook themselves and twisted their necks. Then, as if part of some ballet, not Bach, but Tchaikovsky maybe, they raised themselves in unison and extended their wings to dry.

The children watched the ducks. This was their big step backward, the cause for all the alarm, and yet, Nolan and Elsa didn't think the buffleheads looked inconvenienced by having to perform this practical task. They did not seem hindered by the evolutionary trajectory that had deprived them of past generations' convenient waterproofing. If anything, the children thought the buffleheads looked purposeful. At ease.

After all, they were ducks.

What else did they have to do but these small things? The business of everyday life was not so dreary. It was the stuff a day was built of. It was what kept you alive.

The buffleheads shut their eyes and sat in the sun to dry.

Look, Nolan said. He pointed at the ducks' newly exposed ankles, rubbery pink beneath the dripping fringe of belly feathers. There was a pale green band around almost every one. He lifted his field glasses and began reading off the numbers.

Elsa was staring at her dirty boots again. He's not there, she said.

Nolan lowered the field glasses. You're right.

Elsa said, When we find him, I really think we'll know.

Park Rapids

I
t's only a game, Keiko called. Nolan, it's only a game.

They'd come to Minnesota for Elsa's fifteenth birthday. The mothers were sitting with margaritas in lawn chairs, and they held hands, swinging their arms. Elsa was splayed in the grass at their feet, plucking the tallest blades and knotting them together in a chain. The daisy chain grew ominously longer until it began to resemble a great length of rope.

But Nolan was not paying attention to them. Elsa's yard was a long alley of untrampled grass and Nolan wanted to be master of it. His yard. His legs. He loped and cartwheeled desperately, as if to use the yard up by inhaling every gust of grassy air. And there was his father next to him! Ian loped easily, his legs long and so white. Nolan happily smacked at his father's thighs, and Ian tried to snatch him up from the grass, but Nolan, little rabbit, was too fast and darted away. He knew his father was pretending that he could not catch him when really he could, and this was what Nolan loved most of all. To be free but confident in the knowledge that should Ian need to scoop him up, in a second, he could. I'm going to get you I'm going to get you. Nolan tumbled, forward-rolling out of Ian's grasp. He was laughing, evilly triumphant, when Ian proposed the race.

Elsa, come race, Ian said. She popped up.

So, Ian said, you'll race from the parents to the tree at the far side of the yard and back again.

Ian was still out of breath, wiping his glasses on the tail of his shirt. He sat, taking Elsa's place, and leaned against the knees of his women. Elsa snorted at this, skeptical of the trinity of parents. How happy they seemed together. How unlikely it was. It had taken a while for the dust of the divorce and remarriage to settle, but since then, the parents had loved each other.

Ingrid and Keiko in particular loved each other. They first met over dinner at an Italian restaurant that served slabs of garlic bread and red wine in carafes. There were posters of Marlon Brando on the walls and bunches of dusty plastic grapes on a fake arbor. At first, both women were formal, deferential, not wanting to impose on each other. This lasted half an hour, until Ian excused himself to the bathroom in what was obviously a need for relief from the social awkwardness. As soon as the door swung closed behind him, Keiko and Ingrid laughed at his obviousness and squeezed each other's hands and started to talk in earnest. Ian returned, warily, and found the women imitating his way of squinting at the television remote like it was some strange artifact. He smiled, as if he had orchestrated all of this perfectly.

Ian and Keiko were happy together. And Ingrid was happy single, sometimes dating. But the three of them were never as totally happy as when they were all together. Any number of times Keiko had asked Ingrid to move to San Francisco. Nurses were needed everywhere. They could share a neighborhood so Ian could see Elsa more. But Ingrid shook her head. She was a lake person. For her to leave Minnesota would be the end of her happiness. And in truth, Keiko was relieved. Not because of Ingrid, but because of Elsa. Keiko had forgiven Elsa for the events of five years ago, leaving Nolan in the old well like that. She had been a child, and it was understandable she was jealous.

Still, Keiko sometimes had what she called Bad Dog Feeling around Elsa. When she was a young girl in Kyoto, she had seen a beautiful snowy dog on her walk home from school. When she looked at the dog, something in her gut had told her that it was bad news, not a nice dog at all. But she'd ignored the feeling because the dog looked so soft and white with its fringed white plume of a tail, its large dark eyes, and soft muzzle, and she wanted, of course, to grasp his fur. But she had barely approached the dog when it growled and snapped at her, biting her cheek. It was the smallest wound. A nip so barely there that her mother said it was probably the mark of a single tooth. A one-tooth wound, she called it.

Keiko would never say so to Ian, but there was something about Elsa that reminded her of that dog. Elsa gave her the same inexplicable warning feeling that she knew was unfounded but had served her well enough in the past that she could not totally discount it. And so perhaps it was for the best that these other-Greys stayed away.

Okay, Ian told the children. This is the starting line. He drew his naked toes across the lawn.

Nolan did not know why his father was doing this. They'd been so happy a moment ago and now suddenly this was very serious. But he and Elsa took their places by the parents.

Ian said, Ready, steady, go!

Elsa wheeled across the yard. She gave herself over to the race with the confidence of a human who does not fear that to give all will be too little. Nolan pumped across the yard trying to keep up with Elsa, six years older and many inches taller. He pushed his legs to do more.

It's only a game, Keiko called, only a game.

The parents were alarmed by the frenzy with which he chugged along. They were distressed by the intensity of his small face.

You're doing great, Nolan, Ian said.

Nolan heard them worrying for him and so he worried for himself. They saw he didn't have enough to give.

(Sometimes Nolan thought he must have been happy as a child, carefree and zipping across the garden, but no, even then he'd been worried that for his parents, for anyone, he was not enough. And why had they made them race each other? Why set them up to compete in this way? They had been racing for years. He had always thought this Elsa's doing, but maybe it wasn't. Maybe it was the parents who taught them that their love was a thing to be angled for.)

And so, pushing himself to run faster across the lawn, when the parents called out to Nolan in their worried voices, he began to fear that if he pushed any harder he might run up against the exact limits of his self and strength. And he didn't want to know. So Nolan stopped running, his thin legs flecked with bits of mown grass, still damp from the morning's rain. Nolan sat. The ground was spongy and the cold damp of it seeped into his pants.

He did not move, not even when his father shouted, Run! Nolan! The race isn't over! Come on, Nolan, run!

Elsa bulleted toward the parents, legs wheeling gracefully. And Nolan watched her do it.

Leap's Island

They'd crossed the island, hiking toward the second site, the sinkhole in the middle of the island, but the center kept eluding them. It was five o'clock and they still had not arrived. They'd been trying to avoid the obvious trail routes, where they might be seen by Mitchell, who would want to know what they were doing. But this had proved more difficult than they'd anticipated. The dog was hot and exhausted. They'd been lost twice already and blamed each other for the loops they'd traveled, walking so long only to trek back to their beginnings.

Desperate, they followed what they thought was a trail but became a flooded stream bed full of mud that sucked at their shoes. They walked face first into spider webs invisibly knit across the pathways. They turned their ankles on root after root after root.

The third time they arrived at a lichen-y rock they had seen too many times before, Elsa shouted and Nolan groaned and Jinx yipped to be a part of things. They were disheveled and sweaty. They were furious. They wanted to punch the trees. They wanted to bite each other. They wanted to find the fucking Paradise Duck and wring its neck, because it could not be worth all this.

It has to be that way, Nolan said. We can't be so far.

What if we can't find our way back from here, Elsa said. What if we're stuck out here for days and we miss the post boat.

Shh, Nolan said.

They heard a woman's laughter. They smelled a fire. They heard the same man's voice coming from two directions. The ground was marshy around their ankles. Gwen Manx's shack. The brothers. The good news was that they'd found someone. The bad news was that if they were close to Gwen, they were lost again. Almost an hour from the site. They'd done another circle.

Jinx woofed and ran out ahead of them, and the Greys followed.

When they broke through the bushes, into the clearing, they found Mick with his arm around Gwen and Jim rolling on the deck, telling a story about the highest he'd ever been in his life and how he'd thought he'd been transformed into a beetle and could not get up and so missed an entire day of specimen collecting in Peru. A fire burned in a small pit dug just beyond the deck. And beyond that, three domes, pupae under construction for the ducks.

The Greys presented themselves, their faces streaked and scratched, their legs bitten.

Children! Gwen said, standing. What happened to you?

Nolan and Elsa thought it was strange how everyone on the island thought of them as children. They were Ian's kids, but they were old. They were millennials. They were young. They were ex-siblings. They were ex-lovers. They were technically nothing to each other anymore. Maybe the shared loss of Ian had allowed them to be something again or maybe the island had. *The children.* Like much the Reversalists said, it wasn't technically correct, but sometimes it felt right. So when childless Gwen called Nolan and Elsa out of the woods again, they went to her and let their scrapes be tended to.

Gwen cleaned their wounds with iodine that ran down their calves like rusty water. They loved the firm way she patted on their Band-Aids.

Where were you trying to go? Gwen asked.

Elsa said they were on a trek across the island to process their grief.

I get it, man, Jim said, patting her arm.

What are you guys doing out here? Nolan asked.

Domes for ducks, Jim said, gesturing at the enormous pupae. This is going to be the new nesting ground.

We put in some garden satellites, for good measure too, Mick said. The muck back here is fertile if you can keep it dry enough.

In a raised bed behind Gwen's house, there were lines of green shoots. A horseradish plant with huge fanned leaves. Small radish foliage. Mick pulled a white-and-pink bulb so perfect Nolan could not believe it. Bloody pink stripes across its skin, a dandyish flourish of style—what would Ian make of the elegant radish? Once, Nolan knew, he would have thought its beauty beside the point. He would have thought of its nutrients, its life cycle. But that was before Ian came to Leap's. Nolan was not sure what Ian would have made of the radish now. Something different. Something new.

Eat it, Mick said, holding the radish out.

It's not washed, Nolan said.

Dude, Mick said.

Nolan wiped the radish on his shorts and ate it. Watery, fresh, and bitter.

Good? Mick asked. Nolan nodded.

Are you going back to Ian's tonight? Gwen asked.

We're camping, the children said.

Camp with us, Gwen said.

The brothers said, Party!

They drank tea on the deck, in folding chairs, facing the ocean and far distant mainland. They ate more radishes from the garden. Gwen sliced fruit she'd been saving from her last post-boat delivery, oranges and melon. Jim rolled a joint and they passed it around.

Everyone was merry and telling the good kind of stories. Not the sad "let me explain why I am the way I am" kind, meant to excuse or explain. Tonight, they told small stories, the kind you collect like marbles, odd or pretty. Travel stories and epic feats of wildness from Mick and Jim, funny animal stories from Gwen's days as a vet. Nolan talked about the absurdity of his job and the inappropriate things people posted to the Giants' page. Elsa told children-say-the darndest-things stories about her students. The fire had crumbled to an ember-bright glow and smoke drifted up around them. They settled into peaceful silence. Jinx lay inside the shack with water and food, legs twitching in her dreams.

Gwen picked up her pack of Virginia Slims and tapped one out. Mick cast his arm around her shoulders and drew Gwen to him. It was such a familiar gesture. Elsa saw in it a man confident of his own charms but well aware that a woman had no need of him. The kind of gesture that had endeared Dylan to her in that Minnesota cowboy bar a million years ago. It had seemed a trait unique to him at the time. Elsa found herself relieved to see it again. To know it existed elsewhere, in the wild. The fire popped and she sucked the last flesh of her cantaloupe. It was obvious they were sleeping together. Or was it? Because now Jim was squeezing Gwen's hand. Maybe it didn't matter which of the brothers Gwen slept with, or both. Gwen was being offered something she deserved, and Elsa hoped she accepted it.

Nolan was eating oranges. He stuck a wedge in his mouth and smiled at Elsa horrifically, lips full of pith. Elsa cracked up. Stupid. Little brother.

Fireworks screamed up from the mainland, and Nolan jumped in his chair. Spat out the peel. He had always startled easily, and now he was worried about the Paradise Duck. Would the sound of the fireworks spook it away? What if it swam or flew off on some new, untraceable course?

The five of them sat up in their deck chairs and watched the show above the tree line. The bulb-heads of flame burst in satisfying pops. The air smelled of gunpowder. Jinx woke up to bark at the distant explosions, then went back to sleep.

When Nolan thought of going back to the mainland, he could not bear the idea of sitting in his office chair and designing promotions about free soft-serve ice cream in miniature collectible baseball helmets. He felt the island protecting him from the acid dread he felt in his stomach when he would turn on his computer and watch his inbox counter populate. It protected him from taking Janine out to romantic trendy restaurants where they laughed and drank too much, even though the whole thing felt like a show they were putting on for an unknowable audience. It protected him from the news, the news, the news, on his computer, on his phone, on TV, on monitors in waiting rooms and in airports and in the backseats of cabs—the intractable seriousness of the news revealing the farce of Nolan's days. How mild Nolan's own perceived troubles truly were.

Yes, the island had stripped Nolan of Janine, and his apartment, his job, his Twitter, his pornography, his brunch friends, his news-feed, and his culpability for doing nothing about every rotten thing wrong in the world.

Without these things, Nolan felt something like good.

Had Ian felt this way? Had he been running away? And were he and Elsa on the list of things that Ian had been running from?

The fireworks had finished and they'd eaten the last of the fruit. The smell of gunpowder rolled over the breeze.

Thank you, Nolan said to Gwen, for all of this.

Gwen was staring intensely out at the water. She was no longer smiling, though she still leaned into Mick. She didn't reply. Her arm jerked. Mick leaned away, as if realizing himself unwelcome.

I'm sorry, Mick said. But when Gwen's arm jerked again, her gaze was unbroken. She hunched forward, then began to convulse.

Jesus, Mick said. Jesus. They leapt up. No one did anything. Gwen groaned. Elsa fluttered her hands and took tiny steps in place.

Gwen flopped in the chair.

She's epileptic, Elsa said. Isn't she epileptic?

She's having a seizure, Nolan said. He waited for Elsa to take control of the situation, but she looked panicky.

Jim ran from the deck to the tree line. A stick, he said. We need to put a stick in her mouth.

No, Nolan said, that's wrong. But Jim was gone, looking.

It occurred to Nolan that he was waiting as if he were everyone's last draft pick to do anything. The New Baby. But who had decided that? Nolan knew what to do, and no one was going to come along and tell him to go ahead and do it.

Gwen fell from her chair and lay on her back, still convulsing.

Should we— Elsa said.

I've got it, Nolan said. He knelt down and cleared the chairs away. He slid Gwen's body away from the deck railing. He grasped her shoulder. She had said to wait with her. He remembered this. Just to wait and to watch her.

Gwen's jaw was locked and she clucked, drooling slightly. It seemed to Nolan that she was intensely suffering. He hoped he was wrong. Gwen's arm shot out and she held it there, a clenched open fist. It was as if she were grasping something invisible in the air.

Nolan squeezed Gwen's shoulder. You're okay, he said. You're okay. Her body was stiff but racked with small tremors. She blinked furiously and then her eyes locked open, rolling so far back they were milky slits. Nolan squeezed Gwen's shoulder again and hummed. You're okay.

Elsa was biting her fingers and Mick was pacing around the deck. Jim was still searching for a stick.

We have to do something, Mick said. Something.

I am doing something, Nolan said. I'm doing this. He kept humming.

It lasted for almost thirty seconds. It lasted forever. And then Gwen took a deep breath. She gasped, wetly, and tried to get up, as if she were going to run from the deck.

Hey, Nolan said, hey. He guided her back to the floor, turned her on her side. You're okay.

Where? said Gwen.

You're at home, Nolan said. She breathed as if she'd run miles, and her eyes rolled, focusing nowhere. Where, she said again.

Home, Nolan said. He squeezed her arm. You're okay, he said. Gwen's body slowly relaxed and gave up its stiffness.

————

After fifteen minutes, Gwen assured them she would be fine. She just needed to rest. The brothers fell all over themselves offering her water and aspirin and help.

Once she was resting in the bed, Gwen asked Nolan to describe what the seizure had looked like, and he told her.

Thank you, she said. You did good.

Jim told her he'd tried to find a stick for her to bite on.

Jesus Christ, Gwen said, squeezing her eyes shut like it hurt terribly. Maybe you should stay, Nolan. We need someone smart around here. She pointed at the brothers. I'd trade both of these boy geniuses for one calm smart person.

————

As Nolan and Elsa rolled out their sleeping bags on the deck, Elsa said, You did do good.

Thanks, Nolan said. What he wanted to ask was, Was it how Dad would have done it?

Elsa said, You get that from Keiko. She was always very calm in a crisis.

Elsa was thinking about the time she'd left Nolan in the hole. Keiko hadn't lost a minute to her own panic and fear. She'd just begun looking for Nolan and had not stopped moving until they'd found him.

I think Ian loved that about her, Elsa said.

She was right about his mother, Nolan knew. When he and Elsa had been found in bed together, there was yelling and screaming from Ingrid and Ian, but not from his mother. Keiko had just sat there. She cried a bit, but she was very calm. And when Ian and Ingrid had exhausted themselves with their fury, his mother was the one to say: So what are we going to do?

Elsa squeezed Nolan's hand very hard before drawing herself deep into her sleeping bag.

He listened to Elsa, asleep and breathing in gravelly rasps. It would have sounded monstrous to anyone else, but to Nolan, they sounded like the snores of a small, congested child. Nolan lay in his own bag. He was so tired, but he could not fall asleep. He could not stop seeing Gwen grasping her invisible something out of the air.

Park Rapids

The music was coming from the office. Ingrid never used the desk but felt every house should have one, just in case. Elsa stood outside the door and listened.

It was the third of the *Gymnopédie*. The piano notes were plodding but purposeful. They always reminded Elsa of someone walking in the rain. Perhaps someone carrying a newspaper walking home from the house of someone they loved in the rain. Things had not gone well at the house. The person was melancholy.

It was one of Ian's visiting weekends and he'd come without Keiko and Nolan. It was Saturday and Ingrid was working a double shift at the hospital, giving them time alone. But Ian had just a little bit of work to do, and so he'd settled into the office. After he was through, they'd go to the mall for some shopping, Ian said.

Now that she was fifteen, everyone assumed Elsa always wanted to go shopping, but she hated the mall and liked her ratty t-shirts just fine. What she really wanted was for her father to take her to the Lakeside Diner where they served their milkshakes in elegant, tall glasses and for Ian to blow his paper straw wrapper at her.

Elsa went in and lay on the office carpet like a starfish. The rug was a soft bloodred Oriental with ochre patterning. The wood molding smelled like lemon polish. Ian did not look up; when he worked he was a million miles away. The music shifted to a new movement.

There is a man, Elsa said.

This was a game they played when Elsa was small. Back when they all still lived together in the farmhouse, before Ian had cut them loose and drifted away. The game was that Elsa would tell Ian what was happening in his music. Satie was her favorite because it sounded like it had the most stories in it.

Ian looked up from his laptop.

The man is wearing a gray trench coat, Elsa said. He is walking by a canal. The canal is flowing gently and it smells a bit like trash.

How do you know about canals? Ian asked.

Everyone knows about canals, Elsa said. He is bringing flowers to a woman, but they are not very fresh, and he is worried about them.

Ian closed the computer and inspected his daughter's upside-down face on the red-and-ochre rug. He did not ask what she knew about the reasons a man brought a woman flowers.

What is he worried about?

That the flowers are already half dead and so she won't like them.

Would you like them?

I'm not the woman.

You're almost a woman, Ian said.

I am a woman, Elsa said. Just not this woman.

Her father rocked back in his chair. I suppose you are a woman, Ian said. Will you forgive me for not noticing?

Elsa shrugged.

Ian *tock*ed his way to a new track. How about this one?

Langgaard began. *The Music of the Spheres.* Ian watched Elsa carefully as she listened. The music was awesome and frightening. A high-pitched shuddering string section. Rumbling drums.

Elsa said, It's something that doesn't know how big it is yet.

(Ian was so often gone in those days that even when he was

there, Elsa could not help but anticipate the pain of his going again. And so she knew that even on this day, even this far back, she had not been happy. Still, when she would think of Mars, years from this day, filling out her application to be an Origins colonist, Elsa would remember those opening bars of Langgaard. Someday, she was sure, she'd imagine it playing as she looked out on her new, red planet through a thick pressure-proof window and dust tumbled over the surface.)

Leap's Island

When they woke, they found Gwen nestled between the brothers. Nolan and Elsa whispered good-bye and the three grumbled but did not wake.

Morning at Gwen's smelled like skunk cabbage and fresh mud. They were sore and scabbed from yesterday's endeavors, and as they faced the woods again, the children's packs were heavy. Jinx was not eager to follow after being so poorly shepherded the day before, but they tugged her along.

Elsa said, I think we should head—

Please, let me navigate, Nolan said. Elsa gave him the side-eye.

Nolan insisted. I think I know where we got offtrack.

Fine, Elsa said.

Nolan looked up to get his bearings, then set them on a new course.

Thirty minutes later, they'd found the second site: a geological sinkhole, surrounded by forest, at the heart of the island.

There were great staircases of limestone rock descending to the water line. The Greys descended almost ten feet, arrived at a flat plateau of rock, and took off their packs, which had pressed sweatily against their backs.

The water was the clear mineral green of a soda bottle. Great planks of stone, like steps, led into its depths. Ten feet in, there was a ledge, the edge of an underwater cliff, off which it seemed you could step into the darkness of the deep water beneath it.

They gave Jinx a bowl of water in the shade. They stripped to their bathing suits and sat with their feet in the water.

They watched and waited for the duck.

With binoculars, Nolan inspected the far side of the shore. He inspected the knot of Elsa's bikini, very close up. The shore again.

There were small fish, flat like skipping stones, black darts marking their backs, which came and nipped at their legs and feet. They could see a turtle coming toward them, from a distance, emerging from the depths and into the sun-filtered water. She had blunt-clawed flippers and a long pointed nose that emerged, periscope-like, from the water. She looked at the children, then swam away, the knockable dome of her back breaching the surface just once as she lifted then plunged under a constellation of floating algae blooms.

Elsa lowered herself silently into the water, slipping beneath until she sat on the stone shelf, her chin just above the water's surface. The sinkhole's water was so clear in the shallows that her whole body was visible beneath the surface as she sat cross-legged.

Elsa dunked and made an underwater face. Opened her eyes and saw Nolan's underwater feet. Dead men's feet. Still underwater, she motioned for him to join her. Wavery, his limbs all warped, she could see him shake his head and lift the field glasses again. Elsa swam and grabbed his ankle. Tried to drag him down with her. Nolan kicked her. Not hard, but in the temple.

Elsa sputtered up. What the fuck, she said.

Stop, Nolan said. You're making too much noise and the duck won't come.

Come in.

Lakes are gross.

You came swimming at Potato Lake once.

I didn't swim.

You ate three sandwiches on the porch with the crusts cut off of them and drank so much orange soda you peed yourself.

I didn't pee myself.

You cried.

Because I came close to peeing myself and I couldn't find the bathroom.

Because it's at the back of the kitchen.

I'd seen a *NOVA* special about water snakes.

What?

The night before. I was convinced the lake was full of snakes.

Ian was so strict about TV. I wasn't allowed to watch anything.

Except Discovery, Animal Planet, and *NOVA*.

Like there's nothing horrifying there, right? Like *90210* was going to ruin my life but Shark Week was a-okay.

Exactly.

Come in?

Nolan descended the elegant rocky stairway so he was in ankle deep. Water-walkers, Jesus beetles, skittered by, joyful and defiant.

Nolan hated swimming in dark water, where you couldn't see your way. But he pushed off and dove all the same. The temperature dropped as he swam deeper, his lungs growing tighter. He opened his eyes but saw only motes, shadows. There was no bottom to push off of and so he thrust his arms until he surfaced again.

The children stared at each other, blowing bubbles, eyes just above the surface of the water. Elsa dunked. Nolan followed.

Floating, Elsa extended her legs down into a deeper gradation of green, her elbows out. She circled her fingers and stuck her pinky out, brought her hand to her mouth and pursed her lips. Underwater tea party.

Nolan pretended to butter an imaginary scone and eat it. Came up for air. Purposefully gasped. Plunged again. Pretended underwater note writing. Underwater dance party. Underwater fistfight. Underwater baseball. Underwater blowjob. Underwater apology. Underwater meditation. Pretend, pretend, pretend until it was underwater crying, water all around, mock turtle tears. Underwater apology, apology, apology.

They emerged again, panting.

The duck's not coming, Elsa said.

Maybe he's moved on.

———

Once they were dry and had eaten, it was three o'clock.

Move on or camp here tonight? Elsa asked.

The post boat would arrive tomorrow afternoon. They had a day left to find the Paradise Duck.

Camp here, I think.

Okay.

We're really close to Remy St. Gilles's shack.

Nolan.

We could drop in for a minute maybe, just see—

See if he's writing the next book and would he let you read it?

I just want to talk to him.

You're such a fanboy.

You know you want to ask him about Mars.

He's a writer, Nolan.

A writer with a degree in cosmology.

Everyone I know is insane for those books. I don't get it.

They're amazing. In the first one, the crew is all—

I didn't really want—

Dad loved them too. He read them to me.

St. Gilles was a total dick before. Do you remember this?

Maybe he's seen the duck?

And Elsa knew this was an excuse. But it was a thing Nolan wanted. And at this point, it felt like the least she could do.

———

The door opened, and St. Gilles stood there, his glasses on top of his head, looking simultaneously tremendously disappointed and not at all surprised to see them.

Oh, absolutely not, Remy said.

We were just wondering if you'd seen a particular duck, Elsa tried to get out. Our father—

I have nothing to say about your father, Remy said, and he began to shut the door in their faces.

Actually, Nolan said, we wanted to ask you about Mars.

What? St. Gilles opened the door again, intrigued in spite of himself.

Mars, Nolan said. Elsa is going. He pointed at her and Elsa looked as if she wanted to die.

Bloody hell, St. Gilles said, and gestured for the Greys to come in, as if he knew it would not be worthwhile to try to push them off.

The dog stays outside, he added.

The shack was full of books. They were crammed onto make-shift shelves nailed into one wall and piled several feet high along each of the others. There was a desk and a bed.

Elsa patted a stack of books. You read a lot.

I'm retired, Remy said. And old. He settled into a chair. Are you enjoying our island of Lotus Eaters?

Nolan saw a stack of journals on the desk. Surely, they must be drafts of the last Asterias book.

Are you writing these days? Nolan asked.

No, Remy said.

I just always wanted to find out what happened to the crew, Nolan said. After book eight it sounded like maybe they thought there'd be life on Europa and—

There's not going to be any life on Europa, Remy said. And there's not going to be much left on Earth if they get back. I thought you wanted to talk about Mars?

Nolan said, Wait, like you've written it and that's not what's going to happen or—

Remy said, In the end there's not going to be life left anywhere but Earth. And we're bollocking up what we've got here so it's not looking great for them, is it?

————

Remy St. Gilles grew up in London. His father, born in Haiti, taught biosciences at King's College. His mother worked in the civil service and came from a long line of pudding-pale London East Enders. They were both tremendously proud that Remy was on course to become a scientist like his father. He'd gotten a masters in evolutionary biology, and then shifted course to pursue his doctorate in cosmology, writing about the plausibility of microbial life on Mars.

But the dissertation went poorly. He was going blind from the footnotes. He wrote page after page and found himself sick of explaining things that he already understood. Remy was drawn to what he didn't already know. To the *what if?* In short, he was bored.

And so Remy began procrastinating by writing a story about a ship of explorers. The Earth explorers traveled the universe in a spaceship called the *Asterias* seeking out other habitable planets. When they arrived on Mars, they found a race of sentient and matriarchal insect-like creatures who had evolved from the microbes Remy was discussing in his dissertation.

When is that dissertation of yours going to be done? When do I get to call you Dr. St. Gilles? his mother asked. Remy only shrugged.

His first book, *The Great Space Sea*, was published that summer, and sold over ten thousand copies. He was heralded as the lovechild of Samuel Delany and Terry Pratchett.

Remy started the next book, this time set on Jupiter. He called it *Stardrift* and sent it off to his editor. They marketed it as Book Two of the Asterias Series: A Nine-Planet Exploration.

Stardrift was a best seller. Remy never finished his dissertation. He set about writing the Asterias series in earnest.

In each book, the *Asterias* crew encountered a new civilization on another planet, and in each case Remy based the species on the evolutionary possibilities of the given planet, allowing for freak occurrences and leniencies. He allowed himself to be broad and sloppy with his science, and people loved it. The year Pluto's planet-hood was revoked, there were hundreds of people who showed up to Comic-Con dressed as its ice-moss beings. He won Hugo Awards for books three and five, about Neptune and Uranus, and the books had been made into two feature films of a promised trilogy, the last installment of which would be filmed once there was an ending to the series.

Remy's father had bemoaned his turn toward novels.

Papa, Remy would say, Isaac Asimov had a PhD in biochemistry. H. G. Wells had a degree in biology. Arthur C. Clarke had degrees in math and physics.

But think what they might have done if they weren't writing stories! Remy's father said, poolside, an arbor of bougainvillea behind him and a glass of red wine in his hand. They were at the small summerhouse in Spain that Remy had bought his parents after the first *Asterias* movie check came in.

The crew of the *Asterias* were beloved characters, especially the captain, Angie Clarke, and her chief science officer, Gerald Lewis, who readers wildly speculated would fall in love and settle down in book nine, which would be set on the final planet St. Gilles had not written about: Earth. For eight books, the crew had marveled at the cities and cultures of the other planets. And in every book, they had realized they could not settle there. The pull of Earth was too strong. After all their explorations, Remy needed his characters to return home in book nine. Earth was the only way to complete the series.

But the crew of the *Asterias* had been voyaging for two hundred sixty years (in his father's least favorite part of the series, Remy had invented a state of cryo-like suspended animation for the crew that allowed them to survive the many long years of their journey without much aging, which even Remy admitted was scientifically desperate). Two hundred sixty years was a long time. And when

St. Gilles sat down to write the final book and imagined the crew returning to a changed Earth, he had to consider, for the first time, what that might look like.

He could imagine a million far-from-plausible ways life could happen elsewhere, but he knew Earth too well to play fast and loose with its possibilities.

Earth's long game was terrible.

Every time Remy wrote a draft of the new book and the crew of the *Asterias* touched down on Earth, they found something awful. Dystopian societies with enslaved underclasses. Drought-ravaged wastelands. Corporatized cultures with barely sentient men. Super-violent police states. Nuclear wastelands. Skeletal cities reclaimed by radioactive mosses and vines, no men to be found. This would not do.

Remy wanted his characters to find something better. This was what his readers wanted too: some approximation of a happy ending. He used to believe that was possible.

Then, Remy had what he thought of as The Bad Year.

It was the year he began receiving threatening notes from his publisher asking where the book was. The year his parents died, two months apart. The year, in an act of desperation and willfulness, that he donated almost all of his money to the Green Alliance, over the wails of his financial advisor. The year Remy threw away draft after draft.

It was near the end of The Bad Year that he gave an interview to BBC Radio in which he admitted that the last book was stumping him because he was unsure of Earth's future. The clip immediately went viral. Remy received hundreds of angry emails from fans. Just write the bloody thing! most of them read. Some of them were nastier and suggested what Remy could do if he failed to finish the series, most of which was anatomically impossible. Should we talk? the movie studio asked.

Remy ignored all the emails and letters, except for one. It came via airmail, from the United States. It had the insignia of a bearded man with a walking stick in the corner of the envelope. In it, Mitchell Townes let Remy know that if he ever needed a quiet place to write, the Reversalists would be happy to host him. He could live in the company of other scientists who shared his worldview. He could be their writer in residence. That was ten years ago.

———

So you are writing the last book? Nolan asked again.

Everyone is writing the last book, Remy said. Do you know how many dystopian novels were published last year? He gestured at the stacks on the floor. Everyone is writing about how we'll die. There's no point in me doing it too.

But— Nolan said. Couldn't there be, like, a glimmer of hope?

Why does everyone come knocking on my door for answers? Remy said. Why don't you solve your own problems instead of tracking down exhausted people to do it for you? He moved toward the door, showing them out.

We really did come to ask about Mars, Nolan said.

We didn't, Elsa said.

Again, Remy hesitated. They had a window.

I mean, do you think we're going? Elsa asked in a burst. Will we colonize Mars?

Assuredly, Remy said. In a hundred years or so. The first missions will fail, but we'll get there.

But what about Mars Origins? Elsa said. What about colonization within our lifetime?

Remy laughed. Even my books are more scientific than the Mars Origins mission.

She's a finalist to be part of the Mars One Hundred, Nolan explained, and Elsa slouched.

Well, Remy said, softening.

Elsa said, It just seems like we need an exit strategy.

Just because we need one doesn't mean there is one, Remy said.

Our father seemed to think the buffleheads meant we were going back to when things used to be better and we didn't need an exit strategy, Nolan said.

Remy laughed. And when exactly was that?

What? Nolan asked.

When things were so simple, Remy said. When you want to go back to. When do you think that was?

Nolan shrugged.

Remy said, How well do you think I'd do on the mainland in, say, 1910? How about you? He pointed to Elsa. Fond of birthing children and marrying whoever your father decides, are you? And you—he pointed at Nolan—you want to go back to California in 1942? I'm sure you could find some excellent internment camps.

Nolan said, That's not really—

Remy shook his head. My mother lived through the Blitz. My father grew up with Trujillo next door. Would you tell them to go back?

Well, not literally back to those times, Elsa said. Maybe Ian meant more like, just making life simpler?

There were a whole lot of ways things were simpler for certain people back then, Remy said. I doubt any of us would have found them helpful.

They had nothing to say to this. Outside, they heard Jinx whining.

We are going backward, Remy added.

What? The Greys looked at him.

All the way back, Remy said. Once everything else dies, Earth will be left with a bunch of extremophile microbes. And then we'll have to see if life happens again.

Remy was pointing toward the journals heaped on his desk.

Wait, Nolan said, is that what happens in the last *Asterias* book?

In the latest draft, Remy told them, the crew of the *Asterias* died on the first page. Every character readers had known and loved was reintroduced for one page only before the whole ship succumbed to a viral plague that killed them all within twenty-four hours.

The following one hundred twenty-five pages followed extremophile microbes sloshing about in a warm and shallow sea contaminated by nuclear waste. The microbes were bumping into one another and bumping into one another, the reader's hopes pinned on their merging and evolving into something greater. Life! And each instance of two microbes bumping together was written in a spirit of great hope and promise. But in each case, nothing happened. And the microbes drifted away.

How long will that part of the book go on? Nolan asked, horrified. Before life starts again? Will there be a new ship? Will you bring the crew back? Or a new crew?

As long as it takes for new life to occur. Remy laughed. Hundreds of pages. Billions of years. Forever.

San Francisco

The first time Nolan ever witnessed his father be wrong was the day his namesake punched Robin Ventura in the head. It was a rainy Wednesday, and Ian was sitting on the couch reading, half watching the game, which Nolan had put on. Nolan had a particular investment in the Rangers because of his namesake and because rooting for a team other than the Giants made his parents crazy, which was already something he'd realized was optimal. Keiko was working in her office with the door cracked, David Byrne thumping softly. Nolan lay on his stomach on the rug.

It happened quickly.

Ryan was pitching. Ventura was up to bat and the ball came in too close. He twisted away, but it hit him.

He hit him! Nolan said to his father, jumping up. He hit Ventura!

Ian looked up from his book. He pushed his glasses down his nose so he could make out the screen.

The last thing Ian said before the brawl began was, I'm sure he didn't mean to hit him.

Nolan had never before known his father to be wrong. But even then, Nolan knew he was wrong about this. Children are always being told that no one meant to hit them when they know that this is not true.

Ventura seemed calm as he turned from the plate. Even as he

took his helmet off to confront Ryan, even as he ran toward the mound, it was as if he were not sure this was what he meant to do. The young White Sock, handsome and open-faced, tackled Ryan as if hugging him round the middle.

Nolan immediately got his arm around Ventura's neck, a fatherly headlock, and then concertedly punched Ventura in the face. *Bang, bang, bang.* Ryan's hat flew off as he turned toward the world, then pivoted in to strike Ventura's face again.

Nolan said. Why is he doing that?

Both teams began brawling. Ventura was eventually spat out of the throng of people who'd rushed the mound. Ryan didn't emerge until almost a minute later.

Look at this, the announcer said.

Ryan was rumpled. Without his hat, his dark hair visibly sparser than it used to be, balding in the middle. His shirt had come unbuttoned around his thickened waist. The cameras panned to Ventura, who pouted, as if he could not believe this had happened. They panned back to Ryan and his lined, Texan face was unsurprised: this was exactly what the world was like.

Summoned by the noise, Keiko stood watching from the door to her office, leaning against the frame, arms crossed. The crowd by this point was chanting: Nolan, Nolan, Nolan.

He looks so old, Keiko said, and Ian smoothed his own thinning hair.

(There'd been a time, before Leap's, when Nolan thought this might have been the day his life turned unsatisfactory. His father's wrongness, the violence of his namesake. But he gave up on that now.

Nolan was starting to think there was no such thing as one moment when everything went wrong for you.

Leap's had taught him that. The Reversalists' pat, explanatory origin stories were meant to exempt them from looking at the world head-on. They were all looking for the same thing he was: permission to give up.

But of course there was no single thing that could happen to you that would excuse you from living the rest of your life, no matter how horrible a thing it was.)

On the day of the Ryan–Ventura fight, the announcers had related the long backstory of the Sox and the Rangers, as if this explained Ryan's behavior.

But no amount of history could excuse the fact that Ryan would rather punch some young player in the face than play baseball.

If such a thing as the Moment It All Went Wrong did exist, it was a moment you made yourself. It was having the audacity to leave the ballpark before the game was through because you thought you knew what the next innings held. It was the moment you decided to give up and spend the rest of your life explaining why you were giving up, instead of just playing the goddamn game.

Which meant, despite searching for it everywhere, Nolan's moment, if it existed, hadn't happened yet.

It was out there somewhere in the future, threatening to fall, but not yet fallen.

Nolan still had a chance. If he wanted to, he could still play ball.

Leap's Island

That night, in the tent by the sinkhole, Elsa dreamed of Duck Twelve.

In her dream, she and Nolan floated in the Gulf with the duck. They plunged their faces into the water, feeding on larvae, bubbles glistening like soap around their mouths. When they were full, they floated in the sun. Breathe in, breathe out, the duck said. Meditate on your breath. Don't you feel better?

Elsa woke up and rolled in her sleeping bag to face Nolan.

I have crazy dreams out here, she said.

Nothing is worse than listening to people talk about their dreams, Nolan said.

It was seven. They had not slept well. It was cool and there was a soupy fog that tumbled low over the black morning water.

The post boat comes today, Elsa said. We can go home.

Yes, Nolan said.

What they were both thinking was: there was not much time left if they wanted to find the duck.

What they were both thinking was: what would home feel like?

Nolan's body ached. He was dirty and smelled after days of tramping through the forest. He wanted to crawl back into Ian's bed and keen, to roll in it like a dog. He wanted to swim until he couldn't anymore, then fall asleep exhausted. He considered that in only a week, he'd been de-civilized. All his manners and defenses and useful bullshit were gone. He felt wide open. He couldn't bear the thought of speaking to anyone but Elsa.

When he imagined himself back at work, all he could think of were the dead birds. Nolan's office had plate-glass windows and almost every day a bird would smash against the glass with a small burst of dust and sometimes a trickle of fluid. Most of the heads in the office would turn to look when this happened, but some wouldn't. Often, if it got to be four o'clock and if this had not happened yet, it began to seem inevitable, and Nolan would find himself looking up from his screen and toward the slice of glass warping the city beyond it, anticipating the crack and puff of a small life going out like a firecracker.

Jinx whined and nosed at Elsa's sleeping bag, urging her out. Elsa watched the fog dissipate and lift.

Elsa said, If the boat comes at three, do we have time to check out the third site?

Nolan checked the field journal, his watch. We do, he said. If we're leaving, we do.

Of course we're leaving, Elsa said. Let's just check out the site.

———

The exact location of the third site was unclear. According to Ian's notes, it appeared to be near Gates's and Esther's houses, which was strange, because they knew the cove there to be small and sandy. It was not a place the ducks were likely to be.

Nolan led them swiftly. When the terrain got rocky, Elsa took Nolan's hand and allowed him to guide her. When they arrived, they found the cove empty, except for Mariana Gates.

She had a blanket stretched out on the spit of sand and was walking the shoreline, feet in the water, tallying in a notebook the small crabs that scuttled away from her. There was a green morning smell off the water. Her hair was pulled back and she wore a sweater over a striped red t-shirt. She approached a small device on the shore with a long rubber tube stretched into the water. She stooped over the readout on its face, then returned to the blanket. On the blanket was a shotgun.

Jinx trotted over to see her. Gates startled. She looked as though she wasn't sure whether to put down her notepad or continue what she was doing. She looked as though she knew she ought to hide the gun, but that it was too late. She took in how dirty the dog was.

What are you doing? Nolan asked.

Measuring water salinity. Counting food sources, Gates said, even though it was clear she knew this wasn't what Nolan meant.

What's with the gun? Elsa asked.

The gun is for safety.

Not really.

Gates looked around, scanning for other people, maybe Esther.

Safety and hunting, she said.

Hunting? Nolan said.

Holy shit, Elsa said. Because Gates was on the beach near Site Three with a gun, which meant that Gates was looking for the same thing they were. She was looking for Duck Twelve.

Like you care, Gates said.

Elsa said, You're the only legitimate scientist left on this island and you're hunting the Paradise Duck?

Don't call it that, Gates said. Only your father called it that.

You're going to kill it? Nolan asked. You're going to duck-hunt your own research?

Just one duck, Gates said.

Why? asked Nolan.

Duck Twelve shows the reversal isn't so bad, Elsa said.

Your father never proved anything. Gates scanned the far edge of the beach.

He messes up your article, Elsa insisted.

Twelve doesn't fit, Gates said. The only way we're getting published in *Nature* is if we put out one clear theory. All the other data we've got hangs together.

So study him! Nolan said.

If we don't get that article published we're going to lose the island. She tossed down her notepad and picked up the shotgun.

Maybe that wouldn't be the worst thing, Nolan said.

I know your father took DNA samples, Gates said.

Doesn't that mean it's pointless to kill the duck?

Not if you give me the lab results, Gates said, squinting out over the water, jostling the gun. That duck represents a series of weird fucking mutations I can't even begin to understand without the report.

We don't have any lab results, Elsa said.

Nolan said, So Duck Twelve is actually—

Proof of a reversal that goes beyond the undowny feathers. A reversion back to multiple traits common in distant past generations that we have no way of proving are necessarily disadvantageous.

He's special, Nolan said.

Happy, Elsa said.

He doesn't fit, Gates repeated.

Elsa shook her head. So you're just going to wipe it out?

Maybe eventually we'll figure this thing out and be able to publish properly with a different specimen but... The sun was coming over the trees, shining right in Gates's eyes. She shielded them with her hand. Right now, we just need more time, she said.

Publish Ian's work in *Nature*, Elsa said. We're not going to stop you.

Gates laughed. *Nature* will take our theories for a soft piece, because they sound halfway plausible and the crazy factor sells copies. But Ian's work? Rejecting unidirectional progress? Ducks improving their quality of life by meditating? His being right sounds even crazier than us being wrong.

They won't take it, even if it's true? Elsa asked.

There's a difference between what's true and what people will believe, Gates said. And the thing they'll believe is more useful.

You don't really think that, Nolan said.

Elsa said, She's just afraid to leave the island.

———

Mariana Gates grew up in Texas. Her mother was Greek and her father was a Texas oilman, and so they sent her to cotillion, taught her to cook lamb, insisted on attendance at the orthodox church, and showed her how to shoot a shotgun, just in case.

The first time she saw the cranes, Gates was seven, playing alone in her yard in a very nice dress and patent leather shoes, excavating mica shards from the dirt and wishing her mother would deliver on her promise of a baby brother. Before she saw them, she felt them: the air around her shifted. When Gates looked up she saw twelve migrating whooping cranes. It was like the underside of one of her mother's tapestries, their bellies smooth and white, their wings fit into tessellation. They had stern faces and dark bills and were each allowed one splash of red feathers. They were silent as they flew, and this was the first time Gates fell in love.

Gates got her PhD in biological sciences. Took a position at Sam Houston State as an aquatic ecosystems ecologist. She confounded her parents by never marrying and spending all her time in the mud, watching her birds.

When she wasn't teaching, Gates facilitated a program called Operation Migration that bred the cranes in captivity. When the chicks were born, Gates wore a white full-body suit, one arm painted to look like the face of a mother crane, and fed them. They played the chicks the sound of an aircraft engine so they would not be frightened when they needed to be taught how to migrate by a small plane.

Without the generation before them as guides, the cranes didn't know what migration route to take or where to winter. And so, when they were ready, Gates piloted the small, open craft with wide white wings along the old crane route to the Gulf, showing the adolescents which way to fly. She wore her white suit, steered with her crane hand, and she and her cranes flew in formation. A woman at the center of a flock of birds; a humming mother in the sky. She was never happier. She taught the birds how to be themselves.

But success was unpredictable. One generation of adolescents forgot their route home and died down south. Another group thrived for a whole year before a lightning strike knocked the birds out and they drowned in their own waters. It was hard work, and it hurt when it went wrong.

Gates spent twenty years trying to save those goddamn cranes.

When she was asked by an ecotourism company to run a trip for nonscientists to aid in data collection about the cranes' habitat, she said no. She preferred to work alone when possible and could think of nothing worse than shepherding a bunch of know-nothing tourists through the disappearing wetlands the cranes called home.

But then they told her they would fund her research, so she started running trips for tourists to the Aransas National Wildlife Refuge.

Three years and a dozen expeditions later, the thing that confused Gates most about the experience was how, even though the volunteers got teary when the trips were over; even though they would friend the ecotourism company on Facebook and post snapshots of themselves in waders with the hashtag #savethecranes and little heart emojis; even though they would buy bumper stickers and baseball hats and key chains that read GIVE A WHOOP!; even though they loved the cranes, once they left, they did nothing to advocate for preserving the cranes' habitat. Made no contributions, signed no petitions, and changed their habits not at all.

It was easy to get someone to care about something beautiful. Impossible to make them protect the muck it relied on. Gates found herself operating from a place of low-grade fury at all times.

It was on her last trip—she swore it would be her last—that she met Esther Stein, and this was the second time Mariana Gates fell in love. The first day of data collection, Esther walked straight into the muck and settled in to patiently await the data she would log in her notebook. She was beautiful the way a woman with a sense of purpose can be. Beautiful like a well-formed bowl. Beautiful like a smooth ax handle. The utter peacefulness of Esther in the mud, chin tilted skyward, was almost enough to restore Gates's faith in people.

A few days into the trip, two of the tourists had been found smoking weed in a nesting area, which they'd specifically been told not to go near, and now the territory was spoiled and the cranes would refuse to return to it, a clutch of eggs lost. Gates was outside her bunkhouse that night, wearing a headlamp to fill out a report to explain the spoiled nest. Her bird sighting scope was still set up next to her, optimistically pointed at the ruined nesting ground, and this was when Esther marched over and said: Everyone on this trip is a moron. Doesn't it seem like people are just becoming awful? How can you stand it?

It was such a relief to hear someone else speak these words out loud.

Gates gestured for Esther to sit with her. The tourists had bought a sack of oysters off a passing boat and from the next bunkhouse over they could see them cracking the shells open, yelping as the shucking knife slipped into the meat of their palms. A half-dozen feral cats padded around, licking the spent shells.

Gates said, Sometimes I think I'll just become a hermit.

This was when Esther explained to her about the island.

You should come see it, Esther said.

At first, Gates thought she was joking, so she laughed. But when she realized Esther was serious, Gates was frightened by how much she wanted to agree with anything the older woman said. She demurred, saying that after the trip she had to get back to campus to start prepping a grad seminar on coastal ecology she'd not taught before. But Esther gave her a business card that read LEAP'S ISLAND

INSTITUTE FOR REVERSALISM and told her to think about it. Esther stood up as if to leave, but then took the handle of the sighting scope, pivoting it toward the sky.

It's too dark to see anything, Gates said. Esther waved her over.

Gates bent over the scope, and when she looked into the sight she saw that Esther had framed for her the moon. It was all but full, and through the lens Gates could read the whole swing of time and accident on its face.

When she looked up from the scope, the nearer world rushed up to meet her: Esther was still staring at the moon, blue bandana around her neck, smelling of lemongrass, wire-rimmed glasses slipped down her nose. Gates envied how sure of herself she looked. So certain.

The moon is good tonight, Esther said.

She returned to the tourists' cabin and left Gates alone with the moon.

Gates had been using that scope for years, had framed hundreds of birds in its sight. She brought them close. But she had never thought to twist the thing upward. It had never occurred to her to look at something so large as the moon.

And maybe it was the bigness of the moon, the bigness of Esther, that she wanted to give herself over to. Because after that last trip, Gates did migrate south, following the older woman's trajectory to Leap's.

These days, Gates often wondered why she'd come to the island, and why she'd stayed. Gates had been young. She had been frustrated, but she hadn't been out of options. She could have kept rehabilitating the cranes. She could have kept teaching her students. She could have done any number of things. What she did instead amounted to running away.

That first day when Gates's boat approached the island, she saw Esther standing on the dock, hand cupped to her mouth.

She was whooping. Specifically, Gates recognized the call the cranes made when they assembled to migrate.

Everyone on Leap's had a story about why they came, and sometimes Gates felt like hers didn't stack up. Gates had followed Esther. Like the cranes following her small humming aircraft, she had followed the path laid out for her and not questioned it until it was too late.

Now she was here. Had been here for too long. Long enough that she could not bear to go back.

———

It's not just me, Gates said. Do you think Esther wants to leave the island? Remy certainly doesn't. The brothers. Gwen. Can you imagine sending them back to the mainland after all these years? It'd ruin them.

It's not that bad out there, Nolan said, hoping someone would tell him if this were true.

And you don't seem particularly happy here, Elsa said.

Gates laughed. She sat down on the blanket and began drying her feet. Putting on socks. The gun lay next to her.

No one is particularly happy ever, Gates said. But at least out here, you don't have to pretend.

Our father was happy out here, Elsa said. Wasn't he?

It was such a stupid question, Elsa hated herself for asking it. Because the Ian Grey who had lived on the mainland, who had lived *with them*, had never seemed particularly happy. But the Ian she found in the field journals and Reversalists' stories sounded, to Elsa, positively ecstatic. He had been swept up in the novelty of his discovery, and that was part of it, but it also sounded as if there was something to the way he was spending his days, traipsing through the woods, living like that duck. Wading and hiking and scrounging food and catching naps and listening to Bach and bedeviling Mitchell. Dragging along the boys. Being kind to Gwen. Bothering Remy about his writing. Elsa barely recognized the man in those journals. The kind of Ian who would rush naked into the warmth of the sea without bothering to fold his clothes on the shore.

Was he happier out here than he was before? Elsa asked.

Before, Gates said, was before I knew him. Listen, all I need are the lab results—

Whatever you want, we can't give it to you, Nolan said. He was alarmed by how desperate for answers Gates sounded. He'd thought she had it all figured out. And Nolan had placed her among the ranks of omniscient adults he was always trying to impress.

But maybe there were no adults in charge of anything. Maybe it was just children above children, all the way up the chain.

Greys! came a voice. It was Esther. She was trundling down the path from the Lobby, headed home with a grocery bag in hand. She appeared shrunken, wearing an enormous pair of rubber boots. A green kerchief held back her frizzled hair. She took in the scene, Gates with the gun on the shore.

Put that away, Gates, Esther said, scolding, and Gates's face faltered.

Children, are you leaving? Esther said.

Yes, Elsa said, on the post boat at three.

We're leaving, Nolan said.

Won't you come in for a minute before you go? Esther said. She shuffled up the steps to her shack, turning back to say, I'm making sandwiches, before she disappeared through the door.

Gates stood up. She collected her gun, her instruments, her notebook.

You really don't have it? she asked the children one last time. You would tell me if you did?

Elsa said, Everything out there doesn't get any less bad just because you don't have to see it.

Safe travels, Gates said, and headed toward the Lobby.

The children followed Esther into her shack.

————

Esther enlisted them in making sandwiches. From the bag of supplies came apples and cheese and wheat bread and mustard. She poured glasses of iced tea and put everything on a turquoise platter, along with a large pair of clippers.

Out of knives? Nolan said.

That's for later, Esther said. Let's see if we can rustle up any company on the deck.

Outside, they sat around a small patio table and ate. Across the deck was a second table with the baby pool on it. The water level was lower than it had been a week ago, and the breeze rippled across its surface.

I'm sorry you didn't find what you were looking for, Esther said.

What were we looking for? Nolan asked.

I can't bear to see Gates bullying that poor duck, Esther said. A shotgun. Really.

Have you seen it? Elsa asked. You said before—

Esther hushed Elsa. The crusts of her bread remained on the plate. She got up and placed it on the railing next to the baby pool.

Nolan was still holding his sandwich. He put it down. Then he picked it up again and ate the remainder in two large bites. Then he flipped open the field journal and looked at the notes for the third site where Ian had seen the duck.

No way, Nolan said. Is this—

Ta-dah! Esther pointed at the baby pool. The buffleheads lived in the lobby pool when they were first introduced, she said. I've wondered if that's why they find this one homey. She inched the plate of bread crusts closer to the baby pool. The third site.

Elsa stood. She couldn't quite bring herself to curse out an old lady.

Oh! And here he is, Esther said.

The children heard the flapping of wings.

The Paradise Duck splashed into the baby pool and shook himself all over. He snatched one and then two bread crusts from the plate

Esther had left out. He raised his head and shook it, choking down the sandwich crusts.

He looks, Nolan said, just like all the other fucking ducks.

Oh, but he's sweet, though, Esther said.

Elsa and Nolan slowly inched toward the pool so as not to disturb the duck, though they needn't have worried.

The duck did not pay them any attention at all. He dunked himself in the water, disappearing his whole body in the shallow pool. Then he came up shaking and honking, lolling his squat, bulbous head from side to side. He seemed to delight in this. He lolled again, honking as if showing off. Around his ankle, they could see the green plastic band with a Sharpie marker *12* penned in their father's hand.

A dragonfly buzzed above the baby pool, but the duck did not snap at it. He watched it, his head following the insect's arc and swimming in small circles to follow its course. When the dragonfly landed on the rim of the pool, the duck slowly paddled toward it. As if, the children thought, he meant to sneak up on it. Number Twelve paddled, occasionally casting glances back the children's way, they were sure, until his beak was an inch from the quivering blue dragonfly.

Honk! he erupted, and the dragonfly startled upward. Honk honk! he called after the insect, then buzzing, then gone.

The Paradise Duck honked at the sky another moment, bereft, and almost toppled himself in the pool by looking up at the blue nothingness. Nolan almost reached out for him, concerned. But the duck quickly forgot about his lost friend and started splashing himself, chasing the water droplets that coursed over his back before sinking into his pregnable feathers.

Elsa got closer and held out her hand. The duck swam over and pressed his cool, blunt beak into the soft place where Elsa's life-line bisected her palm. Finding it empty, the duck butted her hand with his soft head. A chirruping noise came from low in his throat.

The children had watched the buffleheads for a week now. They had seen them glide stoically, and hunt efficiently, and mate violently. Their father was right about one thing: this duck was different. He was not like the regal birds on the deck, bearing their dampened underwings nobly. Was not like the buffleheads assembled on fallen trees, arching and posing to dry themselves. In fact, Duck Twelve seemed to not even notice his dampness, though he was very wet.

He's retarded, Nolan said.

Don't say that, said Elsa. She had been a second-grade teacher long enough to know that no one should ever use that word. And yet, Elsa also knew that Nolan was right.

She didn't want to believe it.

She looked at Esther. Is he tame? Did you tame him, Esther?

Esther shook her head. Born that way, she said.

But you're feeding him, Elsa said.

Your father started feeding him first.

Dad would *never*, Nolan said. Ian Grey, feeding table scraps to a study subject?

Esther shrugged. Your father loved this duck. She stroked Twelve's back. He had this trick, she said, where he'd squeeze the insides of a dinner roll into a ball in his hand. The duck would chase it around his palm for ages, nosing it for fun before he finally decided to eat the thing.

That's hardly a trick, Elsa said, as she considered everything she'd ever done to try to earn Ian's attention or delight. She had been ready to go to Mars, for Christ sake. A dough ball.

So he was training him to do it? Nolan said. It was unprofessional. It was silly. It was the indulgent play of a father, and Nolan found it impossible to imagine Ian doing such a thing.

You father seemed to think there wasn't any risk of us influencing his behavior, Esther said. Ian claimed the duck didn't retain learned behaviors. Didn't seem to apply things that had happened in the past to his present situations. Like he wakes up wiped clean every day. The bread ball thing was a kind of test, I think. Every time your father offered his hand, that duck lost his tiny head for it like it was the very first time.

Elsa's throat caught. What the fuck, she said. The duck quacked at her. He tilted his perfectly round head, as if asking what the problem was.

Nolan laughed. He sat down on the porch, knees crooked, and held his own head in his hands and laughed.

Elsa ignored him. I thought the mutations were about bringing the duck back to some purer state or something, she said. Improving quality of life.

Esther nodded. She was patting Nolan's shoulder with one hand, and dandling the other in the pool, Twelve chasing her fingers around. Yes, she said. Your father thought this was it. Look at him! Duck wakes up happy. Everything delights him. And he doesn't seem to be concerned with anything, not even meeting his basic needs.

But that makes him lousy at survival! Doesn't it? Elsa was trying not to shout. If the duck left now, she'd be sure she'd hallucinated it. She insisted, If he's not paying attention to, like, food? The weather?

Backward, Esther said. Ian said he was proof of things gone backward because he's less focused on survival. He doesn't even mate at the right times for his mates' ovulation.

What is he mating for? Nolan said, out of breath.

Seemingly it's whenever the mood strikes him, Esther said, patting his shoulder once more.

This is crazy, Elsa said. He's an aberration. It's nuts to see significance in one retarded duck.

Nolan stood up. I love him, he told Elsa. I love this fucking duck.

Aberration can be another word for bellwether, Esther said.

Elsa tried to take a deep breath, but felt tight-chested and jumpy.

Esther, she said, was he right?

All of us think we're right, Esther said. Was he any more right than the rest of us? She shrugged.

The duck swam from one side of the baby pool to the other in a tight serpentine. He pressed his beak to the colorful beach balls printed on the pool's plastic, investigating, but in such a way that it seemed to Elsa he did not even take his own investigation very seriously. He was, Elsa thought, cavorting.

And this duck, Elsa said, to no one, to Nolan, to her father, this is supposed to be a good thing?

Nolan put a hand on her shoulder and pointed at the duck. Paradise! he said.

Their father had spent months following this duck across the island. Watching it swim and play. Watching it care about and get distracted by the wrong things. Watching it eat and breed for the unproductive joy of it. Watching it fuck and love wrong too. Naturally speaking, the duck was an abomination. It was doomed. It was delightful. It had filled Ian with glee and even hope. It seemed, in his journals, that Ian had loved the Paradise Duck. And if this was possible, the children knew, it was also possible he had not forgotten them, stupid blundering disappointments that they were. They'd amounted to so little.

They were not scientists or giants or Mars colonists.

And still.

Esther came over. She offered Elsa the clippers.

Do it, she said.

What? Elsa said.

Nolan reached into the pool and picked up the Paradise Duck. He did not resist and let Nolan hold him, loaflike, to his chest. Nolan tugged the green ID band away from the duck's scaly ankle.

You're going undercover, Esther said, stroking the duck's belly.

Elsa took the clippers and snipped the ID band free.

Nolan lifted the duck, expecting it to fly away with its newfound freedom, but it only tilted its head backward at him and quacked delightedly.

Elsa pocketed the green band.

Nolan returned the still-quacking duck to the pool. Afloat now, the Paradise Duck began investigating the colors of the beach ball pattern all over again, as if it were for the very first time.

Park Rapids

THIRTY YEARS BACK

Before Ian found out Elsa was not his, before he left, before Ingrid had to sell the farmhouse and the animals, before they moved to Potato Lake, before Nolan existed—

It was summer on the farm and the days melted into one another and the stream of time carried Elsa along so carelessly that it felt as if time was not moving at all.

Elsa's only job was to help Ian feed Sweet Jane, a milk goat, and Snyder, a fat pony. In the morning, Ian and Elsa forked hay into the animals' feeders, and then they mucked the stalls and pen. Elsa had her own pitchfork. She and Ian made the rounds, shoveling manure into a red plastic wagon hitched to a four-wheeler.

What did the wise man say? Ian said.

Never shovel manure into the wind, Elsa said.

When the pen was clean, Ian climbed on the four-wheeler, and Elsa got on behind him, hugging his waist. Ian ripped the engine and drove it down to the manure pile where they'd shovel out the wagon. On the ride back, he drove fast, and Elsa pressed her face against the back of Ian's shirt, warm from the sun, and felt the diesel-smelling world rip itself to pieces as the four-wheeler shook and they climbed the hill to the barn.

Ingrid took days off, and they went to the lake to swim, and when Ingrid lifted the hair from Elsa's neck with one hand and rubbed sunblock onto her shoulders with the other, Elsa sat very still.

Elsa opened her eyes underwater in the lake and spied on turtles and fish and rocks and reeds, and if she found a white rock, she would bring it to Ian and he would throw it for her, and Elsa would have to dive and search for it glowing in the sand and then carry it back to him.

In the evening, Elsa gave the animals their hay. Sweet Jane chased her, bleating insanely, trying to nibble the hem of her shirt. Snyder was old for a pony but still glossy and black. He trotted after her slowly, knowing the hay would come in good time.

(It would have been easy for Elsa to tell herself that this had been her idyll—the last farmhouse summer before Nolan, the summer before the day it all went wrong, but wishing away Nolan wasn't something she wanted to do anymore. And really, Elsa realized, even this was not far back enough. To undo the hurt that came later, Ingrid would have had to not sleep with the Quaker in the first place, a thing Elsa had not known about but had still been true, even when she was small. Not knowing wasn't the protection she'd thought it was. Which meant that to spare herself that later pain, Elsa would have had to never be born at all. Would have to unmake herself completely. The very creation of her world was the same day suffering came into it.

Which was a kind of relief. Because it meant that she could stop staring over her shoulder at everything that had come before, searching for the day that came before the pain. There was no place further back to go. To find any kind of happiness, Elsa would have to turn around.)

Still, on that summer day, when Elsa slid open the door to the hay room and climbed to the top of the stack, halfway to the ceiling, where she'd spread a blanket, and lay there, drunk on the smell of alfalfa, she was happy.

Because Snyder whickered over his food. Because the motes

of dust that hung in the illuminated air seemed frozen as if by an enchantment of Elsa's own making. Soon, her parents would call her in for dinner and she would race across the lawn. But not yet. For now, she was warm and still upon the hay. For now, she was weightless, and time did not move at all.

Leap's Island

The children were going home.

They stood on the dock, hands shielding their eyes, watching the postman approach. Jinx gave him two short barks and reared up.

Pretty rough out here, didn't I say? he called, taking them in.

They were slumped in their packs. Their hair was twisted and slick. Elsa's pits were furry. Nolan was purplish beneath the eyes. Their legs were scabbed over and dirty. The dog smelled. They were pretty rough.

As the children loaded their bags onto the boat, the postman went about slipping a few slim envelopes into the cubby slots for the Reversalists. He returned with one envelope left in his hands. The children were already sitting in the boat, ready to leave, the dog panting between them.

You want this? he said. It's for your dad.

Sure, Elsa said. It was junk mail. A glossy brochure for an academic conference it was a miracle Ian was still invited to.

And we're off, the postman said. He revved the motor and they drifted away from the dock.

The motor whined, and they picked up speed, everyone's hair whipping around. Jinx tossed her snout in the air currents.

Elsa unzipped a side pouch of her pack to tuck in the brochure and found that there were already envelopes in there. The mail from a week ago. She pulled it out and opened the letters. A report from a lab in Louisiana. Another from Georgia. She held the pages up to get a better look and the wind almost snatched them.

Nolan, Elsa said. She handed him the letters.

Nolan skimmed the reports on the Paradise Duck, struggling to understand their meaning. The boat shifted beneath him.

No one had believed Ian. Nolan hadn't. His family and his friends and his colleagues, they'd all written him off. Even on Leap's, Ian's theories had been unwelcome. But Ian believed in what he was looking for. Had wanted to believe that the world he was leaving for Nolan and for Elsa was worthy of them. That they would be okay. Would be better, even, than their parents.

It was enough, for Nolan, that Ian had wanted this to be true. The sheer optimism of the enterprise floored him. The totally unscientific hope. If this was Ian's hypothesis for their outcome, Nolan could live with that.

Over the roar of the motor, it was too hard to tell his sister everything, so he just handed the envelopes back. She nodded, zipping them into her pouch.

Elsa watched the wake of the boat. The way it channeled deep, then foamed itself shallow again. Her father, she knew, had been down there somewhere. Soggy, sodden. She imagined an underwater tea party with the fishes. Underwater explanations. Underwater eulogy. Underwater apology, apology, apology. She wished they had not found his body. Ian would have liked to have wound up back in the primordial soup of the sea.

The postman shouted over the motor, You get a sense of the folks out there?

We did, Nolan said.

That place gives me the creepers, he said.

It was just a week, Elsa shouted. But she and Nolan both knew this was not true. A week had almost been long enough for them to make the same mistakes all over again. A week had almost not been long enough for them to find what they were looking for.

They were just fifteen minutes off the shore, and Leap's spell had been broken.

From this distance, the children could see the whole of the island.

It looked small.

Up close, you can't tell that an island is finite. Up close, an island seems like everything, because you are on it. It can feel as if it will go on forever. But the drag of a boat across the space of waves and time can help you see. With time, most things grow smaller. Trees and rocks become less articulated and significant. You draw away and the island narrows to become just one thing, among many. The farther you go, the more an island blurs, until it looks less like a place you lived and more like a muddied landscape. Just someone's landscape. Maybe not even yours.

———

As they approached Watch Landing, Nolan felt anxious at the noise and bustle coming upon him. Music from the bars. Boat engines. A popcorn machine. People happily shouting at each other over the noise of their own drunkenness. Mitchell, he remembered, had spent his whole life on the island before going to the mainland as a teenager. How frightening this must have seemed to him. How too-much.

They thanked the postman and gave him a forwarding address for Ian's mail.

When they disembarked, Jinx hesitated, nervous to jump out of the boat.

You're a wolf, Elsa told her. You're a ferocious wolf. Jinx leapt and made the dock.

As the children walked along the boardwalk, several young girls stopped to coo over Jinx, petting her despite the smell.

As they reached the end of the pier, Nolan turned to Elsa. We could find someone to show them to. The reports.

They could lose the island.

I know. But I mean, that's not our problem.

But can you imagine?

If Mitchell was forced to sell the island and send the Reversalists away, where would they go?

The children saw Esther in a cheap condo, installing twelve bird-feeders on the patio and ignoring complaints from her neighbors when the spilled seed drew rats.

Mick and Jim would work at some urban food co-op, or buy back their farm, but they would get trapped in a feedback loop of their brotherhood and brilliance until it drove them to loneliness.

Gates they imagined living in some college town where she'd teach a required intro bio class to apathetic undergrads for the rest of her life, drinking instant soup from a thermos and writing cruel things on their papers.

St. Gilles could write the final book of the *Asterias* series and receive ungodly amounts of money, but he wouldn't. They imagined him in a small London apartment, writing and rewriting, trying impossibly to solve for the future of Earth.

Mitchell would take the money from the sale and build an enormous house somewhere remote. Somewhere he could wall off and live in, as if it were an island.

This was what the children imagined for the Reversalists if they were trying to be hopeful.

Hopeful and honest didn't always go together.

If they were trying to be honest, what the children really imagined was that, if the Reversalists were kicked off the island, very few of them would survive the next five years. The children would google the Reversalists late at night (they would not be able to resist googling) and they would find news of their deaths, that they had killed themselves, one by one, or maybe all at once in a kind of Jonestown Kool-Aid debacle.

The children imagined this for all of them except Gwen.

Because the children imagined Gwen maybe pregnant. Gwen, if pregnant, maybe happy. Gwen, maybe a vet again, traveling late at night with her baby strapped to her chest, to barns where she'd catch cows warm from the womb. Snipping the cords between them and their enormous lumbering mothers. Setting them loose on the world.

When does the bus get here? Nolan asked.

Elsa looked at her watch, the black rubber crusted with salt. Four, she said.

I think we should stay, Nolan said.

Nolan—

He gestured at the Landing, the bars and restaurants. For one night.

This place is awful.

Then go.

What could we possibly want to do here?

Everything, Nolan said, and Elsa sighed.

Nolan hugged Elsa. Her pack made it difficult, but he stepped in and threw his long arms around her full circumference.

———

That night, Nolan and Elsa walked the waterfront with Jinx on her lead and they ate everything. They ate fried dough and sausage and peppers. They ate candy apples and a bag of garlic boiled peanuts. Nolan thought of all the times he and Janine had resolved to eat clean because they needed to detox themselves. Their food was poison! They were afraid of chickens with fat breasts and of Monsanto genes in cornflakes. But today Nolan was ravenous. He would eat it all. He ate fried alligator on a stick, and Elsa ate a sack of deep-fried Oreos. They both ordered enormous plastic cups of lemonade with bendy straws and walked around sipping.

Jinx grinned and panted, her pink tongue lolling out. She sniffed and pissed on things, and this seemed like a joyful kind of thing to do. Her way of saying this is mine and this is mine and this is mine.

It was dark out, but there was neon everywhere. On bar marquees and waterfront stands and boardwalk games. There were clubs that thumped noisily, and as they passed by them, they felt waves of body heat from the collective human pack inside. Elsa squeezed Nolan's hand, because they were here, among people, and it was awful and glorious and they were not ruined by it.

There was an outdoor bar on the thin spit of beach at the north end of the landing, and Nolan and Elsa sat on bar stools there. Nolan looped Jinx's lead around the stool leg and she lay down and set her chin on his foot. Was she was afraid he would leave her? Could she smell that he was like Ian? A man who disappears. Nolan was careful not to move his foot. To let her chin rest just so.

Just look at this, Elsa said.

The place was kitsch. A string of seashell Christmas lights ran the length of the bar, and a glowing orange scallop covered the electric outlet next to Nolan. There were TVs showing ESPN, and the bar was a mix of men watching sports and nomadic young people getting smashed for a hot instant before they moved on to another stop. The bartender mixed Elsa a Dark and Stormy. He made Nolan a vodka tonic. Nolan squeezed his lime and stared at the orange scallop light until he saw spots.

What are you going to do when you get home? Elsa asked.

Nothing. I don't know, Nolan said. He considered his job, Janine.

I'm sure Ingrid would love to see you sometime.

Yeah? Nolan said.

She'd be embarrassingly happy if you visited. Holidays or summer. Whenever. The lake isn't full of snakes. You could swim.

Nolan nodded. But won't you be on Mars? he said.

You've made it very clear that you don't believe in Mars, Elsa said.

I believe in Mars, I just don't believe in you going there. He sucked his drink. In fact, Nolan said, I'd definitely prefer it if you stayed. I'd like to share a planet with you, I think. The occasional Thanksgiving.

Okay, Elsa said.

So what about now, Nolan said.

What about now?

I think I'd like to visit Ingrid now, Nolan said.

Now is good, Elsa said. And it was not impossible to imagine. The three of them together in the lakehouse.

Elsa people-watched. Nolan sipped his drink. The lime tasted off, but it was sweet. He rummaged in his bag and pulled out his phone and charger. The bartender was tending to a group of young men who were all competing for the attention of the one girl with them, and Nolan pulled the scallop light from its outlet. He plugged in his phone.

So soon, Elsa said. Nolan let the red battery symbol blink at him as he drank.

There was a bang, and Jinx started, jumping up and barking. Elsa shushed her. You are a ferocious wolf, she reminded her. The fireworks had begun. Pale violet flower bursts. Streaking red tails. Nolan pushed Jinx's rump down and patted her head and told her it was alright. Jinx settled into a crouch and projected a low wookiee rumble of displeasure.

From the island, the fireworks had seemed violent. An interruption of their peace. But here, they were brighter. Gleefully loud. A celebration.

It's quite a show, Elsa said. She ordered another drink and set off for the bathroom.

Nolan's phone came to life, bleeping furiously. A week's worth of texts, alerts, updates, emails, and voicemails made themselves known. Scrolling through the screen of things he'd missed, Nolan felt tight and anxious in his chest. He wanted to chuck the phone into the sea. But then there was the little green blink of Janine having called. Having called several times. Nolan scrolled through and saw that there were exactly seven calls and messages. One for each day he'd been gone.

He listened.

Janine's messages were calm. They said she was calling to see how he was doing. They said he didn't need to call back until he was ready. They said that she missed him and wished he wouldn't do this, but she got it. She said she would be there when he came out of his cave. That she hoped she could go with him to the funeral. To let her know if he needed anything.

There were bursts of music and scuffling in the background of these messages, and Nolan knew Janine was calling from dance rehearsal. Their new show was opening this weekend.

A welling up. A little gasp that got choked in his throat and was drowned out by the fireworks. And then it was over. Jinx nudged his ankle again, worried over Nolan's failure to notice the explosions in the sky.

Two drunk men in jerseys began whooping from down the row of stools. Loudly ordering more drinks. Nolan looked up at the TV. The Rockies had just beat the Giants, 8–7. The Giants were at home, and they panned over the stadium. Dejected fans were standing and shaking their heads. But Nolan knew it was only June. The lights played over the field and even on the tiny screen, Nolan could make out a bird swooping past the glow of the lamps. As the leftfielder walked off, the lights cast a long shadow behind him in triplicate. A giant's shadow. Nolan watched the spot he had left. His spot. He felt the pull of it.

San Luis Obispo

Nolan looked up from the well shaft's bottom. The opening was a wide oval of light. It had been a while since Elsa had disappeared with his tennis balls. He wished she'd left him one. He sat hugging his knees and playing with the stones at the well bottom, stacking them into cairns, then knocking them down again like a small god. Nolan had assumed that Elsa went to get help, but as the oval above him grew dimmer, that began to seem less likely. He shouted her name a couple of times. He whistled.

Nolan used one of the stones to dig in the dirt. He could, perhaps, build himself a staircase. He scratched dirt from one side of the hole and packed it into a ledge on the other. He looked up. It would take a lot of stairs. They might have to spiral.

Once, someone had worked very hard to dig this hole. To make this well. It had seemed a good idea at the time. It had been a good idea, for them, back then.

For hours Nolan dug and built his muddy staircase, ascending slowly. And though years later his parents would convince him that this was the most terrifying experience of his life, that this was the day their lives spun off course, at the time Nolan was not frightened.

It never occurred to him that he would not find a way out. If it had, he might have stopped building. He was absorbed in his work. Nolan tested the first packed dirt step with his sneaker, and one edge crumbled. He spat on it, packed it firm again, and continued digging. He hummed as he dug. "Greensleeves," a song his father had tried to teach him on piano.

He packed the mud. He worked, happily.

He counted how many steps were left to build.

Park Rapids

The airport taxi dropped them off at the lakehouse. The house was built with red wood shingles and wide upper windows. Purple salvia grew bushy by the door. The yard was mown in strips, light and dark like carpeting. But at the perimeter, Ingrid left long shaggy alleys where false indigo and thimbleweed volunteered itself. She could not bear to mow it down.

Jinx peed on some wildflowers.

I've always loved this house, Nolan said. When I was little, it felt like visiting a place in a storybook.

That's a ridiculous thing to say, said Elsa. You complained there was nothing to do here.

I loved that too, Nolan said.

Stop rewriting history, Elsa said. I hate it when people pretend pretty things about the past.

What if I'm just outing the truth, Nolan said. I couldn't tell you I liked it here back then. You were superior enough as it was.

I was never, Elsa said, but of course it was true. She had been, she was sure, insufferable.

Elsa breathed deeply. The smell off the lake was enough like home to make Elsa think she would never leave again. That she must cling to this good place while it lasted. But maybe things weren't so tenuous. Maybe there was no reason to suspect it would disappear on her.

Ingrid came jogging down the gravel path.

I have missed you, missed you, missed you, she said, and hugged Elsa. She was wearing her apron and an old purple t-shirt. Jeans and Tevas. Her blond hair was pulled back messily.

I thought you'd be at work, Elsa said.

I took a bit of time off, Ingrid said.

No.

Ingrid nodded.

You never take time off.

I thought it would be nice to spend some time as a family, Ingrid said.

Hullo, Ingrid, Nolan said.

And Ingrid's eyes welled up. You are enormous, she said. She opened her arms and Nolan hugged her, lifting her from the ground. You are so welcome here, Ingrid said.

You're acting weird, Elsa said, as Ingrid began pulling the backpack off of her. Over her shoulder Elsa repeated, This is weird.

Everything good is weird, dearest. This is so heavy, let me take it, Ingrid said, shouldering Elsa's pack. Just come in, I'm making lunch!

Nolan was beaming. Elsa followed her mother into the house, flexing her shoulders.

Ingrid bustled around the kitchen. Nolan sat at the kitchen table. After the past week Elsa knew him so intimately, the way he sat with his elbows on a table, leaning into his hands, the downy place where his earlobe connected to his jaw, the stupid way he looked around this room, as if it were so wonderful.

Ingrid was setting out the sandwiches and salad and pouring lemonade and with each pass, she tweaked Elsa's waist or patted Nolan's shoulder and it made Elsa crazy to see her acting like there was nothing better than the two of them here like this.

Elsa, Ingrid said. Sit! Sandwiches! Ingrid sat at the table next to Nolan.

The sight of them together at the table made Elsa dizzy. It was as if the world had tipped to one side and everything that used to be over there, separate and away, the whole past part of her life with Nolan and Ian and Keiko, had slid across the landscape to squash together with her real life, over here, with Ingrid. She had kept them separate for so long, the past and the present. But now things were jumbled, mixed, and it seemed impossibly unreal.

You hate Nolan and me together, Elsa said, then stopped. She was speaking the unspeakable, and yet, she found it was easier to talk because Nolan was there with her. He was the one who had opened all this up again and now it would have out.

Ever since you walked in on us, years ago, Elsa said. You didn't talk about it, you wouldn't let us see each other, you pretended it didn't happen but everything was wrong.

Elsa— Ingrid said.

She's right, Nolan said.

We could both feel it, how wrong it was, and we didn't know how to fix it because we were *children*. That was your job. And none of you did anything. You just ignored it forever and then we had to fix it ourselves, Elsa said. It took us this long to fix it ourselves and we did and now, what, you're not even going to notice that? We're just going to eat sandwiches?

Elsa had to say it, before Ingrid painted a rosy tint over everything that had happened. Before she erased the past completely.

You did this to us! Elsa said.

All three of you, Nolan said.

You hated us, Elsa said.

Ingrid was placid. Don't be ridiculous, she said. No one has ever hated you.

You did, though, Elsa said. You all did and you're forgetting everything.

Ingrid got up and squeezed Elsa's shoulder. I'm not forgetting, she said. I just think that maybe we could eat sandwiches together now. Just because we couldn't back then doesn't mean we can't forever, she said.

Ingrid was letting the past slip away as if it were nothing. It wasn't fair. Elsa and Nolan had lugged their own personal sorrow around for years, not because they wanted to, but because it felt important. Ingrid couldn't just make things good and easy because she willed it so. Elsa could not just make herself good.

You can yell at me, Ingrid said. Yell all you want. It's good for you. Someday I'll be gone and who else will you have to blame? It's healthy for young people to yell at old people. Ingrid settled into her place and smiled. But let's eat, she said. The past is no reason not to have sandwiches.

Elsa sat down.

They ate sandwiches.

When she was small, Elsa had wanted to put her family back together like an unshattered vase, Ian and Ingrid and the farm and her pony. And now here were Nolan and Ingrid and Elsa. That this iteration of happiness would be offered had not been foreseeable, but Elsa decided she should not balk.

Ingrid, Nolan, Elsa.

It was a surprise that made time feel more malleable than Elsa had considered possible. Made it feel less like their lives were some sad equation strung out from left to right with a blinking equal sign at the end. And if she could untether herself from what seemed inevitable, from her own inevitability, maybe Elsa would find other possibilities. Surprise herself. Maybe there was a difference between ignorance and forgetting. Maybe the past was no reason not to do anything at all.

———

That night, Nolan slept in Elsa's room and Elsa slept with her mother, who spooned her aggressively. The sheets smelled like cedar and lavender.

Ingrid had always fallen asleep quickly, exhausted from work.

Was there something of Duck Twelve about Ingrid? Her calm acceptance and good cheer had always infuriated Elsa. But no, Ingrid wasn't ignorant.

If anything, she was the opposite.

Every day, Ingrid tended to the dying of Earth. She cleaned pockets of rotten flesh, and stripped beds wet with shit, and was often yelled at for the trouble. Ingrid stared the dying and their mistakes in the face and refused to believe in an afterlife because of her conviction that what we had here was enough. In spite of the meanness and squalor doled out to the lives she saw in hospice, this planet, she thought, was worth it. Eating your second-favorite ice cream flavor the day before you died young was worth it. Loving someone and then having him hate you and leave was worth it. Changing bedpans and holding people who tried to claw at the soft yellow bruises around their own IVs was worth it. Because there was also the tenderness of the vein. The years before he left. The child who came of strawberry just as she would have from chocolate.

Elsa knew that tomorrow they would make margaritas and watch the birds on the lake—the one Ingrid called Potato Lake, which was what the settlers had called it, because it looked like a potato, though obviously the Ojibwe had called it something else, and before the Ojibwe it had existed with no name at all, because it was a fucking lake. When developers bought the lakefront they renamed it Peeper Pond, which was what it was called now, and all the little houses the developers had built were laid out in orderly flat-roofed rows. The old houses—the Eriksons', the Michaels', her mother's—had roofs extremely peaked, ready to shed snow in great, tumbling sheaves that parents warned children away from in winter. The relative flatness of the new houses' roofs meant they would cave in on themselves come wintertime. If not this year, then next. When the new people's roofs did cave in, it was Ingrid who would show up with a shovel, ready to dig them out.

There was always some good work to be done, so why not do it and fall asleep exhausted? Why not make that look easy to a person like your daughter?

Or maybe it was easy.

If you chose it, maybe the gravity of the present moment was irresistible.

———

Nolan sat up in bed, hair in his face. Elsa was sitting on the floor. She had the plastic tiger float out and she was blowing into it.

I was sleeping, he said.

Up now, Elsa said.

People always say that the newly awoken look like children, but Nolan did not. He was shirtless and there were creases on his face and lovely purple swaths beneath his eyes, as if all the exertion of the island were only now catching up with him. He slid up and leaned against the washed-wood headboard.

Elsa put her mouth to the rubber stopper and blew again.

What are you doing?

Elsa shrugged as if it was obvious and kept blowing.

Do you need help? Nolan said.

Come outside, she said.

———

They stood by the lake. The moon was swollen and battered-looking. She hung brightly above the water as if to admire her own reflection, all pocks and cratered scars. There was a wooden life-guard's chair up the beach, a sign nailed to its back informing them that no one was on duty to save them. From the grasses along the shore, one cricket trilled, an embarrassed, lonely sound. *Anybody. Anybody.* The sand was coarse and stuck to the children's feet as they left prints in the smooth expanse of the shore.

Nolan finished inflating the tiger. Heaving his breath into it so the animal was full of him and full of Elsa too. His limbs grew, his claws and face popped free, his neck straightened. The tiger's pink and orange and purple stripes seemed less garish in the moon-light.

Nolan plugged the rubber stopper in the tiger's side.

Elsa wore Ian's Beethoven shirt and cotton shorts. Nolan was in a hoodie and boxers, his hair tied back. Elsa took the tiger. The sand was silty and cold. The way into the lake was shallow but she didn't have to wade very far to push the tiger in. She released him, and he drifted out. Nolan pulled Elsa back to shore. He led her to the lifeguard's chair and hoisted her up. From their new height, they could see the tiger being pulled toward the heart of the lake.

A real Viking's funeral, said Elsa.

This is better.

He would have hated it.

Well, I love it, Nolan said. And funerals aren't really for the dead anyway. Who cares what they want.

That's true, Elsa said.

They watched the tiger getting sucked out to where he was head-ing, a circuitous route full of tangents and diversions. Nolan fum-bled in his hoodie pocket for his phone. He woke it up and the tiny light seemed crass to Elsa.

Put that away, you fucking millennial.

I want to show you something.

Seriously, now? Elsa said. The stars seemed alarmingly close. The bugs were rattling. Their father was dead. Not now.

I saw it right before I went to bed. We missed less news than I thought, Nolan said. I thought there'd be so much to catch up on but it was mostly the same old things. Except for this.

Elsa took the phone from him.

It was a video. A rocket launch. Elsa watched as the shuttle vaulted into space. She'd seen launches before, but soon she real-ized it wasn't the shuttle she was meant to be watching. It was the rocket propelling it.

While the shuttle was still going upward, soaring off, the detached rocket, instead of dropping away like so much spent trash, turned back on the same fiery trail it had traced in ascent. It looked like a bomb or a fairy in a cartoon—a glowing orb, plummeting—and as it approached, Elsa felt sure she was about to see an explosion.

What is this? I don't want to see this, Elsa said, shoving the phone at Nolan, but he shoved it back.

Watch, he said.

The rocket was returning. It had reversed course by design and was headed for a landing pad set out in the sea. And as the rocket came home, a chrysanthemum of flame, half menacing, half celebratory, blossomed from the pad and then slowly dimmed. The rocket on the landing pad came into focus once more, standing whole. There was cheering. The video cut out.

What the fuck was that? Elsa said.

Reusable rockets. Space-Gen has been making them. Their first successful launch was this week.

Elsa tapped and watched from the beginning again, the screen of Nolan's phone glowing softly over her face.

Why are you showing me this? Are you teasing me?

They'll send it back up again. That exact same rocket. They say it's going to cut the cost of space travel by ninety-five percent.

Rockets falling along their own paths, then launching out again.

Elsa laughed.

Ninety-five percent meant, sure, she wasn't going to Mars, but someone was. Someday.

She read the article below the video. In the photos, Space-Gen's CEO looked tired but young. Hardly old enough to run a business. But there he was, saying they would have manned missions to Mars by 2035. Maybe sooner. Construction of the tunnel systems in which the colonists would live would start via robotic builders in the next five years. To settle Mars, the young CEO said, was the obvious choice. It was an expansion of the human experience. And it would happen in his lifetime.

Elsa's lifetime.

I wonder if St. Gilles will find out about this, Nolan said.

Elsa thought of St. Gilles out on the island, surrounded by his books. Destroying the Earth in his pages over and over again. He would not hear about this, and Elsa thought that he might never even imagine it. Despite being the creator of whole worlds, despite being a famous and culturally beloved establishment, Remy St. Gilles would fail to imagine something so simple as this: a rocket not undone by its journey.

This was how Mars would happen, and it wasn't Remy who had done it, or Mitchell, or their father. It was the young CEO. It was Nolan and Elsa. It was all of them, miserable millennials, who understood that it wasn't about going forward or back. Who wanted to blow the whole thing open. To make the world a wider, greater vessel with room to hold more and different things.

Most of them would stay on Earth and fail at fixing it the best they could, but some of them *would* go to Mars. James Peacock maybe, Elsa thought.

James would travel in a Space-Gen shuttle, flying as high as the school jungle gym and higher. And when James Maxwell Peacock ascended as far as Mars, he would not plant a flag, Elsa thought, but he would cry all their names out loud.

The tiger was now bobbing out toward the center of the lake. Elsa told Nolan about the sounds the spheres would have made had she gone to Mars. The cozy claustrophobia of her bunk. The packets of food they would have rehydrated. How she imagined it would have felt to be weightless. Not unlike floating in the Gulf, maybe. Buoyant in her body.

Nolan told Elsa about sneaking into the stadium at night. The long shadows of giants. The turfy smell and red clay like blessings.

They talked about these things and they did not talk about Ian.

As the unbound tiger drifted, the children let each other forget him. Not forever, but for tonight. They forgot his dog snoring in the house and they forgot his crooked nose and forgot the way he twirled his pencil when he listened to music. They forgot what he had told them was true about the world and how to be in it. Because those things were heavy, and they did not need to carry them all the time. Older people were always handing younger people things to carry, things they said it was important to bring forward. But maybe if Nolan and Elsa Grey could lay these down, if they could forget for just a little while, they might finally be able to get somewhere.

Acknowledgments

Meredith Kaffel Simonoff is a marvel. Thank you for sending me into the dark forest of this book time and again, and for giving me flashlights to carry with me. Thank you for mailing me Darwin's diary from London. Thank you for your unquantifiable brilliance and warmth.

I probably shouldn't say that I fell in love with editor Lee Boudreaux that first day we talked about phantom duck vaginas, but that's the truth. Thank you for your wise edits, your incredible vision, and for implicitly understanding this swampy gulf-world.

I'm terribly grateful to everyone at Defiore and Company for their support.

I'm also very thankful to Bill Thomas for making Doubleday an incredible home for this book. Many, many thanks are also owed to Cara Reilly, Lauren Weber, and Emma Joss, for getting all my ducks in a row. Many thanks to Caitlin Landuyt for steering the paperback ship.

Thanks to Diana Sudyka, whose art I have loved for so long, for her magical illustration, and to Emily Mahon, for designing this cover which I love so much.

Jeff Wozniak and Lindsay Tiegs of Earthwatch are responsible for any real science that appears in these pages and are not responsible for any of the pseudoscience. Thank you for teaching me about the whooping cranes and the muck they rely on too. Thank you for being good scientists and enthusiastic teachers and bird nerds. Thank you for showing me the moon up close and for letting me drive the boat.

Thank you to Eric Schlich and Hasanthika Sirisena for our conversations about omniscience at Sewanee which gave me the opening to this book. While I'm at it, thank you to the Sewanee Writers' Conference for the Peter Taylor Scholarship in Fiction and for those magical two weeks: you made me feel like art was important again. Alice McDermott and Jeffrey Renard Allen's feedback on this manuscript was invaluable.

Kate Sparks and Will Root helped me understand reversible rockets, and why a girl might go to Mars, and so, gave me my ending.

Thanks to Colin Farstad for seeing this book with x-ray vision through early drafts and offering such excellent notes. Niki Keating gave me my title. Sean Towey offered scandalous alternative titles (and helpful notes too). Cora Weissbourd is always my first reader. Teddy Casper is a luck dragon. Rachel Hanson knows baseball. Pat Caputo walked me around McCovey Cove three times. Randall Joyce knows the best bookbinders in Belgrade. Gary Sheppard reminded me that Nolan Ryan once punched Robin Ventura in the face.

I traveled through many texts while writing this book, but I am particularly indebted to the following: The story Nita's mother tells her is inspired by a real Choctaw story called "Little Ants Help Turtle." Charles Baxter's essay "Regarding Happiness" shaped my thinking on movement, happiness, and time. The history of Itasca comes from a wonderful article in the *Star Tribune* by Curt Brown.

Thank you to all my fiction students, the Chicken Squad, for inspiring me with your passion and voices. Thanks especially to the members of the Write-In, alongside whom I revised these pages. Thank you too to the students in my "Dysfunctional" Family Novels class at FSU and at Colgate for all our conversations about how writing about family can be writing about the world. These conversations have informed this book deeply.

I am grateful to Colgate University for their support of my research with grants and enthusiasm both. The community of friends and scholars I have found in Hamilton, New York, is more than I could have hoped for. I'm especially grateful to my creative writing colleagues: Peter Balakian, Jennifer Brice, and Greg Ames.

I remain so fond of the Brooklyn College MFA and Trout House crew.

I drafted this book while living in Tallahassee, Florida, and might have never known the gulf at all if the Florida State University PhD program hadn't brought me there. Thanks to all my teachers and fellow writers under the oak trees. Huge thanks to my committee for their help with the earliest draft of this book: Mark Winegardner, Elizabeth Stuckey-French, Alisha Gaines, and Lisa Ryoko Wakamiya.

I am so grateful to my writer family and drag house, the Firefeet, for being confidantes and motivators throughout this whole process: Emily Alford, Charlie Beckerman, and Olivia Wolfgang Smith.

I am, as always, grateful to my family of origin: Tom Hauser, Brenda Hauser, and Leslie Caputo. Thank you for believing in science. Thank you for believing in stories.